THE GHOST
AND THE SILVER SCREAM

The Ghost of Marlow House

The Ghost Who Loved Diamonds

The Ghost Who Wasn't

The Ghost Who Wanted Revenge

The Ghost of Halloween Past

The Ghost Who Came for Christmas

The Ghost of Valentine Past

The Ghost from the Sea

The Ghost and the Mystery Writer

The Ghost and the Muse

The Ghost Who Stayed Home

The Ghost and the Leprechaun

The Ghost Who Lied

The Ghost and the Bride

The Ghost and Little Marie

The Ghost and the Doppelganger

The Ghost of Second Chances

The Ghost Who Dream Hopped

The Ghost of Christmas Secrets

The Ghost Who Was Say I Do

The Ghost and the Baby

The Ghost and the Halloween Haunt

The Ghost and the Christmas Spirit

The Ghost and the Silver Scream

The Ghost of a Memory

HAUNTING DANIELLE - BOOK 24

THE GHOST AND THE SILVER SCREAM

USA TODAY BESTSELLING AUTHOR

BOBBI HOLMES

The Ghost and the Silver Scream
(Haunting Danielle, Book 24)
A Novel
By Bobbi Holmes
Cover Design: Elizabeth Mackey

ISBN: 978-1-949977-59-2

To fellow author and friend, Cameron Lowe. Thanks for suggesting The Ghost and the Silver Scream book title, and thanks for letting Lily and Heather read your book, A Ghost at His Back, Book One of the Rankin Flats Supernatural Thrillers.

ONE

Of all the ways he imagined his life ending, he never considered murder. After all, people adored him. He was not only handsome, he was generous, loving, and undoubtably the life of the party, any party. But murder? It was an insult, a blot on a life well lived. Plus, in his craziest alcohol-induced dreams, he had never imagined one of the people closest to him might be the one to pull the trigger. How had he missed the signs?

Trigger was just a metaphor. A firearm hadn't been the murder weapon. Although, he was as dead as if he had been shot through the heart.

The impressive Victorian, with its intriguing mansard roofline, loomed over him. Looking up at the house, he guessed it had three floors, considering the number and position of the front windows. Turning his attention to the sign posted out front, he silently read: *Marlow House, Established 1871*.

"I guess I'm at the right place," he murmured.

He started toward the front door, but then changed directions and made his way to the downstairs windows to look inside. Standing in the shrubbery bordering the front edge of the house, he peeked in one window. It appeared to be a living room. No one was inside. Moving to the next window, he found a bedroom. Once again, the room was empty.

Deciding not to enter through the front door or windows, he went to investigate what he could find by entering along the front gate to the side yard. A few minutes later he stood by what he would soon discover was the kitchen window. Peering inside, he was happy to find three people sitting at the kitchen table, having coffee and chatting.

One was an attractive woman, with dark

wavy hair falling just beyond her shoulders. He guessed her age to be late twenties or early thirties. She wore a navy blue, long-sleeved T-shirt and plaid pajama bottoms. He was fairly certain she was Danielle Marlow.

The two men at the table with her were similarly dressed, each wearing what appeared to be dark jogging pants or pajama bottoms with T-shirts. The dark-haired thirtysomething man to her right, he recognized him immediately—Walt Marlow. It was Marlow's bestselling novel, *Moon Runners*, that had gotten him into this mess.

If it wasn't for that book, he wouldn't be playing Peeping Tom in some little beach town along the Oregon coast. He also wouldn't be dead.

He turned his attention to the third person at the table, a blond man whose back was to him. At least, he assumed it was a man, considering the broad shoulders stretching out the T-shirt. By the length of his wavy blond hair, barely touching the shirt's collar and in desperate need of a comb, he admitted it could possibly be a woman, albeit a rather huskily built one.

Motion from the doorway leading to what he assumed was the hall caught his attention. It was then he noticed a black cat strolling into the kitchen and trailing behind him, a pit bull.

DANIELLE LOOKED up from the table and watched as Hunny followed Max into the room. The pit bull kept a respectable distance behind the black cat, not wanting to get a swat on the nose for coming too close. What the pit bull, Hunny, didn't know, Max the cat had long since realized the puppy had grown into a muscular dog who could easily take him down if she felt inclined. Hunny's temperament prevented her from hurting the cat, yet Max hadn't managed to last this long by using up his nine lives being overly cocky.

"I think Max is going to miss Hunny," Danielle said as she watched the pair. A moment later Max curled up by her feet while Hunny made her way around the table, greeting everyone with a wet nose before settling between Walt and Chris on the floor under the table.

"Not sure about that. But Sadie will," Walt said, referring to the golden retriever who lived across the street. "Those two have become quite the pair, always running around in the side yard or on the beach together."

"I think it was those bones they dug up next door," Chris said with a snort. "Partners in crime, those two dogs."

The bones in question were the remains of a couple who had been murdered in the forties and had been put to rest almost six months earlier, after Hunny and Sadie's discovery.

"I feel a little guilty having you move out before your house is done," Danielle said.

"Ahh, don't be silly." Chris gave a shrug as he picked up his coffee cup. "It's going to be a few weeks before I can move into the new house, so I can deal with staying at the foundation office until then. Heather tells me the bed she ordered is being delivered this afternoon. Anyway, I think I'm starting to annoy Walt."

"No more than usual." Walt smiled and sipped his coffee.

"Plus," Chris continued, "you guys are going to need the room for all those Hollywood people. It's going to be like having the B and B up and running again."

"Yes, but this time Joanne will be doing most of the cooking," Walt said.

"I'm playing lady of the manor." Danielle grinned.

Before Chris could respond, Hunny jumped up from her place under the kitchen table and began to bark. The three turned toward the kitchen door leading to the side yard, to see what had set the dog off, and to their surprise they found a young man standing in the kitchen by the closed door. He looked to be in his early twenties. While it was shocking to find a stranger standing in the room with them—one they hadn't heard come in—the vibes he gave off were anything but threatening.

"I know that door was locked," Danielle muttered, her eyes wide as she stared at the stranger. Neither Walt nor Chris had gotten up from the table, but instead remained in their chairs, turned toward the intruder.

The man glanced around the kitchen curiously, unfazed by the pit bull still barking at him. After taking full inventory of the room, he looked to Danielle and smiled. "I didn't come through the door." He then reconsidered his words and laughed, adding, "On second thought, I suppose I did."

The next moment the man abruptly took several steps backwards, disappearing through the door, and then in the next moment he reappeared.

"See?" he said cheerfully. "The lock was no problem."

"You're a ghost," Danielle blurted.

Hunny, now silent, sat down and stared at the ghost, cocking her head from side to side, while Max looked up, annoyed, his sleep having been disturbed by the canine barking.

"And you can see me," the stranger said, sounding surprised. He looked from Danielle to Walt and Chris. "And you can too. I hadn't expected that." He walked over to the empty chair and sat down, which fortunately for him had already been pulled out from the table, since he had not yet learned to harness energy and move objects.

"Who are you…and why are you here?" Walt demanded.

Instead of answering the question, the ghost looked from Walt to Chris, then Danielle and back to Walt. "I have heard there are people like you who can see ghosts, but I've never encountered one before. Are all of you alive? I know Walt Marlow is alive." He turned to Danielle and added, "and I just assumed you're Danielle Marlow, but maybe I was wrong. Maybe you are someone else. A dead someone." He turned to Chris and asked, "Are you a ghost?"

"No, we're all alive. But how do you know who I am?" Walt asked.

"You're the reason I'm here," the stranger explained.

"Me?" Walt frowned.

"Who are you?" Chris asked.

"Who I am is not as important as why I'm here," the man explained. "And since you all can see me, then there is no reason for me to stick around once I tell you why I had to come."

"Why is that?" Danielle asked.

"I want to prevent a murder," the ghost said.

"Murder? Whose murder?" Danielle asked.

The man shrugged. "That's the problem. I'm not sure. It could be several of them. Or none of them. But who knows, maybe all of them, considering I certainly didn't see it coming."

"Didn't see what coming?" Chris asked.

The ghost looked at him. "Why, my murder, of course."

"You were murdered?" Danielle asked.

"Didn't I just say that?"

Danielle frowned. "And there's going to be another murder?"

"I certainly hope not. That's why I'm here."

"And what does any of this have to do with me?" Walt asked.

"Just tell us who you are," Chris insisted.

The ghost started to say something but then stopped. "I don't know if I should say who I am. I don't want to get anyone in trouble."

"Who would get in trouble if you told us who you are?" Walt asked.

"My killer, obviously."

Danielle arched her brow at the ghost. "Your killer? You come and tell us you've been murdered, and then say you don't want to get your killer in trouble?"

"It's too late for me. I don't want to see anyone go to prison over a little misunderstanding."

"Your murder was a little misunderstanding?" Chris asked.

"Please, we're getting off track here. I don't want anyone else to get hurt," the ghost insisted.

"Whose murder are you trying to prevent?" Danielle asked.

"Like I told you, I'm not quite sure," the ghost said.

"Do you at least know who the would-be killer is?" Chris asked.

"Of course. The same person who killed me," the ghost said.

"And who is this killer?" Chris asked.

"I told you, I can't say. I don't want to get anyone in trouble."

"Then I don't know how you expect us to help you," Danielle said impatiently.

"What does any of this have to do with me? Why are you here, and how did you know who I am?" Walt asked.

"Because they're all coming here," the ghost said matter-of-factly.

"Who's coming here?" Walt asked.

"The possible victims, of course." He then looked at Walt and said, "And I would probably still be alive if you hadn't written that book, and I wouldn't be standing in your kitchen right now."

Before anyone could respond, the ghost of Marie Nichols—the image of an elderly woman—popped into the kitchen. She said a cheery hello; the other ghost looked at her in surprise and then vanished.

"Was it something I said?" Marie asked, glancing around the kitchen. She turned to the table. "Who was that?"

"Some guy who said he had been murdered," Danielle explained.

"Murdered?" Marie repeated.

"Yes, and he seems to believe there'll be more…here," Chris said.

TWO

Marie sat quietly at Marlow House's kitchen table, listening to Danielle explain their odd encounter with the apparition minutes earlier. When Marie had first arrived, she had been wearing a straw hat with her sundress—a dress made from a brightly patterned poppy fabric in red, orange, green and yellow. At least it looked as if it were made from the cheerful floral fabric. The dress was only an illusion, like the elderly woman wearing it and the straw hat, which had vanished the moment after Marie had sat down at the table with her friends.

Danielle finished with the telling, and

Marie leaned back in her chair and let out a sigh.

"And you have no idea who the young man was?" Marie asked after a moment of pondering what she had just heard.

"None. The only thing he really told us, someone might be murdered," Danielle said.

"We also know this has something to do with Walt and his book." Chris glanced briefly to Walt and then looked back to Marie.

"That's the most ludicrous part of all of this," Walt grumbled.

"More ludicrous than a ghost randomly popping up in our kitchen and foretelling a murder? Of whom, he didn't know, and a killer—his killer—whom he refused to name," Danielle asked.

"I'm just saying it's ridiculous to imagine my book is responsible for getting anyone killed. It is a book of fiction. And while many of the events did actually happen, they occurred a hundred years ago," Walt argued.

"It has to have something to do with that movie crew," Chris said.

"The movie crew?" Danielle asked.

Chris looked at her. "That has to be it. The ghost talked about someone coming here and then talked about Walt's book. The only people coming here in the immediate future—at least as far as we know—are the people making the movie."

"It still doesn't make any sense," Danielle argued.

"I wish we could have gotten that ghost to tell us more," Walt said.

"I'm sorry I scared him off," Marie apologized.

"It wasn't your fault," Danielle said. "Maybe he'll come back."

"I'll go down to the cemetery and check around," Marie offered. "Perhaps someone knows who he is. Spirits often check into the local cemetery when they hit town—to get an idea what type of lingering spirits are nearby and if there might be any mediums in the area that can help them."

"Oh, please," Danielle groaned. "The spirits at the cemetery haven't been giving out our names, have they? Like some Ghost Chamber of Commerce? If so, please take our names off the list."

Marie chuckled. "It doesn't quite work that way, dear. And would you want us to turn away a spirit in need?" Before Danielle could respond, Marie vanished.

LATER THAT AFTERNOON, Pearl Huckabee, Marlow House's neighbor to the south, stood at her upstairs bedroom window, peering out the narrow opening between her curtains. She stared down into the driveway next door. The only car in the drive belonged to Chris Johnson. Walt and Danielle Marlow normally parked in their garage located to the rear of the property. Yet she knew only one car was currently parked there. Fifteen minutes earlier she had seen the Marlows drive off in their Packard.

She watched as Chris carried several suitcases to his car.

"Is he going somewhere?" Pearl wondered aloud. She glanced around the yard, looking for Chris's pit bull, Hunny. She had once been terrified of the dog; she had even plotted to find a way to have it permanently banned from the neighborhood. But then the dog did something unexpected—it had saved Pearl's life. She still did not like her neighbors and would prefer the house next door be vacant, as it had been when she was a child. However, Pearl now had a soft spot in her heart for Hunny.

She watched as Chris walked to the gate at the end of the driveway and opened it. A few moments later she spied Hunny coming outside through the doggy door. Chris opened his vehicle's passenger door for the dog, who then jumped into the car. Pearl continued to stand at the window. She watched Chris back his car out of the driveway a few minutes later, taking his dog and suitcases with him.

She turned from the window and picked up the newspaper she had set on her dresser earlier that morning. Turning to the article about her neighbor, she reread the piece. It was an interview with Walt Marlow. Apparently his book was actually being made into a movie, and in a few days the producer, director, several movie stars, and others were coming to Frederickport and staying at Marlow House.

"I don't know why I bothered getting that darn bed and breakfast closed down," Pearl said angrily as she tossed the newspaper in her wastebasket by the dresser. "They keep finding loopholes and continue to bring more unwanted traffic to the neighborhood."

She looked back to the window, thinking about those suitcases she had seen Chris load into his car.

OFFICERS BRIAN HENDERSON and Joe Morelli sat in the police car, preparing to go out on patrol. Brian was about to slip the key in the ignition when Joe said, "There's the Marlow Packard."

Brian looked up and spied the vintage black Packard pulling into the police department parking lot. He sat there and watched as Walt and Danielle got out of the car a few minutes later. From what he could tell, they had not noticed him and Joe sitting in their vehicle.

"Why does he dress like that?" Joe asked in disgust.

Brian chuckled and glanced to Joe and then back to Walt and Danielle, who were now walking to the front door of the station. "I assume you're talking about Walt Marlow?"

"For one thing, that hat. What is that about? Who wears hats like that anymore?"

Brian shrugged. "You have to admit it looks good on him."

"What kind of hat is that, anyway?" Joe asked.

"I think it's called a fedora."

"And doesn't he ever wear jeans like a normal person?" Joe asked.

"Jeans would look silly with a fedora," Brian said. "Although, I'm fairly certain I've seen him wear jeans before."

"Maybe. But most of the time he's wearing a suit. Who wears a suit all the time if they don't have to?"

"He's not always wearing a suit."

"Practically," Joe grumbled.

"Why does it bug you so much? You don't still have a thing for Danielle, do you?"

"No!" Joe snapped.

"Then what is it?" Brian asked.

After a moment of silence, Joe said, "It's Kelly."

"Kelly?"

"Yeah, the last time we went shopping in Portland, she dragged me into a shop selling men's suits. I told her I didn't need a new suit, and then she suggested I start dressing a little less casual when I'm off work."

Brian started to laugh.

"Oh, shut up," Joe snapped.

When Brian finally stopped laughing, he said, "You have to admit he always looks so natural—comfortable—dressed like that."

"Looks like a gangster from the twenties."

"Kind of reminds me of my grandfather," Brian muttered, shoving the key into the ignition.

"Your grandfather? Your grandfather was a gangster?"

"No. My grandfather was a sharp dresser. He was probably born around the same time as the original Walt Marlow."

"You're calling Walt Marlow a sharp dresser?" Joe asked, sounding incredulous.

"You've got to give the guy credit; he's playing up this author role to a T. Remember when we first met him, before his accident? He certainly didn't dress this way back then."

"So that's what you think this is, him dressing for a part?" Joe asked.

"Maybe, it also goes with the Packard," Brian said as he turned on the ignition. "Or maybe Clint has been possessed by the spirit of the original Walt Marlow."

WALT AND DANIELLE sat in Police Chief MacDonald's office with the door closed. They occupied the two chairs facing the chief, who sat behind his desk.

"A murder?" MacDonald repeated.

"He said there might be a murder—or several," Danielle told him.

"Let me get this straight…" the chief began, his hands now folded on the desk before him as he straightened in his chair. "A ghost—of someone you have never seen before—barged into your kitchen this morning and told you someone—or several people might be murdered, yet he didn't know who they might be, and that he himself had been murdered, but he didn't want to tell you who the killer was—or who he is—because he didn't want to get the killer in trouble?"

Danielle nodded. "Yeah, pretty much."

The chief groaned.

"Chris is convinced this has something to do with the people who'll be staying with us," Danielle explained.

"The movie people," the chief muttered.

"According to the ghost, this all started with my book. But none of it makes any sense," Walt said.

"No, it doesn't," the chief agreed. "And I'm not sure what you expect me to do with any of this."

"We wanted to give you a heads-up," Danielle told him.

"I think you just want to torment me," the chief grumbled.

"I'm sorry, Ed," Walt said. "Danielle felt she needed to say something to you, but I told her there wasn't anything you could do."

"I figured we owe it to you to keep you in the loop," Danielle argued.

"And this is pretty darn loopy," the chief replied.

Danielle slumped back in the chair. "I wish there was something we could do, in case he's right."

"You could always ask them not to stay with you. But I doubt that's the answer," the chief said.

"No, it isn't," Danielle agreed. "Walt and I already discussed it. I don't think we have enough to warrant canceling their trip—after all, this is only Chris's theory. And how credible is the ghost?"

"And we also realize that if someone is intent on killing someone, they don't need to be at Marlow House to do it. If we come up with an excuse, saying they can't stay with us, it doesn't mean we prevent a murder," Walt added.

"Tell me again, who all are coming?" the chief asked.

"The producer and her husband, along with the director and his wife," Walt began.

"The producer is a woman?" the chief asked.

"And why shouldn't she be a woman?" Danielle asked.

The chief shrugged. "No reason."

"Seraphina Bouchard," Walt continued.

"Ahh yes, you mentioned that before." The chief grinned. "She has an amazing voice."

"I know. Walt's agent was thrilled they got her to play the jazz singer. This will be her second movie," Danielle said.

"Who else?" the chief asked.

"Beatrice Adair. She's backing the film," Walt explained.

"Birdie Adair?" the chief asked. "No kidding."

"You've heard of her?" Danielle asked.

"Who hasn't?" the chief said.

"I know nothing about her other than she has money and is backing the film." Danielle looked at Walt and asked, "Do you know anything about her?"

Walt shrugged. "Not really."

"All I know is that her parents were wealthy—not as rich as Chris's. But old money," the chief explained. "But like Chris she was an only child, inherited everything. From what I recall, she was married twice, had only one daughter, but they're all gone now. Her daughter died years ago when she was fairly young, drugs. Her last husband died a couple of months ago."

"Her husband died? Can you tell us what he looked like?" Danielle asked.

"I doubt he's your ghost. For one thing, he was well into his seventies. He'd had a heart condition for years. Didn't you say your ghost was in his twenties?"

Danielle let out a sigh. "It was worth a shot."

THREE

Heather's calico, Bella, would be celebrating her fourth birthday in a couple of months. Compared to Max, she was a petite feline, about half his size. Despite her small stature, she didn't feel inferior or inadequate. While Max thought himself a panther, Bella was a courageous lioness. At the moment she stealthily stalked her prey.

Crouched behind the sofa, she peered out into the dimly lit space. The sofa concealing her from her victim was the only piece of furniture in the room. She assumed Hunny had arrived when she had been napping in one of the rooms down the hall. But now the dog was sleeping, curled up on the floor next to the front of the sofa, unaware of the imminent danger.

Bella could hear the music playing from another room in the house, yet her focus was on the hapless canine. Stretching one front paw out from behind her hiding place, careful not to wake Hunny, Bella took her first step… and then a second.

CHRIS AND HEATHER made their way down the long corridor to one of the rooms that hadn't been converted to office space. Chris reached the open doorway leading to his would-be bedroom and stopped abruptly, grabbing Heather's wrist, bringing her to a silent stop with him. Startled at the gesture, Heather looked at Chris, who nodded into the room.

Together the pair stood silently just outside the open doorway, looking in at Bella, who was creeping around the sofa while Hunny slept. They watched as the cat effortlessly jumped onto the sofa and made her way closer to where the dog slept nearby on the floor.

Chris watched as Bella positioned herself on the edge of the sofa cushion, preparing to pounce down on the unassuming sleeping dog. While he found it amusing, Heather did not.

"Bella!" Heather called out as the cat prepared to leap on her prey.

Startled by her human's unexpected shout, Bella's leap did not go as she had imagined. Her four paws went out wildly in all directions, making her look as if she were trying to hold onto some imaginary platform. Below, the dog jumped up and managed to avoid her assault.

When the cat landed on the floor, she darted from the room while the pit bull started barking.

Chris walked into the bedroom, gave his thigh a pat, and the dog immediately quieted and went to his side, happily licking Chris's hand.

"That cat is going to get herself killed," Heather said as she walked into the room.

"Hunny won't hurt her," Chris said, giving his dog another pat.

"I can't say I'd blame her if she did. Bella is always tormenting her."

Chris walked to the sofa and plopped down, resting his right arm along the back cushions, while Hunny curled up by his feet. He glanced around the room. "You think I should leave this couch in here?"

"You might as well," Heather said with a shrug. She glanced at her watch and then looked at Chris. "They should be here in about fifteen minutes with the bed. What wall do you want it on?"

Chris pointed to the far wall.

"You know, you and Hunny could have stayed with us," Heather said.

"I appreciate the offer. But I figure Hunny and Bella spend enough time together during the day. They need a break in the evenings."

Heather joined Chris on the sofa. "You're probably right. But I did think it would be fun to see Pearl's expression, just as she thought Hunny was leaving Marlow House, only to discover she was staying with her other neighbor."

Leaning back in the sofa, Chris propped one ankle over an opposing knee. "I don't know about that. She doesn't seem to have a problem with Hunny anymore. I actually caught her talking baby talk to her through the fence."

"Pfft…she was probably trying to coax her over so she could do something evil. You keep Hunny away from that crazy neighbor of ours."

"By the way, we saw a ghost this morning."

"Umm, the way you say that, I have to assume it was not Marie or Eva," Heather said.

"No. It wasn't." Chris went on to tell Heather about the strange encounter with the mystery ghost.

"Well, that is just creepy," Heather said when Chris finished the telling. "And you have no idea who he was?"

"No. But if you happen to run into a strange ghost in the neighborhood, see what you can find out."

"Wonderful," Heather grumbled.

Glittering snow began falling from the

ceiling, halting their conversation. It vanished as it hit the floor.

Heather, Chris and Hunny nonchalantly glanced upwards. If any of the three found snow falling from the ceiling an unusual occurrence, they didn't show it.

With a sigh Heather said, "I guess it's better than glitter."

"And you always say you hate it when they pop in unannounced. I'd say this could be considered an announcement." Chris watched the snow swirl in front of them, taking on the form of a woman's silhouette.

Heather shrugged, her eyes focused on the emerging apparition. "True. Marie does it all the time. I swear, one of these days she is going to give me a heart attack the way she just appears unannounced. Disappearing snow is a nice touch."

In the next breath the spirit of Eva Thorndike materialized. Onetime silent screen star and childhood friend of Walt Marlow during his first life, she bore an uncanny resemblance to Charles Dana Gibson's drawing the Gibson Girl.

"I came to see Chris's new home!" Eva announced.

"You have been here before—a million times," Heather said dryly.

"True, but it was never Chris's home before." Eva glanced around. She looked back to the sofa and frowned. "Surely you don't plan to sleep on that thing, do you?"

"I ordered a bed for him," Heather told her. She glanced at her watch and then looked back to Eva. "It should be here soon."

Eva waved her hands dramatically, and all evidence of snow vanished. A chair appeared, and she sat down.

"Are Walt and Danielle ready for their guests? I'm so excited!" Eva squealed. "Being among my people again!"

"Technically speaking, only one is an actor," Chris told her. "I think."

Eva shrugged. "They're all in the business. If I had lived long enough to be in talkies, I would have been famous."

"You were famous," Chris reminded her.

"Who remembers silent film stars these days?" Eva asked.

"I'm sure you would have been amazing in talkies," Heather said.

Eva flashed Heather a smile. "That's very sweet of you to say."

"I'm rather looking forward to meeting Seraphina Bouchard," Chris said. "I'm a huge fan of hers. She's got one hell of a voice."

"She's the one playing the jazz singer?" Eva asked.

"Yes," Chris told her.

"Didn't Walt say the jazz singer in the book was based on a real person?" Heather asked.

"Yes, on Desiree Davis," Eva said.

"Did Desiree Davis really have a sister who was a silent screen star who passed for white?" Heather asked.

"Yes, that part of the story was fairly accurate. In fact, I knew the sister."

"Did you know she was black back then?" Chris asked.

"Yes, a few of us did. But I never said anything. She was beautiful and a talented actress, and there weren't leading-lady roles for black actresses back then. I didn't blame her;

of course, Desiree didn't see it that way. She felt her sister was betraying her people."

"Wasn't she part white?" Heather asked.

"Yes, their father was white. But Desiree took after her mother's side of the family, while Charlene took after her father's side," Eva explained.

"That's so lame," Heather grumbled. "They were of both races. Why are you black because one parent is black? What about the other parent?"

"It didn't work that way back then," Chris told her. "If someone had just a drop of black blood, they were considered black. I find it sometimes amusing when a white friend gets annoyed at someone who identifies as black when they're part white, taking insult. When the fact is, that whole—you are black if any of your ancestors were black—is a notion our slaveowner ancestors came up with."

"And it is lame," Heather reiterated.

"True," Chris agreed.

"I've watched much change since I passed to this side," Eva said. "The fact Seraphina Bouchard can stay with the others at Marlow

House without raising a brow is a notable stride forward."

"I suppose." Heather sighed.

"When Marie and I stopped in the library the other day, they had an article about Seraphina Bouchard, and they mentioned *Moon Runners*. I would have loved to have taken the article for Walt, but Marie refused to help me."

"What did you find out about her?" Chris asked.

"She's single, which might interest you." Eva flashed Chris a smile.

"I thought she was dating someone. I remember reading about it," Heather said.

"She was in a long-term relationship, but according to the article, they broke up last month, after she found him cheating on her with her assistant."

"Why is it always the assistant?" Heather asked. "As I recall, he wasn't in the business. Some trust fund guy."

"That's what the article said. But I don't think it's going to work out for the assistant," Eva said.

"Why do you say that?" Chris asked.

"Two weeks ago he was killed. Drowned in his own spa. According to the article, drugs and alcohol were involved."

Chris sat up abruptly. "Do you know if he was white?"

"Yes, why? Are you interested in Seraphina and are afraid she won't date someone white?" Eva asked.

"No. I was wondering if we found our ghost," Chris said.

"Ghost? What ghost?" Eva asked.

FOUR

Across the street from Marlow House resided Danielle's best friend, Lily Bartley, who lived with her husband, Ian, and their six-month-old son, Connor. Lily sat in her living room reading a book while Connor played quietly nearby on a blanket on the floor with their golden retriever, Sadie. Connor busily explored a small rubber ball, passing it from hand to hand while periodically mouthing it. Sadie waited patiently for him to drop the ball so she could retrieve it should it roll away.

Sprawled lazily on the sofa, Lily peeked over the book and checked on the baby and dog. She smiled at the pair and refused to think of the dog germs when the baby gummed the ball Sadie just had in her mouth. Lily smiled again when she heard Connor giggle with delight as Sadie pushed her nose along the baby's cheek.

"You look comfortable," Ian said when he walked into the room several minutes later.

Lily tucked a bookmark between two pages, closed the book, and set it on her lap. She smiled at Ian. "I could get used to this. Sadie does a wonderful job entertaining Connor."

Ian glanced over at his dog, who had just snagged the ball and was returning it to the baby. "I'm not sure who is entertaining whom," he said with a chuckle before joining Lily on the sofa. As he sat down, he lifted her bare feet from the cushion and then dropped them on his lap as he took his seat next to her.

"You don't seem to miss teaching," Ian noted.

"You're right. As much as I loved it, I don't miss it. I'm surprised at how content I am right now. In fact, I've been giving that some thought."

"When I'm content, I just enjoy it and don't think about it too much," Ian teased.

"What I mean, I have a better support system than most. If I had a husband who believed I should be solely responsible for Connor and taking care of this house, I don't think I'd be as happy."

"Ahh, I'm responsible for your happiness," he gloated.

Lily laughed. "That's not exactly what I meant. But I do appreciate that you don't think it's solely my job to care for Connor—even though I'm not teaching right now. But it's not just you. It's our friends. Marie has been great. How many people have a ghost who doubles as a nanny?"

Ian laughed. "I don't imagine many."

"Having Dani and Walt across the street is so convenient, and even Heather has been awesome. I feel blessed having such a great support system. Plus, it is never boring on Beach Drive. Although, I could do without some ghostly visits."

"You're talking about the ghost Danielle told you about this morning?" Ian asked.

"I wish they could figure out who he was before those people show up in a few days."

"I did a little research on everyone who'll be staying at Marlow House," Ian said. "The only thing I found for recent deaths of men about that age within that social group was Seraphina's ex-boyfriend. I could only find a couple of photos of him online—not terrific pictures and none straight on. I emailed them to Walt. He said they could be him, but he can't be sure."

"Why recent deaths?" Lily asked.

"According to their mystery ghost, his death had something to do with *Moon Runners*. I looked for deaths after the book came out. But it was just a quick search, and there was limited online personal information on the people coming. And who knows, maybe this has absolutely nothing to do with them. It's all a shot in the dark."

"And maybe the ghost is some practical joker," Lily suggested.

The doorbell rang. Ian looked up. "That's probably Kelly. That's why I came in here, to tell you she was on the way over." He lifted

Lily's feet from his lap and stood up, while she picked up her book and opened it again.

A few minutes later Ian returned to the living room with his sister, Kelly, at his side. She wore denims, jogging shoes, and an oversized pale blue hoodie over her blouse.

"What are you reading?" Kelly asked as she walked into the room.

"*A Ghost at his Back*, by Cameron Lowe. I love a good ghost thriller," Lily said with a grin as she once again closed the book and set it on her lap.

Kelly walked over to Connor, leaned down, and gave his waving hand a gentle squeeze. He smiled up at his aunt, but turned his attention back to Sadie, who had just returned with the ball. Kelly wandered over to an empty chair and sat down as she dropped her purse by her feet. Ian took a seat on the floor near Connor's blanket and leaned back against the sofa.

Kelly watched as Sadie shoved the ball at Connor, who managed to take it from her mouth and then immediately mouthed it.

"Ewww, he's putting it in his mouth!" Kelly shrieked.

"He puts everything in his mouth," Ian countered.

Kelly wrinkled her nose in disgust. "But Sadie had it in her mouth."

"We gave up trying to get them to stop sharing spit," Lily told her.

Kelly shuddered at the thought and looked away from the baby and dog. "I imagine Danielle and Walt are all excited for their Hollywood guests. I can't believe Seraphina Bouchard is staying at Marlow House! Joe has such a crush on her."

"He's going to have to stand in line. Heather told me Chris is rather taken with her himself," Lily told her.

"Since Joe already has a girlfriend, he'd better not be standing in any lines," Ian grumbled.

Kelly laughed. "I love that protective side of you, big brother. But I'm not worried about Joe. Heck, I have a few celebrity crushes myself." She turned to Lily and said, "I heard Chris moved out of Marlow House. It's a shame he wasn't able to stay, especially with Seraphina Bouchard staying there. Heck, with Chris's money and looks, he would actually have a shot with her."

"It would have been a little crowded," Lily told her. "They have all the rooms booked up. No place for Chris to bunk."

Lily stopped talking when she heard a suspicious sound coming from her son. She looked down at him and wrinkled her nose. "I know what you did," Lily told him. Tossing her book on the sofa, she leaned down and picked up her son; he began to wiggle.

"Sheesh, you stink!" Lily said with a laugh as she held Connor out from her.

"You want me to take him?" Ian asked.

"Nah, I've got this. Visit with your sister."

Connor began to kick his legs exuberantly. "Oh, please don't do that." Lily laughed as she made her way to the nursery, holding the baby under his armpits and keeping him at arm's length.

"CONNOR IS GETTING SO BIG," Kelly said wistfully as she sat in the living room with Ian and Sadie.

"You're telling me," Ian agreed.

"Did the baby quilt Mom made get here?" Kelly asked.

"Yes. Lily put it over the rocker in the nursery."

Kelly stood up. "I need to see it. I've only seen pictures of it."

Moments later Kelly walked into her nephew's nursery. She found Lily standing at the changing table, putting a new diaper on the baby.

"I wanted to see the baby quilt Mom sent you," Kelly announced as she made her way to the rocking chair.

"It's adorable. Your mom is so talented," Lily said as she grabbed a clean pair of pants for the baby.

Standing by the rocking chair, Kelly examined the quilt for a moment and then glanced around the room. She spied a dry-erase board hanging on one wall near the crib. She hadn't noticed it before. Someone had written *goodbye* across it in a red dry-erase pen. She didn't recognize the handwriting. It wasn't Ian's and it didn't look like Lily's.

"When did you get that?" Kelly asked, pointing to the dry-erase board.

Lily glanced up at the board, licked her lips nervously and shrugged. "A while ago."

"What's it for?" Kelly asked.

"For shopping lists, that sort of thing," Lily lied. "You know, if I need to pick up diapers or wipes. So I don't forget."

"Umm, why does it say 'goodbye'?"

"I don't know." Lily shrugged. "Ian was just goofing around."

Kelly frowned. She glanced from the unfamiliar handwriting to Lily, whose back was to her as she redressed the baby. Kelly's cellphone began to buzz. She fished it from the hoodie pocket and looked at it.

"It's Joe," Kelly said after she read the message and put the phone back in the pocket. "I need to get going. I dropped Joe off at work this morning, and I need to go pick him up."

"He's off already?" Lily asked.

"He was supposed to have today off," Kelly explained as she walked over to the changing table. "But he went in to cover for someone." She leaned over and gave Connor a kiss. "See you later, big guy."

Lily remained standing near the dressing table, watching her sister-in-law leave. A moment later she walked with her son to the rocking chair and sat down. He yawned.

"I think you're about ready for your nap, aren't you?" Lily said softly as she cradled him in her arms. "You had a busy afternoon with Sadie, all that ball tossing—or more accurately dropping."

The baby yawned again.

A soft knock came from the wall. Lily glanced up and watched as the eraser sitting on the ledge along the bottom of the dry-erase board floated upward and wiped away the goodbye. It settled back on the small ledge. A pen then floated upward, and off came its cap. The cap floated in the air as the pen wrote in a flourish on the board: *I am here!*

"Hi, Marie," Lily greeted her in a whisper.

The pen recapped itself and settled back on the ledge.

"Can you hand me Connor's Winnie, please," Lily asked.

The Winnie the Pooh stuffed bear floated up from the crib and drifted across the room. Lily snatched it from the air and gave it to Connor, who hugged it tightly.

"He always has to have his Winnie," Lily said softly. She then looked up, guessing where Marie might be. "Kelly was just here. She asked about the dry-erase board." Lily chuckled. "I couldn't very well tell her we put it up so you could communicate with me."

The next moment Kelly barreled into the room.

Lily immediately stopped talking and rocking. She looked to her sister-in-law, who froze in her tracks.

"I'm so sorry," Kelly whispered apologetically. "Did I wake him?"

Lily shook her head. "No. That's okay. I'm just trying to get him to sleep."

"I'm sorry. But did I leave my purse in here?" Kelly asked, glancing around the room.

"No. I think it's on the floor by the chair you were sitting on."

"I looked. It wasn't there."

"Did you ask your brother? He doesn't

like leaving purses on the floor—afraid Sadie might get in them. He probably moved it. He has this new paranoia about sugarless gum."

"Sugarless gum?" Kelly frowned.

"Yeah. The sweetener they put in them now, it can kill a dog. A good friend of his recently lost his dog that way." Lily almost added, *Walt has already talked to Sadie about not eating gum, but Ian is still paranoid,* but she caught herself.

"I didn't ask him. I just assumed I brought it in here with me. Thanks. See you later." Kelly started to turn from Lily when she froze, her attention riveted on the dry-erase board. The *Goodbye* had been cleaned off, and in its place someone had written, *I am here!*

FIVE

Chris Johnson and Heather Donovan were an odd pair. They had some things in common. They could both see ghosts. Both lived on Beach Drive. They both worked for the Glandon Foundation—or more accurately, Chris, whose real name was Chris Glandon, was the man and fortune behind the Glandon Foundation, while Heather was his faithful assistant.

Because they spent so much time together, some people around Frederickport assumed the pair was a couple, which Heather found wildly hilarious. It wasn't that Heather thought Chris so far out of her league that she could never imagine him being interested in her—it was more she made a practice of never dating someone who was prettier than herself. Perhaps he wasn't pretty, exactly. But it grew weary seeing how women reacted to Chris's appearance upon first meeting him. Fortunately, Chris managed to maintain a sense of humility and had kept his ego in check. Heather suspected it had something to do with the influence of his adoptive mother, to whom he had been especially close.

Heather couldn't imagine what those fawning women would do if they knew billions came with that pretty face. The thought made her shudder—she could see it now, women breaking into his house—if he still had one—and—well, she had read romance novels with similar plotlines.

The new bed had been delivered, and Chris had helped Heather put the sheets on the mattress. She had purchased the sheets for Chris and had washed them at her house before bringing them with her today. When helping Heather make the bed, it had dawned on Chris there was no longer a laundry room in the building. Technically speaking the room was still there, but it was empty, as the washer and dryer had been removed during the renovation.

"You can use my washing machine," Heather offered, "until you move into your house. But I'm not going to do your laundry. The sheets were a onetime thing."

Chris laughed and said, "Deal."

Later that afternoon Chris sent Heather home early, considering all the hours she had been putting in recently. She happily accepted the early release. While she went straight home, she didn't stay there. Instead, she dropped Bella off at her house and, after feeding the cat, left again to feed herself.

KELLY BARTLEY BORE a striking resemblance to her older brother, Ian. Tall, fit, with an all-American look, she was the softer version of her sibling. She sat with her boyfriend, Joe Morelli, in Lucy's Diner, planning to have an early dinner after picking him up from work minutes earlier.

Only half listening to Joe while he rambled on about his short day at work, Kelly silently studied his features. She inwardly sighed at his dark good looks—the friendly brown eyes, dark wavy hair and chiseled features. She never understood how Danielle had cast him aside so carelessly. Sure, he had arrested Danielle for murder, but Joe had also thought Kelly might be guilty of murder before they had hooked up, and she never held it against him. After all, that was Joe's job.

She also didn't understand the fascination Joe once had for Danielle—a fascination she believed had lingered after she and Joe started dating. Danielle was nice enough, but she had a penchant for attracting trouble. And it wasn't that Danielle was some raving beauty—oh, she was cute, but she was a little on the overweight side, although recently she had dropped a few pounds. Kelly wondered if Walt Marlow might be the reason for the somewhat slimmer version.

Walt Marlow—Kelly had to admit she did find him attractive. She didn't always, and originally she thought it odd how he dressed after he started going by Walt instead of Clint. But the look had grown on her, and recently she had been dying to see how Joe might look if he took a little more care with his wardrobe. If he would just be more cooperative…

"So did you have a nice visit with your brother and Lily?" Joe asked, interrupting Kelly's train of thought.

"It was short. I got tied up at home answering emails, so I got there late, and then you texted me."

"I'm sorry."

Kelly fidgeted with her water glass, looking from it to Joe, back to the glass. "No, that's okay. But something strange happened over there."

"Don't strange things always happen at your brother's house?" Joe asked with a laugh.

"True." Kelly then when on to tell Joe about the dry-erase board. When she was done, she said, "I just don't see why she would have erased *goodbye* and then written *I am here.* And she told me Ian wrote the *goodbye*, which he obviously didn't because whoever wrote *goodbye* wrote *I am here*. Which is also strange, because the handwriting was different from how Lily normally writes."

"Why didn't you ask her?" Joe asked.

"I wasn't sure what to ask. It was the strangest thing to write. And I don't even see how she could have done it, considering I was just out of the room for a minute, and she was holding Connor."

"There is probably a logical explanation. I think you should just ask her," Joe suggested.

"I suppose," Kelly murmured. She picked up her water glass to take a sip and then noticed Heather Donovan walking into the diner alone.

"There's Heather." Kelly nodded toward the new arrival.

Heather, who walked in their direction, wore her long ink black hair fastened in two low pigtails, and her straight bangs needed a trimming, as they covered her eyebrows. She wore burgundy—almost black—lipstick, which gave her fair complexion an alabaster glow. She hadn't bothered changing out of her work clothes, still wearing the black dress, its hem falling inches above her ankles, revealing black boots with spiky metal heels. She paused a moment when she reached Joe and Kelly's table.

"Hi, guys," Heather greeted as she stood next to them.

"Hi, Heather, you meeting anyone?" Kelly asked cheerfully.

"No. Just got off work and didn't feel like cooking," Heather told them.

"I know what you mean," Kelly agreed.

"Would you like to join us?" Joe asked. He cringed a split second later when he felt Kelly kicking his shin under the table.

If Heather noticed the pained expression on Joe's face, she reserved comment. Instead she said, "I appreciate the offer, but it's been a long day, and I just need to decompress and have some alone time."

Several minutes later, after Heather took a booth on the other side of the diner, out of earshot, but still in clear view, Joe asked, "Why did you kick me?"

"I didn't want Heather to sit with us," Kelly said.

"Well, kicking me *after* I asked was a moot —and painful point."

"I'm sorry. I didn't want you to talk her into joining us. Heather is…well…" Kelly glanced over to Heather, who sat alone in a booth reading her menu. "Weird."

HEATHER SLUMPED BACK in the booth seat looking over the menu. Nothing looked particularly appetizing.

"I should have gone to Beach Taco," she muttered under her breath.

"Beach Taco, is that near here?" a male voice interrupted.

Heather glanced up from her menu and found an attractive young man standing over her, grinning foolishly. She just stared.

"Well, is it?" he asked, not budging from his place by her booth.

Heather frowned. "Is it what?"

"Beach Taco? Is it far from here? It's been ages since I've had a taco."

"You were eavesdropping," Heather accused.

He shrugged. "You're sitting alone. I don't think it's eavesdropping on my part if you choose to talk to yourself and I happen to walk by and hear you." Without asking, he sat down across from her in the booth.

Heather closed her menu and set it on the table. "Just what do you think you're doing?"

"Joining you. No one was sitting here," he said.

"Go away," Heather ordered, picking up the menu again.

"No."

Slamming the menu back on the table, she glared at the man. "Listen, I've had a long day. Maybe this tactic works with other women, but, well, for one thing, you are way too young for me. So please just leave."

"Hey, I'm not trying to pick up on you. And if I was, I'm not too young for you."

"What are you, barely twenty, if you're out of your teens? Just go away. Do I have to call a cop? I can, you know. There's one sitting right over there." She pointed briefly to Joe and Kelly, only to be met by a perplexed frown from Kelly.

"I'm older than I look," the stranger insisted. "Anyway, you have no idea how hard it is to find anyone willing to talk to me."

"I can imagine," Heather said with a snort.

"No, really. Please, I just need to talk to someone."

Before Heather could respond, the waitress walked up to the table. Heather quickly barked out her order and then added, "He's not having anything."

Heather's comment was met by a confused frown, but the waitress said nothing and walked away to put in the order.

"WHAT IS SHE DOING?" Kelly asked, staring at Heather across the diner.

Joe glanced over to Heather and shook his head. He looked back to Kelly. "Obviously talking to herself. And I have to say, she is having one hell of an animated conversation."

"I told you she's weird," Kelly grumbled. "I don't see why Chris hired her. But probably a charity case."

"Maybe she's talking to a ghost," Joe

teased as he picked up his burger the waitress had brought minutes earlier.

"Ghost?" Kelly frowned.

"Sure, she claimed she could see ghosts, remember?"

"Yeah, well, she also retracted that when I asked her about it once. Said she was just annoyed and trying to pull your guys' chains."

"Maybe she just has an imaginary friend," Joe suggested. "Or is talking on the phone." He took a bite of the burger.

"She's not on the phone," Kelly argued.

After swallowing his bite he said, "Earbuds. She's probably wearing earbuds."

"I don't see any." Kelly stood up.

Joe looked up at her. "Where are you going?"

"I'm going to see if she's on the phone."

WALT FOLLOWED Danielle into Lucy's Diner. They had decided at the last minute to drop in and get something to eat before heading home. The moment they walked into the restaurant, they froze when they spied the ghost they had seen that morning sitting at a booth with Heather.

"He's here—and with Heather," Danielle said under her breath, grabbing hold of Walt's hand. Danielle then noticed Kelly standing up from a booth on the other side of the diner, looking in Heather's direction.

"Yikes," Danielle yelped, holding tighter onto Walt's hand before dragging him along as she quickly made her way to Heather's booth.

Kelly arrived first and was just saying, "You're not talking on the phone?"

"Umm, no. Why?" Heather frowned up in confusion.

The next moment Walt and Danielle arrived at the booth. Danielle's gaze flashed nervously to the ghost and back to Kelly.

"Wow. It's getting crowded in here," Heather said dryly.

"We saw your car outside," Danielle lied, "and thought we would join you."

Heather looked to the ghost and said in a loud voice, "My friends are here, now will you leave?"

Danielle cringed. The next moment the ghost vanished.

"Oh crap…" Heather muttered, looking across at the now empty booth. Swallowing nervously, she glanced up at Kelly, who was staring at her like she had seven extra heads.

SIX

Danielle and Walt sat on the booth seat the ghost had been occupying moments earlier, while Kelly remained standing mute, staring down at Heather.

With a sigh of resignation Heather looked up to Kelly, her expression devoid of emotion, and said dryly, "Don't mind me. I often talk to myself."

"It's one of her endearing qualities," Danielle said cheerfully as she picked up a menu from the table and opened it.

"I…ah…just walked over here to see if everything was okay," Kelly stammered. She then looked back to Walt and Danielle and forced a smile. "How are you doing? I was just across the street from your house a little while ago, visiting with my adorable nephew."

"He is adorable, isn't he?" Danielle smiled up to Kelly.

"I get to babysit him tonight," Heather said.

Kelly turned abruptly to Heather, her eyes wide. "You are?"

"Don't worry, Connor is cool with me talking to myself," Heather quipped.

Kelly smiled lamely and said her good-byes, excusing herself to return to her table. When she was out of earshot, Heather groaned and tossed her head on her arms, which were now folded on the tabletop.

"I had no clue he was a ghost!" Heather groaned again, peeking up from her folded arms.

"Neither did I when he first appeared in our kitchen. I thought he had walked in the door without us noticing," Danielle said.

"So he was the one I was supposed to be looking out for?" Heather asked dully.

"Yep," Danielle said as she closed her menu.

The next moment the waitress showed up at the table and took Walt and Danielle's order. When she left, Walt asked, "Any chance he told you his name?"

Now sitting up straight, Heather shook her head. "No. I'm really sorry. I was trying to get rid of him. He just walked up, started talking to me, and sat down."

"What was he talking about?" Danielle asked.

"Nothing really. I thought he was trying to pick me up." Heather groaned again.

"What?" Danielle asked.

Heather glanced briefly at Joe and Kelly's table. Kelly was looking over at them, but quickly turned back to her own table when Heather's eyes met hers. Heather looked back to Danielle and said, "When he wouldn't leave, I threatened to call the police. You know, go over to Joe's table and get him to make the guy leave."

Danielle started to giggle.

Heather frowned. "It's not funny."

"Yes, it is," Walt said with a grin. "I'd love

to see Joe's face while you insist he remove the guy from your table."

"Oh, shut up." Heather picked up her glass of water and took a sip.

"Aww, stuff like this happens to all of us," Danielle reminded her.

Heather shrugged. "I guess it's no big deal. Ian's sister thinks I'm a wacko anyway."

"That's not true," Danielle argued.

"It's true," Walt teased.

Instead of getting mad at Walt, Heather looked at him and laughed. "You're starting to sound like Chris."

"How is he doing, by the way? Did you get him all tucked in?" Walt asked.

"Yeah, but I wish he would've agreed to stay with me. It's kind of creepy over there at night. That place is huge. Heck, it sometimes creeps me out during the day. Of course, now there's more people around. At least during the day," Heather said.

ON THE OTHER side of the diner, Kelly

picked up her cellphone and dialed her brother.

"Who are you calling?" Joe asked.

"I'm going to offer to babysit Connor tonight."

"What? I thought we were going to the show?" Joe asked.

Kelly frowned at Joe. "Don't you think Connor's safety is more important than seeing some stupid movie?"

"WELL, at least I know who to look for now," Heather said after the waitress brought her food. "What do you know about these people coming to stay at Marlow House, aside from the fact one of them may be a killer—and one a new victim?"

"The ghost never said that exactly. But the way he talked, it was like one of our guests could be in danger," Danielle explained.

"So what do you know?" Heather asked again.

"About their personal lives, not much," Walt said. "There is the producer, Jackie

Stafford, and her husband. I believe he's a photographer. Then there's the director, Teddy Larimore, and his wife. I think she's an actress, Polly Larimore."

"I've never heard of her," Heather said with a shrug. "Actually I've never heard of any of them—aside from Seraphina Bouchard. I'm not into following celebrities—but everyone knows who Seraphina is."

"I have a feeling Seraphina staying with us is going to drive Pearl batty," Danielle interjected.

Heather chuckled. "I assume you mean because of all the fans who're probably going to be cruising up our street to check her out."

"I wish Walt hadn't agreed to that interview," Danielle grumbled.

"I didn't really have a choice," Walt reminded her.

"They aren't even starting the movie for a couple of months, are they? Is this normal for the director and producer and some of the actors to come stay in the area before filming even starts?" Heather asked.

Walt shrugged. "I've no idea what's normal. This is a first for me. But from what I understand, it was a request made by the film's backer—Beatrice Adair, who'll be one of our guests. And as far as I know, Seraphina is the only actor from the film who'll be staying with us next week."

"Which is odd," Danielle said. "Seraphina's character isn't even the lead role."

"Okay, so you have the producer and her husband, that is one room," Heather said, counting on her fingers. "Then the director and his wife, that is two rooms. I assume Seraphina has her own room and then the backer. So that leaves one empty room. Who's going in there?"

"The room with the twin beds," Danielle said. "The producer's assistant is coming, and there might be another person, who'll share the room with him—or her. We don't know."

"WHERE WILL YOU BE STAYING?" Josie asked. She sat on the edge of the bed and watched as her roommate, Phoebe Greda, rummaged through their closet, deciding what to bring with her on the trip up to Oregon.

"With the others, at some place that used to be a bed and breakfast. The guy who owns it, he's the one who wrote *Moon Runners*."

"It must be a big place, if everyone is staying there."

"I have to share a room with Jackie's assistant, Bentley Mason," Phoebe explained.

"Oh, fun, co-ed," Josie teased.

"He's gay," Phoebe said dryly. "But he is good looking."

"Aren't all gay guys?" Josie quipped.

Phoebe laughed and went back to sorting through her clothes while her roommate watched.

Josie thought Phoebe the perfect example of how beautiful girls were a dime a dozen in Hollywood. Phoebe's dream of becoming an actress had not materialized. And while she had managed to associate with some heavy hitters, it was as an assistant through a childhood connection.

But Phoebe was an ambitious girl, and Josie had no doubt she would find a way to make her acting dream come true. Phoebe had that Lolita thing going for her. With the makeup off, her delicate features framed in an oval face, and her long blondish brown hair pulled back in a ponytail, she could easily pass for a teenager instead of her actual age of twenty-two.

Josie envied Phoebe her petite perfect nose, yet Josie knew if she saved her money, she could hire Phoebe's plastic surgeon to give her one just like it. While Phoebe insisted her full pouty lips were her own, Josie suspected she meant *her own* in the sense she had paid for them, as opposed to being born with them. Phoebe's most striking feature—in Josie's opinion—were her light color eyes. Not quite green or hazel, ever changing depending on the eye makeup.

"I can't believe she took you back," Josie said. "Especially after all that stuff that was in the newspaper about you and Barry."

Phocbc turned from the closet and faced Josie. "I told her at the time nothing happened. That it was all Barry's fault."

"But she saw you kissing him," she reminded her.

"No, she thought she saw us kissing. But

he was kissing me; I was not kissing him." Phoebe then added dramatically, "He was forcing himself on me!"

Josie rolled her eyes. "But that's not what happened."

Phoebe shrugged and turned back to the closet. "She doesn't know that. And I do regret it."

"I'm still surprised she rehired you."

Phoebe shrugged and turned back to Josie, now holding several hangers with blouses. "Sera and I go back a long way. Plus, my acting skills are obviously unappreciated."

"I'm not sure why you even want to go on this trip. What do you hope to gain from it?" Josie asked.

Phoebe tossed the clothes she had been holding on her bed and then sat down.

"It's all about contacts. I need to make friends with Jackie. I gave up on Teddy. Birdie Adair will be there. I would like a benefactor like that. I just have to convince her I never betrayed Sera."

"Why is Birdie so enamored of Seraphina? I know she's got a great voice, but they seem like an odd pair," Josie said.

"I think it's white guilt."

"White guilt?" Josie frowned.

"Sure, help out the poor black girl and make Birdie feel good about herself and worthy of that silver spoon she was born with. I told you how they met, when Birdie and her husband discovered Sera singing at a dive, and then the doors started opening for her. If you ask me, it was probably more about Randy Adair trying to score."

"Phoebe!" Josie admonished. "That is a horrible thing to say. Everyone knows Randy and Birdie were the real deal. He wouldn't have cheated on her."

Phoebe shrugged. "Maybe not. But one thing I've learned since moving to Hollywood, things are not always what they seem."

"Like you and Barry never being an item?" Josie teased.

"I said I regretted it. Anyway, I did Sera a favor."

"I know it's a horrible thing to say, but Barry being careless with his booze and drugs was probably a good thing for you. Stupidest thing you ever did was hook up with him."

"I know. You told me enough times."

"I could see the big picture, and Barry was not part of your master plan."

"You're right. I got sidetracked. I allowed Barry to throw me off my endgame. But that won't happen again," Phoebe promised.

SEVEN

Ian sat on the edge of the mattress, pulling on his socks, as his wife sat at the nearby dressing table, applying her makeup. In the nursery Marie entertained Connor while Sadie napped nearby.

"I have to say, I'm grateful Marie isn't anxious to move to the other side. I'm getting rather spoiled having her around to help," Lily said as she unscrewed the lid to her mascara.

"Have you considered how we're going to handle all this when Connor gets a little older—and can talk?" Ian asked.

Lily cringed. "Yeah…there is that. And I

wonder, will he just stop seeing her, like Marie did with Eva?"

"I don't know. Maybe not, since we acknowledge her." Ian let out a sigh. "And then there is the issue of my sister."

Holding the open mascara tube in her hand, Lily swung around on the stool and faced Ian. "Yeah, what was that all about? I thought when she was here, she told you she and Joe were going to the show tonight?"

"I have no idea why she suddenly got the bug to babysit. Maybe seeing Connor today?" Ian suggested with a shrug.

"I'm just glad you told her no. Nothing against your sister, but I just feel more comfortable having Marie and Heather here."

The doorbell rang and Ian stood up. "I'll get that."

A few minutes later Ian was leading Heather into the living room.

"Marie's in with Connor now," Ian told her.

"I kind of expected you to call and cancel for tonight," Heather said as she tossed her purse on the coffee table.

"Why?" Ian frowned.

"I ran into your sister at Lucy's this afternoon," Heather explained as she plopped down on the couch.

"And?" Ian asked, taking a seat on his recliner.

"You know that ghost Danielle wanted me to be on the lookout for?" As Heather asked the question, Lily walked into the room.

"What about him?" Ian asked.

"I ran into him at the diner; he sat down with me. I had no clue he was a ghost, and well, we were having quite the conversation," Heather explained.

"And my sister was there?" Ian asked.

Heather nodded. "Yep, her and Joe. Sitting right across the diner from me, in clear view."

"Ahhh, and Kelly saw you talking to yourself?" Lily asked with a chuckle as she sat down on the arm of Ian's chair.

Heather nodded. "It was embarrassing. I looked crazy."

"It does explain things. She called me late this afternoon, offering to babysit tonight. She was pretty insistent about it, but she never mentioned you," Ian said. "But she did say she and Joe were at Lucy's having dinner."

"Really? I'm surprised she didn't tell you what she saw," Heather said.

Someone yelled, "Hello!" from the entry hall, and the next minute Walt and Danielle walked into the living room. As they did, Sadie came running out from the nursery to greet them.

"Well, that's nice," Heather said with a snark. "She didn't come say hi to me when I got here."

Sadie wagged her tail excitedly and nosed Walt's hand.

"Don't mind Sadie. Other than Ian, we all play second fiddle to Walt when it comes to Sadie," Danielle said as she reached out and gave the dog a scratch behind her ears.

"I'm not even sure I don't come in second with her," Ian grumbled.

"You need to tell Dani and Walt about this," Lily said.

"You mean about my conversation with the ghost?" Heather asked. "They were there."

"Is that what you were talking about?"

Danielle asked. She then told the story from her perspective, and Ian told them about his sister's offer to babysit.

After they exhausted the conversation, Danielle asked, "You guys ready?"

"Where are you going tonight?" Heather asked.

"A play in Astoria," Lily explained.

"Maybe we can stop and get something to eat afterwards," Walt suggested. "Danielle and I had an early dinner at Lucy's, but I think I'm going to be hungry by then."

"You're always hungry," Danielle teased.

"Life makes me ravenous," Walt explained. "That's what happens when you have nothing to eat for almost a century."

"Are you all ready to go?" Marie asked when she popped into the room. She then added, "Connor fell asleep. I think I wore the poor dear out."

Heather conveyed Marie's words to Lily and Ian. They both stood up and Lily said, "Thanks, Marie, Heather, we appreciate you watching him."

"It's my pleasure. By the way, Eva told me

she would meet you at the theater," Marie said.

Heather arched her brows. "Eva is going?"

"She's the one who told us about the play," Walt explained. "It's some community theater presentation, and Eva's been haunting the rehearsals. I think she sees herself as part of the theater group."

"That's only because she's been hanging out with that Gordon Hershey." Marie snickered.

"Gordon Hershey?" Heather asked.

"Yes. He used to be a member of the theater group in Astoria. He died last year. Heart attack or something. Since then he's been haunting the theater and got friendly with Eva."

Heather shook her head and chuckled. "We live a weird life."

"Yes, we do," Lily said cheerfully. "And we'd better get going so we aren't late. But first, one last peek at Connor…"

AFTER IAN, Lily, Walt and Danielle left for Astoria, Heather stretched out on the sofa and picked up the book Lily had been reading earlier and began thumbing through it, while Marie went to check on the baby. Marie returned to the living room a few minutes later and found Heather laughing, book in hand.

"What's so funny?" Marie asked.

"This book has the best opening line." Heather snickered.

"What book is that?"

Heather turned the cover over so she could read it. "*The Ghost at His Back*, by Cameron Lowe."

Marie perked up. "Ghosts? It's a book about ghosts?"

"Yep." Heather turned the book around and reopened it to the first page. She snickered again and said, "Great opening line."

"Are you going to tell me?" Marie urged.

"'Ghosts arc assholes'," Heather read.

"Heather Donovan, that is a rude thing to say!" Marie snapped.

"Hey, you asked me what the opening line was. It's Cameron Lowe's words, not mine," Heather reminded her.

"It's just awful!" Marie said in outrage as her energy tore the book from Heather's hand and sent it flying across the room.

Heather's eyes widened. She remained on the sofa, looking from her now empty hands to the book that had landed on the floor at the base of the bookcase. "Kinda proved Lowe's point," Heather muttered under her breath.

"I wish I could do that. You're a ghost, aren't you?" A male voice broke the momentary silence.

Both Marie and Heather turned and found a young man—the ghost they had both seen earlier that day.

"Don't leave," Heather blurted, sitting up quickly on the sofa.

"At the restaurant you couldn't get rid of me fast enough," he said in a pout.

"I'm sorry. I was having a bad day. Let's start fresh." Heather forced a smile. "My name is Heather, and this is my friend Marie, who, like you, is a ghost. And you are?"

"Nice to meet you. I'm…" He paused and then shook his head. "No. You're trying to trick me."

"At least answer some other questions," Heather urged.

"What?" he asked with a frown.

"This morning you told my friends you wanted to prevent a murder—that someone—but you aren't sure who—might be killed by the same person who killed you," Heather said.

"They told you all that?" he asked.

"Yes. We need to know, these potential victims, are you talking about the people who are coming to stay at Marlow House this week, the ones making *Moon Runners* into a movie?"

"*Moon Runners*," he grumbled. "If it wasn't for that book, I'd still be alive."

"Please answer my question," Heather pleaded.

"Yes. That's who I was talking about," he said after a moment of silence.

"I want to know, how was *Moon Runners* responsible for your death?" Marie asked.

"I can't say, because you might figure out who my killer was, and I don't want to get anyone in trouble. I just don't want anyone else to get hurt," he insisted.

"Goodness gracious, why in the world would you want to protect your killer?" Marie snapped. "I was murdered, and I certainly had no desire to protect my killer, I will tell you that!"

The ghost stared at Marie for a moment and then said, "Wow, your killer must have been a real creep, to kill an old lady like you."

Marie let out a gasp and then said, "I suppose sometimes it is true!"

"What's true?" The man frowned.

Heather chuckled. "You're talking about that opening line in the book you just hurled across the room."

Marie looked sheepishly at the book. "Yes, and I suppose that was not a nice thing to do —I could have damaged it." The next moment said book floated up from the floor and drifted over to Heather, landing on the coffee table, still intact.

Looking from the book to the unidentified ghost, Heather asked, "What makes you think those people might be in danger? Did your killer threaten one of them?"

The ghost pondered the question a moment and then shook his head. "No. But considering what happened to me and the fact they're all going to be here—together—for an entire week. Something could happen. And I don't want to be responsible."

"Is the killer one of the guests staying at Marlow House?" Heather asked.

He began shaking his head. "I have said too much." The next moment he disappeared.

SNUGGLED on the sofa under a lap quilt, her feet tucked under her and *The Ghost at His Back* in her hands, Heather was so engrossed in the story she failed to hear someone unlock the front door and enter the house. Sadie heard the intruder but greeted them with a quiet tail wag. Walt had lectured Sadie on proper barking while a baby was in the house—especially a sleeping baby. Unless there was a threat of danger, resist the urge to bark, he had told her.

Heather about leapt from the sofa when a voice said, "Hi, Heather." Standing at the entrance to the living room was Kelly

Bartley and her boyfriend, police officer Joe Morelli.

"We just got back from the show, and I thought I would stop by and check on Connor," Kelly said sweetly.

Still on the sofa, Heather said, "I could swear I locked the front door."

Kelly held up the spare key in her hand. "I have a key. And I didn't want to knock, afraid it would get Sadie to barking and wake up the baby if he was sleeping. So I just used my key." She smiled sweetly.

"I guess the baby is sleeping?" Joe said.

"Umm…yeah…" Heather muttered. Actually, Connor had been sleeping but had woken up crying a few minutes earlier. Marie was in the nursery changing his diaper and feeding him a bottle.

"I'll just peek in…" Kelly began, only to be stopped by Heather's frantic, "No!"

Kelly stopped in her tracks and looked at Heather inquisitively.

"Umm…" Heather blushed. "I just mean, he's sleeping. I just got him down. I don't want to wake him."

"I'm just going to take a quick peek—I'll

be quiet, promise." Not waiting for Heather's approval, Kelly turned and made her way to the nursery.

MARIE KISSED Connor's nose as she refastened his sleeper. He had been fed, burped, diaper changed, and it was time to put him back in his crib for a lullaby. Tucking her hands gently under his arms, she lifted him up and carried him to the crib. The use of her hands was only for show. She didn't want Connor to imagine himself flying around the room and come to believe that normal. From Connor's perspective, Marie's hands lifted him up from the changing table and carried him to the crib—as opposed to Marie's spiritual energy moving him through the air like Peter Pan flying on fairy dust.

She reached the crib and lifted him up and over it, letting him hover there a moment to give him a kiss, when a chilling scream broke the silence.

EIGHT

By the time Heather and Joe rushed to the nursery, Connor was in his crib, making little gasping sounds, trying to catch his breath after being frightened by his aunt's unexpected outburst. Marie stood by his side, soothing him until he caught his breath. His little mouth turned into a pitiful pout as tears squeezed out from his now watery eyes. Marie glared up at Kelly and then looked down at the baby as she whispered reassuring words to him.

Kelly was no longer screaming but stood frozen just inside the door, staring at the crib, making no attempt to get closer. Joe, thinking something horrible had happened to the baby, rushed by Kelly, straight to the crib, and was relieved to find the baby breathing, yet obviously on the verge of tears. He was about to pick up Connor when Heather pushed by him and shoved him out of the way.

Joe watched as Heather picked up the baby, comforting him in her arms. He then turned to Kelly. When doing so, he failed to notice that Sadie sat quietly by the crib. Had he taken a moment to consider her demeanor, he would have thought it strange behavior for a dog, who would normally be more hyped up after hearing someone screaming the house down. But what he didn't know, Marie had already conveyed to Sadie what had occurred and asked her to stay quietly out of the way.

"What happened?" Joe asked Kelly.

"Silly girl, she scared the dickens out of the poor boy," Marie said, knowing Joe and Kelly had no idea she was even there.

Connor, no longer on the verge of tears, happily snuggled against Heather's shoulder as she glanced curiously at Kelly, wondering what exactly she had seen. Heather could only guess. She knew she would be expected to chastise Kelly for the outburst—considering how she would normally behave when someone let out a shout in the nursery after being reminded to be quiet. Yet Heather knew it was not Kelly's fault—plus she was desperately holding in laughter, imagining all the possible scenarios Kelly might have walked in on.

"What happened?" Joe repeated, now at Kelly's side, placing a reassuring hand on her shoulder.

Kelly pointed at the baby and said, "He was flying."

Joe's expression went blank. "Excuse me?"

"He was flying—over the crib," Kelly said in a small shaky voice.

"And you think I'm weird for talking to myself." Heather laughed and then walked over to the crib and put Connor down.

"What did you see?" Joe asked, ignoring Heather.

Kelly rubbed her temple with the heel of her right hand and shook her head wearily. "Of course he was not flying. That was a silly thing to say. I…my…eyes were playing tricks on me…that must be it."

"Some trick," Heather said.

"I think you're enjoying this a little too much," Marie scolded Heather.

"I think we should go," Joe said, leading Kelly from the room.

"What happened?" Heather asked Marie in a whisper after Joe and Kelly left the nursery.

"I was just putting Connor in his crib when she walked in. Why in the world did you let her in here? You knew I could be in the middle of changing him—or feeding him—or just carrying him across the room," Marie asked.

"You think I could stop her? Short of tackling her, she was determined to come in here."

"Well, you should have figured out some way to get in here before her, to warn me," Marie said.

"I know," Heather grumbled, glancing to the door.

"And you were enjoying her discomfort a little too much."

"You were annoyed with her when she first barged in," Heather reminded.

"Yes, but if things like this keep happening, I'm afraid Lily and Ian won't let me watch Connor anymore," Marie said.

Heather let out a sigh, deciding to take the situation more seriously. "Okay, where exactly was Connor when she walked in?"

Marie told her.

Heather glanced from the crib then to the door. The next moment she sprinted into the hall and then the living room. There Joe and Kelly stood in the middle of the room, quietly talking amongst themselves. When Heather walked in, Joe looked up and announced they were getting ready to leave.

"No, I think we need to talk first. I'm pretty sure I can explain what Kelly saw," Heather said.

"I'm curious to hear this," Marie muttered and then took a seat in an imaginary chair. She hovered above the three.

Heather glanced up to Marie and said, "I hate when you do that."

"What?" Joe asked with a frown.

Heather looked back to Joe and grinned. "See, I was talking to myself again."

"I'm not sure if you're trying to make me

feel better about myself or more crazy," Kelly grumbled.

"Okay, here's the thing…when I'm talking, I know exactly who I'm talking to—even if it's simply to myself. I don't imagine I'm talking to a unicorn or anything. I just like to think out loud," Heather said.

"So you aren't trying to make me feel better—just more crazy?" Kelly asked.

"You aren't very good at this," Marie said. "Danielle is much better at this game than you. If she was here, she would already have come up with a logical story to explain Connor floating over the crib."

"I imagine Ian hasn't told you—but Connor has become quite the jumper," Heather said.

"Jumper?" Joe asked.

"Yeah…you know, how some babies manage to climb out of cribs. Well, Connor doesn't do that. But he does stand up, and when he does, he likes to jump. I bet you saw Connor when he did one of his jumps," Heather suggested.

"Jumps?" Kelly asked.

"Yeah, you know, he manages to stand up,

and then he jumps up and down on the mattress. Gets kinda high. Looks like he's floating over the crib sometimes. I think he's going to be a gymnast," Heather said.

Marie groaned. "That is the stupidest thing I've ever heard."

Kelly seemed to be considering Heather's words for a few moments. Finally she said in relief, "I thought I was going crazy."

"She is crazy if she believes that preposterous story," Marie said.

INSTEAD OF GRABBING something to eat in Astoria after the play, the foursome decided to head back to Frederickport and stop at Pier Café before going home. They pulled into the parking lot and found Joe and Kelly getting out of their car. Ian pulled up next to Joe and parked.

"Coming for pie or a late night dinner?" Ian asked his sister as his foursome met up with Kelly and Joe.

"Pie for me. I think Joe is getting a burger," Kelly said. "How was the play?"

"It was good," Lily told her.

By the time they all reached the diner, it was decided they would sit together.

They had just sat down at the table when Kelly said, "I have to say, Connor freaked me out. Why didn't you tell me he could jump like that?"

No one answered immediately, but the original foursome exchanged glances.

"You were at our house?" Ian asked.

"We were in the neighborhood and had just gotten out of the show," Kelly explained. "I thought I would just stop by and peek in on Connor."

Before anyone could respond, Carla walked up to the table and took their drink order.

"How exactly did Connor freak you out?" Lily asked after Carla left the table. "Is he okay?"

"Yes, he's fine. But when I walked in his room—well, I know this sounds crazy, but it looked like he was flying."

FORTY MINUTES LATER, Walt, Danielle, Heather, and Marie sat with Lily and Ian in their living room. Heather had just finished explaining her version of the encounter with Kelly and Joe.

"Connor doesn't even stand yet," Lily said.

"Like I always say, people believe what is convenient," Walt said.

"I thought I always said that?" Ian asked.

"Whoever said it, it's true," Danielle said.

"I never even considered you would run into Kelly and Joe before I could talk to you." Heather groaned.

"Fortunately we figured something had happened, so we mostly listened and didn't comment on Connor's supposed jumping," Lily explained.

"The next time we go away, you need to use the deadbolt," Ian said. "I don't want to ask Kelly for the key, but at the same time, we can't have her just barging in the house like that. It could have been worse."

"I'm so grateful you're saying that," Marie said. "I was afraid you wouldn't let me stay with Connor again."

Danielle conveyed Marie's words to Lily and Ian.

"But there is some good news to report," Heather said.

"What is that?" Ian asked.

"We saw the ghost again," Heather explained.

"Did you learn anything?" Danielle asked.

"Unfortunately he refused to give us his name or his killer's," Heather began. "But he confirmed who he was talking about—in regard to the possible victim or victims. It's who you thought. The houseguests coming this week."

"And the killer? Is the killer among them?" Walt asked.

"He wouldn't say," Heather said.

"I thought you said you had good news," Lily said. "None of that sounds too good."

"According to the ghost, the killer didn't make any threats against anyone—and as far as the ghost knows, the killer isn't planning anything. He feels that getting all these people together might trigger something," Heather explained.

"We don't know much more than we did before," Danielle said with a groan.

"You now know one of your guests might get murdered. Before, you didn't know for sure if he was talking about your guests," Heather reminded her.

"Like I said, not sure why you think that is good news," Lily said.

NINE

Bentley Mason gave his boss credit, she never seemed particularly upset when a new business contact extended a hand in greeting, believing him to be Jack Stafford. A sure sign the new contact hadn't done his or her homework prior to the meeting. But he had to admit, he looked more the part of producer, with his perfectly coifed dark hair, neatly trimmed at the sides with a pompadour. He rocked the designer stubble. Today he wore a dark suit jacket over his crisply ironed mauve dress shirt, sans the tie. If not a producer, many assumed he was an actor instead of the producer's assistant.

He sat across from Jackie at the table, their lunch meeting had ended ten minutes earlier, and the most recent person to mistake him for his boss had just left the restaurant. Bentley stayed behind with Jackie so they could review some last minute details about their upcoming trip to Oregon.

Silently waiting for Jackie to finish looking over her notes, Bentley studied her features. The word *wholesome* came to mind, with her red hair neatly trimmed, falling just above her shoulders. Freckles dusted her face, and when Jackie smiled, she showed off straight white teeth. Her brows arched perfectly over hazel eyes, and he thought she looked more like a girl off the farm as opposed to the shrewd businesswoman she was.

A sharp pain shooting from his lower back disrupted his mental musing. Sitting up straighter, he reached back and grabbed hold of his right hip and winced. The motion caused Jackie to look up from her notes.

"Did you take something for that?" she asked.

"Yes, before we ate."

"You need to do something about that back," she chastised.

"The doctor says I can either live with it with some good drugs, or get surgery. I opt for drugs." He rubbed the sore area and then relaxed. "It feels better now."

"You're too young to have back problems," she said.

"Tell that to my back," he grumbled.

She set her notes aside and said, "By the way, did I mention Seraphina took Phoebe back?"

Bentley arched his brows. "How did that happen?"

Jackie shrugged. "I have no idea. But she's coming with us and will be staying in your room."

"With me?" Bentley choked out.

"You don't look thrilled?" she teased.

He rolled his eyes.

"Most men would love the idea of sharing a room with the lovely Phoebe."

"Cute," he said dryly. "She's not really my type."

"It's why I was glad they had a room with twin beds. I thought this might happen."

"I can't believe you thought Seraphina would take Phoebe back. You must know something juicy you aren't sharing," Bentley said.

"I just assumed Seraphina might be hiring another assistant—and if she did, she'd want the assistant to come along. Although I have no idea why a singer needs her own personal assistant."

"I heard Birdie paid Phoebe's salary," Bentley said in a whisper.

Jackie shrugged, disinterested. "I heard that too. Frankly, I thought Birdie would lose interest in her little project after Randy's death. But I suppose it keeps her occupied, and as long as she continues to fund this project, she can pay for all the assistants she wants."

"I'M LOOKING FORWARD to it. I think it'll be fun," Polly Larimore said as she chopped the greens for their dinner salad. Her husband, Teddy, sat at the nearby home bar, drinking a gin martini. "I just wish there was some way to see my brother while we're in Oregon."

"You can see him another time. This isn't exactly a pleasure trip. I'm not particularly looking forward to staying in a bed and breakfast with a bunch of people I don't care about." Teddy Larimore, who was a good fifteen years older than his wife, showed no signs of gray in his head of dark brown hair. Which made one suspect considering the tinge of gray along the outer corners of his shortly cropped beard. Like his beard, he wore his hair neatly trimmed, with the outer edges cut short, its back length touching his collar, and the front combed forward, almost touching his bushy brows.

"What are you talking about? We've been friends with Jackie and Julius for years," Polly reminded him.

"Jackie is a business associate. It doesn't mean I particularly want to vacation with her and Julius. And this trip is nothing more than an unnecessary work trip to appease Birdie. I'd rather go up there without all the additional baggage."

Does he consider me part of this additional baggage? Polly asked herself.

Teddy downed his martini. Setting the glass on the bar top, he looked over to the kitchen island, watching his wife prepare their salad. She'd had her dark hair cut that afternoon in a perky wedge.

"Why didn't you get highlights this time?" he asked.

Polly glanced up from the cutting board. "I just didn't. Thought I would try something different."

"You look better with highlights." He fished his gin-soaked olive from the martini glass and then ate it.

"I can get them next time," she told him.

Picking the empty glass off the bar top, he stood up and carried it to the kitchen island and set it down for Polly to wash.

"I talked to Seraphina today," Polly told him, dumping the lettuce she had just chopped into a large bowl and ignoring the martini glass.

"Why are you talking to Seraphina?" he asked.

"We've gotten close. I've been giving her some acting tips," she said.

"Leave her alone, Polly. You haven't had a role in over five years, and if I want your help, I'll ask you."

"She asked me," Polly said in a small voice.

"She shouldn't have. You're the director's wife, not an acting coach."

"You said I might be able to get a part in *Moon Runners*."

"What did Seraphina have to say?" he asked, ignoring her comment.

"You will never guess, but she hired Phoebe back."

"Why would she do that?" he asked.

Polly shrugged. "She said something about it all being a misunderstanding, that there really hadn't been anything between Barry and Phoebe. And that Phoebe had been as hurt as she had been, and she wanted to make things right."

"That doesn't mean she has to rehire her."

"And she's coming to Oregon," Polly added.

"What!" Teddy said louder than he had intended. The outburst made Polly jump.

"I don't know why you're so upset. Anyway, I thought you liked Phoebe?"

"She's Seraphina's assistant. I don't particularly like or dislike her. But we don't need that type of drama."

Polly giggled.

Teddy furrowed his brows and asked sternly, "What's so funny?"

"You know *movie crew—drama*. Isn't drama what you do?" Polly giggled again.

"Don't be obtuse," he snapped.

"I'm not being obtuse! Goodness, Teddy, do you have to be so cranky all the time? You don't like my hair. You don't want me helping Seraphina. You don't like my jokes!"

Teddy let out a sigh. "I'm just tired. I'm not looking forward to this trip. I would rather scout the area without taking an entire entourage along."

"Can't you just try to enjoy yourself?" Polly asked. "It's been so long since we've gone anywhere together. I know it's for work, but the Oregon coast is beautiful, and I'm excited to be staying at Marlow House."

"Why?" He frowned. "We've stayed at B and Bs before, and from what I understand, it's just a house now."

"Haven't you read about it?"

"Read about it? It's the house where the author lives, why would I read about it?"

"It's fascinating. There are lots of articles about Marlow House online. Did you know it was built by the founder of the town, who happened to be one of Walt Marlow's distant cousins? In fact, he was named for the grandson of the founder, and he looks just like him."

"Yes, I've heard all that, so?"

"Did you know some people think Marlow House is haunted?" she asked.

He laughed. "Don't they always say old houses are haunted?"

"I'm serious. And there have been a number of murders at the house." She sounded far too happy to be delivering that piece of news.

"Then I suppose Chase should be staying at Marlow House instead of Bentley. Sounds like the perfect place to inspire a writer," Teddy said sarcastically.

"Actually it is. I never understood why Chase insisted on getting his own place. Surely they could have put Bentley in some nearby motel," Polly said.

Teddy shrugged. "Chase doesn't like anyone around while he's writing. It would be more convenient for him to stay in Marlow House so he could easily collaborate with Marlow. But I suspect it is his way of keeping Marlow at a distance. You know Chase, when he's adapting a book, he sees the final project as his own and doesn't appreciate the original author butting in too much—especially a new author, like Marlow."

"It is Walt Marlow's story," Polly countered.

"And I trust Chase to do an excellent job with the screenplay. He is one of the best."

"Then why has he never even been nominated for an Oscar? Or an Emmy, for that matter," she asked.

"It's the politics. Chase is not that well liked in the industry, and you know it."

"Well, I'm just glad we're staying at Marlow House. I wish you were looking forward to it too."

"Fine, I'll try to enjoy myself," he promised unconvincingly.

"Dinner should be ready in five minutes," she said brightly.

"I'm going to my office to make a quick call."

"Don't take too long. Dinner is almost ready."

"It won't take long," he said before turning away.

A few minutes later he stood alone in his home office, the door closed, and his cellphone to his ear. When the party answered, he asked in a harsh voice, "What are you up to?"

"Oh, Teddy, I was wondering when I would be hearing from you," the female voice purred.

"I'm warning you, Phoebe," he hissed.

TEN

Joanne Johnson spent Thursday putting fresh sheets on all the beds in Marlow House, washing a load of towels, along with cleaning all the bathrooms, vacuuming the house from top to bottom, and dusting. For a woman with a full load of chores she had a cheerful outlook, eagerly anticipating the guests. The housekeeper had missed the B and B. She enjoyed meeting the different people who had stayed at Marlow House, and there always seemed to be something interesting happening, although she could have done without a few of the murders.

On Friday morning she made a trip to the

grocery store to purchase necessary items for the upcoming week. She had already returned and had put everything away, filling Marlow House's pantry and refrigerator, and now sat at the kitchen table, reviewing the upcoming week's menu with Danielle. Danielle was just refilling Joanne's cup with coffee when the back door opened and in walked Lily and Sadie.

"Morning, Dani, Joanne," Lily greeted them cheerfully as Sadie went to press a wet nose against Joanne's hand, and then Danielle's, while her tail wagged. Danielle gave the golden retriever a scratch behind her ears before the dog ran out of the kitchen, looking for Walt.

"Hello, Lily," Joanne said with a smile.

"Want some coffee?" Danielle asked, still standing by the coffee pot.

"I would love a cup," Lily said as she sat at the table and then lifted the lid off the cake pan sitting in the middle of the table.

"Help yourself," Danielle said just as Lily snatched one of the cinnamon rolls off the plate.

"I was going to." Lily giggled.

Danielle chuckled and then grabbed a clean cup from the cupboard for Lily.

"I understand you have your hands full now," Joanne said.

Pulling the sticky roll in half, Lily gave Joanne a questioning look.

"I ran into your sister-in-law at the grocery store this morning," Joanne explained. "She tells me Connor isn't just standing now, he's jumping—and quite high. My, he is a precocious one! He's barely six months. I don't think my niece's son could stand on his own until he was nine months."

"Kelly sure is a chatty thing," Lily grumbled under her breath before shoving a piece of roll in her mouth.

"One of my friend's sons walked at nine months," Danielle said as she brought the coffee cups to the table.

"Fact is, Connor is not doing that much jumping," Lily said. *Or standing*, she thought.

"Little ones certainly keep you busy," Joanne said. "But if he's already standing—much less jumping—I'd say you have a pistol on your hands!"

Lily smiled dully at Joanne as she accepted a cup of coffee from Danielle. She then changed the subject and asked, "So when are your guests going to be here?"

"They should be arriving any time now," Danielle said as she took a seat. Just as she sat down, she glanced at the kitchen window and spotted a man standing outside looking in at them.

"Either that's one of them now who decided to come to the back door, or Seraphina's fans are going to be more annoying than we imagined."

As Danielle stood up, both Lily and Joanne turned around and looked at the window.

"What are you talking about?" Lily asked.

Danielle pointed to the window. "The man."

"What man?" Lily asked.

Joanne stood up and made it to the door before Danielle. She jerked it open and looked outside. Glancing back to Danielle, she said, "There's no one out here. What did you think you saw?"

"ANOTHER GHOST?" Lily asked Danielle after they left Joanne alone in the kitchen.

"I assume that's what it has to be. I saw him standing there, even after Joanne opened the door and looked outside. And then he vanished."

"And it wasn't the ghost you saw the other day?" Lily asked.

Danielle shook her head. "No. It was another guy. Different person. Getting a little crowded around here."

Danielle and Lily headed to the library to tell Walt what Danielle had just seen when the doorbell rang.

PHOEBE HAD DRIVEN the rental car from the Portland Airport to Frederickport, allowing Seraphina to sit in the back seat with Beatrice Adair—or Birdie, as she liked to be called. When Birdie had asked to travel with Seraphina, even offering to pay for all the travel expenses, Seraphina had said yes —and no.

While Seraphina appreciated all that Birdie and Randy had done for her, there was no reason for Birdie to continue picking up the tab. Seraphina could pay her own way—plus she was acutely aware of how much she owed Birdie.

The time had passed quickly from the airport to Frederickport, and they now stood on the front porch of Marlow House, waiting for someone to answer the door. Seraphina smiled inwardly, thinking about the first time they had met. She had thought Birdie the stereotypical rich white lady—or at least, how she had once imagined one might be, before she had met any. At sixty-three, Birdie had only slight creases around the corners of her brown eyes, and Seraphina would describe her as mature as opposed to old looking. If Birdie had ever been flighty or youthful, it was before Seraphina had met the woman.

Fair skinned, Birdie wore her thin blond hair down, its ends turning up into a slight flip at the shoulders. She wore makeup with restraint, plum lipstick and black eyeliner. Slim and tall, Birdie had been fairly active and fit. But after Randy's death she had taken a fall and now used a cane and found it difficult to walk without one. It was one reason Seraphina would not try coming up with an excuse to avoid flying to Portland with Birdie. Birdie needed assistance traveling now, and she and Randy had been there when Seraphina had first started her career. In fact, if not for Birdie and Randy, she would not have landed the role in *Moon Runners*.

Seraphina could tell Birdie was not happy that she had taken Phoebe back, but since she was no longer paying the woman's wage, she didn't think it was any of her business. Fortunately Phoebe seemed to be going out of her way to work her way back into the older woman's good graces. Normally it wouldn't matter, but they would be spending the next week together.

The front door finally swung open and she found herself facing not one—but three people. The man she recognized immediately, Walt Marlow, the author of *Moon Runners*. He was as handsome as the picture on his book jacket. Next to him were two attractive thirtysomething women, both much shorter than herself, with the redhead being the shortest.

Forty minutes later Seraphina sat in the library with Walt and Danielle Marlow. Shortly after arriving, they had been introduced to their hosts, along with a neighbor and the housekeeper, Joanne Johnson. They were shown to their rooms, where Seraphina had eventually left Phoebe to unpack for her.

Birdie had been given the downstairs bedroom so she wouldn't have to maneuver the stairs. The Marlows' neighbor had said her goodbyes and left with her golden retriever, and now Seraphina enjoyed a cup of green tea with her hosts.

"You have a beautiful home," Seraphina said. "I love that it's been in your family for years. I always envy those who have such a strong sense of family history."

Phoebe walked into the library. "Everything is unpacked."

"Help yourself to some tea and cookies," Danielle told Phoebe, pointing to the tea set and plate of cookies on the table.

"When do we get that tour of the house?"

Phoebe asked brightly as she picked up a cookie.

"When Birdie is finished getting settled in her room," Seraphina told her.

"I did offer to help her." Phoebe poured herself a cup of tea. "But she insisted on doing everything herself."

"You know how Birdie prizes her privacy," Seraphina reminded her.

CHRIS DIDN'T BOTHER KNOCKING. Marlow House always felt like a second home to him. He entered through the kitchen door and found Joanne standing at the counter, chopping up vegetables.

"Hi, Chris," Joanne greeted him, looking up from the cutting board.

"Hi, Joanne. I saw a strange car out front. Some of the people get here?" He lifted the lid from the cake pan on the kitchen table and snatched the remaining cinnamon roll.

"I'm telling Walt you took the last one," she teased.

"How about I give you half?" he asked.

"Deal."

With a laugh Chris tore the cinnamon roll in half and handed one side to Joanne.

"So, who's here?" Chris asked.

"The singer. She's in the library now with Walt and Danielle."

"Ohh…Seraphina…I have to meet her. I'm a big fan." He started for the kitchen door but was stopped when Joanne called his name. He paused and looked at her.

"If I were you, I would finish that roll before you walk in there, and Walt sees it."

Chris chuckled. "You have a point." He finished the roll and then licked his fingers as he left the kitchen.

When Chris barreled into the library a few minutes later, he froze in his tracks the moment his eyes set on Seraphina. He hadn't expected her to be so—so—stunning in person. How could it be possible she looked even better in real life, he wondered.

It was not just her appearance and talent that had fascinated him—it was her story. Like him, she had been raised in foster care after her parents had been killed in an accident. But unlike him, she had never gotten out of the foster care system. At least, not until she came of age.

She wore her long black curls down and free flowing, and while he suspected she wore makeup, he couldn't see the makeup—just the results, which were flawless. As much as he was physically attracted to her, it wasn't her celebrity status that pulled in his reins, it was her age—which was even more apparent in person. Seraphina was young—barely in her twenties. With a sigh, he flashed the room his lopsided grin and approached the group.

"Chris, hi," Danielle greeted him.

"Playing hooky from work?" Walt teased.

"The boss won't notice I'm gone," Chris retorted, then turned his attention to Seraphina and Phoebe.

"Seraphina, Phoebe, I'd like you to meet a good friend of ours, Chris Johnson."

PHOEBE SIPPED her tea and silently studied the handsome and hunky Chris Johnson. She had noticed his last name was the same as the housekeeper's. *Must be a son or younger brother*, she thought. He wasn't wearing a wedding ring, and he was far too young to be the housekeeper's husband. Plus, men who looked like that did not settle for women who looked like the housekeeper—not unless she was as rich as Birdie.

Like most of the men they encountered, his attention focused on Seraphina. The celebrity in the room always got first billing. *I will not always be in the background*, Phoebe thought. Someday she too would be walking that red carpet. She listened as Chris peppered Seraphina with countless questions and annoying praises. He didn't even make an attempt to conceal his obvious adoration. Yes, he was ridiculously good looking. But so? Beautiful men were a common commodity in Seraphina's world. Although, Phoebe had to admit, he was damn exceptional in the looks department. Made a woman drool.

Seraphina flashed Chris one of those smiles. Phoebe knew that smile. The foolish woman was interested in the housekeeper's son—or brother. Whoever he was. No, that was not going to happen. The last thing Phoebe needed was a new love interest hanging around while she was trying to rebuild her relationship with Sera. What inevitably always happened, the man grew weary of Sera, and then he turned his attention to Phoebe. Phoebe didn't need that type of aggravation right now, especially since a man with Chris's looks might be difficult to turn down.

ELEVEN

A knock came at the library's open doorway. Danielle glanced over to see Birdie peeking into the room.

"So this is where you're all hiding," Birdie said as she stepped into the library.

"Are you all unpacked?" Seraphina asked.

"Yes..." Birdie glanced around the four walls, a collection of dark paneling and floor-to-ceiling bookshelves housing a massive collection of leather-bound books. "I just love home libraries. And this one is exceptional."

As her gaze washed over the room, it came to an unfamiliar person sitting next to

Seraphina. She paused a moment and just stared.

"This is Chris, Birdie. Chris, this is Birdie —" Seraphina began.

"You're one of the cast members!" Birdie declared. "Teddy and Jackie didn't mention any of them were coming, aside from Seraphina. But you must be the new actor playing Hunter Rage, am I right? Teddy mentioned there was a problem with the original actor cast in the role."

Chris broke into a wide Cheshire cat grin and turned the smile to Walt. "Whatcha say, Walt? Would I be perfect for the main character from your book?"

Walt rolled his eyes. "I would prefer someone who can act rather than just standing there and looking pretty."

"You think I'm pretty?" Chris asked in a goofy voice.

Danielle broke into a chuckle and then said, "No, Birdie. This is a friend of Walt's and mine. Chris Johnson. Chris, I would like you to meet Birdie Adair."

Chris stood, smiled at Birdie, and shook her hand while offering her a cordial greeting.

"You could be an actor," Birdie declared when their brief handshake ended.

Chris thanked her and returned to his seat while Birdie continued her inspection of the room. She stopped a moment later at the life-sized portraits and began studying them.

"Isn't it eerie how much Walt looks like the man in the portrait?" Seraphina asked Birdie.

Still focused on the portrait, Birdie nodded. "It is amazing. If I hadn't heard the story behind these paintings, I would assume it was of Walt."

"If you think about it, it is. Wasn't his name Walt too?" Phoebe asked.

Ignoring Phoebe's comment, Birdie turned her attention to the second portrait. "This is the wife, the one you believe tried to kill him?" Birdie asked Danielle.

"Yes. Her name was Angela," Danielle said.

Birdie turned to Phoebe and said, "You know, she looks a little like you. If they ever make a movie about the gold-digging little opportunist, I think you would be perfect for the part."

Phoebe's expression went blank, and the room grew uncomfortably silent.

"We have some cookies and tea. Would you like me to pour you a cup?" Danielle asked abruptly a moment later.

Birdie turned to Danielle and smiled. "No, thank you. Not right now. But you mentioned a tour when we first arrived. I would love to see the rest of the house."

"There are a lot of stairs. Are you sure you can handle it?" Phoebe asked.

Birdie smiled sweetly at Phoebe and said, "Stairs might slow me down a little these days, but I am persistent. If I really want to do something, I usually find a way to do it."

"If you'd like, we can have that tour now," Walt said as he stood up.

WALT AND DANIELLE led the house tour, with Birdie walking with Walt, and Danielle following them with Phoebe. Chris and Seraphina trailed behind, the two continually chatting it up amongst themselves, lost in their own private conversation. Phoebe continually flashed the pair annoyed glances over her shoulder, but neither one seemed to notice.

They started in the library, where Walt discussed the extensive collection of books once owned by the original Walt Marlow—the one who had been murdered in the attic almost a century earlier. What none of them knew—aside from Danielle and Chris—he was that other Walt Marlow, now residing in what had been the body of a distant cousin by the same name. His cousin had willingly checked out of the body during a coma, wanting instead to move on with his recently deceased fiancée. Walt of today had accepted the gift—and another chance at life.

From the library they went into the dining room, and then the kitchen, and to the parlor. When they returned to the entry hall, Walt asked if they would like to see the basement, and since they had read about the tunnel that ran under the street from the Marlows' basement to a neighbor's house, they all wanted to see—even Birdie who told them it might take her a little longer to get down the stairs, but she could do it. Ten minutes later, the group stood in the basement.

"So where is this tunnel?" Phoebe asked.

"You can't see it now," Danielle explained. She then removed a key from a hook on the wall and used it to unlock a padlock on what appeared to be a low-hanging cabinet door. After removing the padlock, she swung open the door, revealing a dark, damp enclosure.

"This is where the access used to be," Danielle explained. "We replaced the original panel with this door, but we had considered just closing up the wall after we sealed off the tunnel."

The three guests peeked into the dark enclosure.

"But where is the tunnel?" Birdie asked.

"Technically speaking, it's still there," Danielle said. "But it's been sealed off from both sides."

Removing her cellphone from a pocket, Phoebe turned on the flashlight app and used it to illuminate the opening. She looked inside. On its far wall was another door, and like the one Danielle had just opened, it was padlocked. "So this is like a little mini tunnel leading to the main one?"

"I suppose you could describe it that way," Walt said.

"That is so creepy," Seraphina said, stepping back from the opening.

"Can we see inside the main tunnel?" Phoebe asked.

"Honestly, there's not much to see. It's pitch dark," Walt explained. "Even with the light from your phone, you won't see anything."

"Does that key open both padlocks?" Phoebe asked.

"Yes," Walt said.

"Oh, stop, Phoebe." Seraphina laughed. "You're trying to get them to open up the other door so you can see inside the main tunnel."

"Which I can't do," Walt said. "I'm sorry. But it's not safe; plus the door is difficult to open."

"You're never going to open it again?" Phoebe asked.

"No," Walt said. "Not worth the risk. We don't want the tunnel falling down on us."

"YOU ARE SUCH A LIAR," Danielle teased Walt fifteen minutes later. They stood at the first-floor landing while their guests followed Chris to the second floor.

"It's a pain to unlock that door," Walt whispered.

Danielle chuckled. "Well, I did wonder why you admitted the key fit. Once you said it, I thought, *no, Walt, now she's gonna wanna see inside.*"

"I realized that once I said yes. But then I caught myself," Walt said.

"Good save." Danielle stood on tiptoes and kissed his cheek. "Quite creative."

"I've been around you long enough, picked up a few tricks on how to spin a believable lie at a moment's notice."

Danielle giggled and said, "Glad I could help."

Walt and Danielle made their way up the stairs to give the rest of the tour, but Chris was already showing them the other bedrooms, which would be occupied when the remaining guests arrived.

Marlow House, which had been built in 1871 by Walt's grandfather, Frederick Marlow, founder of Frederickport, had changed very little since Walt's death in 1925. The Victorian, a Second Empire with mansard rooflines, boasted wood floors and dark paneled walls. Even most of the furniture had been in the house at the time of Walt's death. The most notable change was the remodeling of the attic into a master bedroom suite for Walt—which Walt and Danielle now used as a master bedroom. Another notable addition were the flat-screen televisions hanging in various rooms, the computer sitting in the library, the modern kitchen appliances, and washer and dryer.

After inspecting the rooms on the second floor, the group made their way up the second flight of stairs to the attic bedroom suite. Walt and Danielle waited patiently for Birdie to make her way up, her one hand clutching the oak rail while the other held onto her cane. Worried about Birdie's safety, Seraphina trailed behind the older woman, Chris by her side. Phoebe was already in the bedroom, having arrived first.

Once they were all in the room, Danielle said, "Perhaps we couldn't show you the tunnel, but would you like to see our secret staircase?"

"A secret staircase? Seriously?" Seraphina asked.

With a grin, Danielle opened the panel leading to the staircase. She flipped on its overhead light and stepped aside so her guests could see. Phoebe walked right into the stairwell, standing on the upper landing. She looked down. Seraphina followed her in, and Birdie stood outside looking in.

"Where does it go?" Seraphina asked.

"The bedroom that used to be mine," Danielle said. "The stairwell goes to its closet. But we also have it locked on both sides, so our guests won't feel someone is going to pop in on them."

"That's the room you're giving to Jackie and Julius?" Phoebe asked.

"Yes," Danielle said, standing next to Birdie, looking into the stairwell.

"I can think of some great practical jokes you could do with something like this," Phoebe said.

Walt walked over to Chris, who sat quietly on the edge of Walt and Danielle's bed, listening to the women discuss the hidden staircase. Walt sat down next to him.

"I remember a time you wouldn't tell anyone about that staircase," Chris said.

Walt shrugged. "After the tunnel was discovered, it was rather difficult to keep a secret, with all that went on. So now, it's an interesting novelty for our guests."

"Do you miss the B and B?" Chris asked, the chatter of the women in the background.

Walt shrugged. "Danielle misses it more than I do. To be honest, I rather enjoy our privacy."

Chris nodded. "Totally get you there."

AN HOUR later Seraphina and Phoebe were back in Seraphina's room. Yet they weren't alone. Marie had just popped in and was curious to get a closer look at the celebrity houseguest.

"You are a pretty thing," Marie said to Seraphina as she watched the young woman take a seat along the edge of the bed. She looked to Phoebe and said, "You're quite attractive yourself. Are you an actress too?" Of course, neither guest could see or hear the curious ghost.

"That friend of theirs was quite attractive," Seraphina noted.

"Yes, and the way he was drooling over you, obviously another fan. I hope they don't allow their friends to keep tromping through while we're here. You certainly don't need to be bothered by them," Phoebe said.

"Come on now, considering how he looks—and he seemed pretty nice—I can't imagine it would be much of a bother to be around him."

Phoebe laughed. "Come on, Sera, men with looks like his are a dime a dozen in our world. And the guy's the housekeeper's son. Seriously, after Barry, didn't you learn?"

"How do you know he's the housekeeper's son? I didn't hear him say that."

"They have the same last name. And I don't think she's his wife," Phoebe said.

"You silly woman," Marie snapped. "Chris and Joanne aren't even related."

"Even if he is the housekeeper's son, so

what? I used to clean houses to make ends meet."

"Well, you aren't that woman anymore!" Phoebe said. "And trust me, you can do a lot better than someone like Chris Johnson. There are lots of handsome men out there."

TWELVE

"Did you stop by for any reason other than to get a look at the beautiful and talented Seraphina?" Walt teased Chris as the two men sat alone in the library.

"That and boredom," Chris confessed. "Living and working in the same place makes me a little stir-crazy. I don't know how you do it, living and working from home."

Walt shrugged. "Considering I was stuck in this house for almost a hundred years, I just appreciate I can actually get out sometimes."

Chris laughed. "I hadn't thought of that."

"I saw how you looked at our guest. I

don't know if you realize how fortunate you are to live during this era," Walt said.

"Why is that?" Chris asked.

"Don't say anything to Danielle," Walt began.

Chris arched his brows. "This sounds interesting."

Walt chuckled. "It's nothing bad. Just something a wife doesn't appreciate listening to."

"Go on."

"When I…during my first life…that character in my book, the jazz singer, was inspired by a real woman."

"Yes, I know. You told us," Chris reminded him.

"What I didn't tell you, I was quite smitten with her. Not that she would have gone out with me," Walt mused.

"I find that hard to believe," Chris said, thinking of Walt's wealth and standing in the community back then.

"No, she was quite proud and would never have gone out with a white man. She never forgave her sister for passing as white to further her acting career. Felt it was a betrayal of her people. We were friends, and she accepted me as one. But to be honest, even if she would have gone out with me, it would have never worked. It would have killed my grandfather."

"He was prejudiced?" Chris asked.

"I wouldn't call him prejudiced—at least not by the standards of his day. He was always fair with his employees and didn't care about their nationality or race. If a person of color did a good job, he would get promoted over a white man if he deserved it. Which was one reason the local Klan had some issues with him. Because of his money and political standing, they didn't go after him the same way they would a more vulnerable white man who they felt was being a little too kindly to people of color. But have his only grandson date—or god forbid, marry—a woman of another race. No. It simply was not accepted back then."

"Would he have disowned you?" Chris asked.

"No. I don't believe so. But the fact is, I

wasn't willing to step that far over what was socially accepted at the time. So I suppose, if I was to be judged back then by today's standards, I would be considered prejudiced too. And if I am honest with myself, I was."

"And now?" Chris said.

Walt smiled. "I think if you're seriously interested, there is no reason you shouldn't try getting to know her better. And if it develops into something romantic that you both want, then there is no reason not to pursue a relationship."

"She's too young," Chris grumbled.

"Now, back in my day, no one would bat an eye when a man much older than you pursued a woman Seraphina's age."

Chris began to laugh.

Walt frowned. "What?"

"*Back in my day*. You old man." Chris laughed again.

THE LARIMORES and Staffords were on the same flight to Portland, along with Jackie's assistant, Bentley Mason. When they arrived in Oregon, they picked up the rental van they intended to share, with Bentley driving. Before leaving Portland, Julius asked Bentley to stop at one of the local pot shops so he could do a little shopping. While there, they all bought something, except for Polly, who never indulged.

When they arrived at Marlow House, Bentley was left to haul all the luggage up from the van to the front porch, much to his annoyance. Polly felt guilty about Bentley handling all the luggage without help, but when she tried to take her own suitcase, her husband chastised her, telling her to leave it; that was what Bentley was getting paid for, he said.

"I don't get paid to tote your suitcases," Bentley grumbled to himself.

Within minutes of ringing the bell, Walt Marlow opened the front door and welcomed them inside. They were introduced to Walt's wife, the housekeeper, and a friend named Chris Johnson, who helped Bentley take the suitcases up to the rooms.

After all the suitcases were delivered to the

appropriate rooms, Bentley went to the one assigned to him and found Phoebe Greda sitting at the dressing table, freshening her makeup.

"I heard we were roomies," Bentley said as he walked into the room carrying a large suitcase and a briefcase.

Phoebe glanced over her shoulder and said, "The bed by the window is mine."

Bentley tossed his cases on the other bed and muttered, "Of course."

"So is everyone here?" Phoebe asked.

"Looks like it. I assume you came with Seraphina and Birdie?" he asked.

"Yes. They put Birdie downstairs. Thank gawd. If her room was next to Seraphina's, she would be driving her nuts."

"I have to say, I'm surprised to see Seraphina took you back," Bentley said as he opened the suitcase and began to unpack.

"Why? Barry's not around anymore. No reason to let him come between us."

"Wow. That's cold," Bentley said.

Phoebe turned back to the mirror and applied some lipstick.

"There's nice scenery here. Did you catch that friend of theirs, Chris?" Bentley asked.

"You mean the housekeeper's son?" she asked.

"Is that why he helped me with the suitcases?" he wondered.

Phoebe shrugged. "Probably. He's all yours."

"Seriously? You aren't interested? I'm surprised."

"I learned my lesson. Don't waste time with someone who can only offer a good time."

"What's wrong with a good time?" Bentley asked, filling one of the empty dresser drawers with some of his clothes.

"Nothing, but I need to focus, and I'm not going to get distracted again." She screwed the lid back on her lipstick.

"Like you did with Barry?" he asked.

"Nothing happened between me and Barry," she insisted. "It was all a misunderstanding."

"Yeah, right," he muttered as he closed the now full dresser drawer.

SNOW BEGAN to rain from the ceiling of Marlow House's foyer. The only one to see it was Marie, who had just stepped out from the living room after noticing the glittering snowflakes through the open doorway. Marie stood in the foyer and glanced upwards, waiting for the apparition to appear. She watched the flakes begin to swirl, and then the vision appeared, transparent at first, with arms extended and sparkling light shooting from her fingertips.

"You know, that is wasted on me," Marie said dryly as Eva made touchdown, her slippered feet landing on the wood floor and any evidence of snow vanishing.

"I do love a good entrance. It's so critical," Eva said.

"It was a good one, I give you that. But you might want to save your energy for when some of the mediums are around, so they can enjoy it," Marie suggested.

"Imagine if anyone could see it? How I would love to make that entrance amongst a roomful of unsuspecting living people!" Eva said.

"They wouldn't be living for long. Would probably all drop dead from a heart attack—shock. Join us all on this side."

"You are such a pessimist!" Eva scolded with a laugh. She then peeked over Marie's shoulder. "Are they in there? All of them?"

"Yes, come. I'll introduce you—so to speak."

CHRIS HAD RETURNED to the foundation office, and Joanne had gone home, but she intended to return in time to finish and prepare dinner. Walt and Danielle sat in the living room with their guests. Danielle noticed Marie and Eva, who stood by the open doorway eavesdropping.

"So your friend Chris isn't the housekeeper's son?" Polly asked after the topic had come up.

"Oh, no." Danielle laughed. "They just happen to have the same last name. No relation. Actually, Chris is also a neighbor. Or he was, until his house burned down before Christmas."

"That's horrible!" Seraphina said.

"Yes, but he's rebuilding," Danielle said. "In fact, the house is almost finished. At the moment, he and his dog are staying over in one of the rooms at the Glandon Foundation Headquarters, where he works."

"That's awful generous of his employer, to let him stay there with his dog," Teddy said.

"Glandon Foundation? That's who he works for?" Birdie asked.

"Yes, are you familiar with it?" Danielle asked.

"Oh, yes. In fact, I was going to mention it. I had read how Christopher Glandon stayed at Marlow House a few times," Birdie said.

"You read about that?" Walt asked.

"Yes." Birdie nodded.

"What is the Glandon Foundation?" Phoebe asked.

"The Glandons were a very wealthy family. Quite well known," Birdie told her. "I never met the son, but I was familiar with the parents. Randy used to golf with the father." She looked at Walt and Danielle and added, "Randy was my husband."

"What do you mean they were? Aren't they wealthy anymore?" Seraphina asked.

"The parents were killed in a tragic boating accident. Their son, Christopher, inherited everything. He's worth billions."

Phoebe perked up. "And he lives in Frederickport?"

"I don't believe he does." Birdie looked to Danielle. "From what I understand, his foundation is located here, but he lives abroad. Isn't that true?"

"That's right," Danielle lied.

"But you know him? He has stayed here?" Phoebe asked.

"I remember reading about that now," Jackie said. "There was a big lawsuit where the uncles contested the will. And then later, after they lost, they tried killing their nephew. They ended up in prison. I think one of them has since died."

"You're right," Birdie said. She turned to

look at Danielle and said, "The uncles tried to kill you too, didn't they?"

"So you read about that too," Danielle muttered.

"Sounds like we have another movie in the making," Teddy remarked. He looked at Walt and asked, "Are you going to write about it?"

"I've never considered it," Walt said truthfully.

"So this Chris we met, he works for this Glandon guy?" Phoebe asked.

"Yes, but more for the foundation," Danielle explained.

"Does he ever come to Frederickport?" Phoebe asked.

"Considering what I've read about his few experiences while in Frederickport, I'm not even sure why he would have his foundation here," Birdie said. "This place certainly hasn't been lucky for him."

"What does the foundation do?" Polly asked.

"The Glandon Foundation does a lot of philanthropic work," Danielle explained.

"He gives his money away," Walt added.

"What's he like? What does he look like?" Phoebe asked.

"You seem kind of interested," Bentley teased. "You don't even know if he's married."

"He isn't married," Birdie told him. "And as I recall, he's sort of a beatnik sort of boy. Shaggy beard. Needed a haircut. Not very attractive. At least not from the few photographs I've seen. There aren't many. He's camera shy."

Danielle resisted the temptation to let out a snort, and by Walt's smirk, she figured he was thinking the same thing as her.

"With his money, who needs to be attractive?" Bentley chortled.

Phoebe looked at Walt and Danielle and asked, "What is he like? You said he gives money away. He must be pretty generous."

Walt considered the question a few moments and then said, "I think it is his desperate need to be liked. Frankly, Chris Glandon is rather an odd, sad little fellow. Socially inept. He might be worth billions, but he's extremely awkward around women. A bit of a recluse. Kind of a klutz."

Danielle giggled. "Walt, that is a horrible thing to say."

Walt looked to her, feigning sincerity. "You know it's true, love. He's a nice guy, but if he hadn't been left all that money, we both know he would probably be living on the streets now."

THIRTEEN

"Have you seen any ghosts yet?" Teddy asked with a smirk as he removed the shirt he wore and tossed it over the nearby chair. He and his wife were alone in their room at Marlow House, preparing for dinner. Alone except for the ghost sitting on the bed watching them.

"I never said I expected to see a ghost," Polly argued.

Standing shirtless in the middle of the room, he pointed at the closet and said, "Get me a clean shirt. Something that will go with these slacks."

Polly scurried to the closet to find a shirt

while Teddy turned to the mirror hanging over the dressing table. Looking at his reflection, his right hand moved over his beard, absently inspecting it, before saying, "Maybe you didn't say that, but I know how you are. You believe all that nonsense."

"I just find those stories fascinating," she said, handing him a clean shirt.

He let out a snort and shoved one arm into the right sleeve, pulling on the garment. "Polly, it's a good thing you're pretty, because you can't act."

Polly furrowed her brows. "What are you talking about? Since when did you think I can't act?"

"Trying to convince me you wouldn't be sucked into believing those ridiculous ghost stories. You are so gullible. I imagine the Marlows, when they ran this as a bed and breakfast, planted all that ghost nonsense. You know, she used to own a marketing company. A haunted bed and breakfast would get quite the draw."

"Whatever, but that crack about me not being able to act, that wasn't very nice. When we met, you told me I was talented."

"I wasn't speaking about your acting." He let out a crude laugh and reached over, giving her a pat on the backside.

Instead of responding, Polly stood quietly, her lower lip quivering, and watched as Teddy began buttoning the front of his shirt. When he came to the second button, he began to struggle, unable to push the button through the tiny hole. A moment later he cursed and yanked his right sleeves' cuff, impatiently tugging the garment from his body. In a rage, he balled up the shirt and threw it at Polly, hitting her in the face. "Find me another shirt to wear. Something's wrong with those damn buttonholes. I want you to return it to the store when we get home. I want my money back."

Now holding the shirt, she shook out the wrinkles he had made and said, "Teddy, you've worn this before. I don't think they're going to take it back."

"They'd better take it back," he snapped. "Those buttons are too big for the holes. It's always a pain to put on. I don't know why you bought it for me in the first place."

"You aren't a very nice man," Marie said

from her place on the bed. "That is no way to talk to your wife." Annoyed that Teddy could not hear her reprimand, Marie watched as the flustered wife hurried to find her husband another shirt to wear.

"And for gawd's sake, find something else to put on. You don't expect to wear that to dinner, do you?" he asked.

Now standing in front of the closet, looking through the shirts she had hung there earlier, Polly glanced to Teddy. "What's wrong with what I have on?"

"I don't need to explain myself. Just put something else on." The next moment he turned abruptly and stomped over to the closet. He pushed her aside and then grabbed a hanger with a blue dress. Turning toward Polly, he shoved it at her. "Put this on."

"You are a horrible little man," Marie grumbled, looking sympathetically to his wife, who looked to be on the verge of tears.

"And I don't want you sitting next to Julius at dinner, do you understand?" he snapped.

Using the cuff of her blouse to wipe away the moisture around her eyes, she asked, "Why can't I sit next to Julius? When we're all together, you're always talking to Jackie anyway. It's like I'm not even in the room."

"I'm talking to Jackie because we have a movie to make. You are my wife, and your job is to sit there and look presentable. It's the only job you have."

"That's not true," she choked out. "I am an actress."

"And when was the last time you worked?" he snapped.

"That is because you…"

"Enough! I don't want to talk about it. Just do as I say. I see how Julius looks at you. I'm not going to have my wife become another conquest of Julius Stafford."

"Julius isn't like that," she fairly whined.

"You're such a simpleton sometimes." He turned from his wife, who stood frozen by the closet, clutching the crumpled shirt and blue dress. Reaching in the closet, he grabbed another shirt.

Several minutes later Teddy stood at the bedroom door and said, "I'm going downstairs. Wash your face before you join us. We don't need everyone to know you've been crying. Let's keep the drama in front of the camera, shall we?"

Polly stood silently and watched her husband leave the room. After he shut the door, she turned around to go change clothes when she noticed something on the floor. With a frown she reached down to pick it up. It was the small paper sack the edibles Teddy had purchased at the pot shop had come in.

Looking at the crumpled empty sack in her hand, Polly shook her head and said, "I thought this stuff was supposed to make you mellow, not crabby." Wadding up the small sack, she tossed it in the nearby trash can.

FUMING, Marie had followed Teddy from the room into the empty hallway, cursing him. Unfortunately, he could not hear her. She stood behind him and watched as he paused a moment, adjusting his shirt collar. Glancing around the hallway, she spied one of the paintings hanging on the wall.

"Oh…I really shouldn't, should I?" Marie asked herself with a chuckle. "Yes, I should."

Teddy didn't notice at first when the painting down the hall unseated itself from the nail holding it in place. Yet it was difficult to overlook as it floated down the hallway in his direction. Frozen in place, his eyes widened as the painting stopped inches before his face, and he found himself looking into the eyes of the girl in the painting. It hovered there a moment in midair. But when Marie heard someone turning the doorknob of one of the other bedrooms, she sent the painting in a quick reverse, rehanging it on its nail just as one of the bedroom doors opened, and Jackie and Julius Stafford stepped out into the hallway.

"Where's Polly?" Julius asked as he closed the bedroom door behind him.

Teddy remained motionless, his eyes on the painting now hanging on the wall.

"Teddy?" Jackie asked a moment later when he did not respond to Julius's question.

Teddy blinked his eyes and then shifted his gaze to Jackie.

Jackie studied Teddy a moment, cocked her head, and then asked, "Are you okay, Teddy? You look as if you've seen a ghost."

TEN PEOPLE GATHERED around the dining room table at Marlow House. Walt sat at the head of the table, while Danielle took her place across from him, at the other end. To Walt's left sat the Larimores and Staffords, with Teddy and Jackie sitting next to each other. To Walt's right sat Birdie, and next to her was Seraphina and then Phoebe and Bentley, who sat to Danielle's left.

"I swear, I think poor Teddy saw a ghost upstairs," Jackie said with a laugh as she picked up her glass of water and took a sip.

Polly, who had just joined the group, looked to Jackie in surprise and was about to ask what she was talking about when Teddy said, "Stop it, Jackie, it was nothing."

"A ghost? I have to hear this," Phoebe urged with a giggle. "Sounds exciting."

"It was nothing," Teddy said.

"You were as white as a sheet," Jackie said. She looked around the table and added, "He was utterly speechless. When have you ever known Teddy to be without words?"

"What happened?" Seraphina asked.

Danielle and Walt exchanged glances, and then each looked around the dining room. There were no ghosts in sight.

"Nothing happened. I was just distracted when Jackie came out of her room," he said. "Can we please change the subject?"

"What is the plan for tomorrow?" Birdie asked. "I would like to do a little sightseeing."

"Since we need to look around the area anyway, I think sightseeing would be in order," Jackie said.

"I was hoping you and I could go over a few things, alone," Teddy told Jackie.

"There is no reason some of us can't go sightseeing while you two do whatever you need to do," Birdie said.

"Is there anything in particular you want to see?" Walt asked.

Birdie turned her smile to Walt. "Actually, there is. I would love to stop by the Glandon Foundation. I don't imagine it's open on Saturday, but do you think your friend might give us a tour? You did say he's staying there."

Walt arched his brow at Birdie. "The Glandon Foundation, you want to see that?"

"Yes. Like I mentioned, I knew the Glandons. He was a good friend with my husband, and while I never met their son, I would be most interested to see what he's doing over there."

"Umm, you do know Chris Glandon isn't in Frederickport," Danielle lied.

Birdie looked to Danielle. "Yes, I understand. But I was hoping I could get your friend to give him a letter from me. I would like to reach out to him. I feel quite negligent, as I haven't tried contacting him since the funeral. We missed the funeral. Randy and I were in Sweden at the time."

"Can I go too?" Phoebe asked excitedly.

Birdie looked to Phoebe and said, "I assumed you would drive."

Phoebe grinned. "Yes!"

"You seem rather excited to go over there," Bentley said dryly.

Phoebe gave Bentley a shrug.

Bentley laughed.

Phoebe frowned at him.

"Come on. Ever since you heard Chris Glandon is an eligible billionaire, you can't wait to find out more about him," Bentley whispered to Phoebe.

"I'm sure Chris would be willing to pass on whatever letter you have for his boss," Danielle told Birdie. "And I'm sure he'll be happy to give you a tour of the headquarters. They've recently done some remodeling over there, converting existing rooms to office space. The building is rather impressive, not my style—very modern and sleek, located right on the ocean. It was once the home—or should I say mansion–of a wealthy family. It's not just the headquarters for the foundation, but for other Glandon business interests."

"Then I imagine Chris Glandon must have reason to visit Frederickport frequently," Phoebe suggested. "Any chance he might be coming while we're here?"

"You would like that, wouldn't you?" Bentley snickered.

"He just sounds quite fascinating—and generous," Phoebe countered.

"I wouldn't mind going too." Seraphina spoke up.

"That Chris Johnson did seem like a nice fellow," Birdie teased.

"Oh, please, Seraphina can do much better than him." The moment the words slipped from Phoebe's mouth, she blushed and looked to Danielle and then Walt. "I'm sorry, I know Chris is a friend of yours. I didn't mean that as it sounded. But you see, in our business, handsome men—like your friend—are rather common. And well, someone like Seraphina has certain standards."

"I didn't know you were in the acting business," Teddy said sharply. "I thought you were an assistant?"

Phoebe flashed Teddy a glare. "You know what I meant."

"I'm afraid I do," Teddy muttered before picking up his wineglass and taking a sip.

"I'm not planning on marrying anyone," Seraphina said with a laugh. "I just think Chris is a nice guy, and I'm curious to see where he works. It sounds like a fulfilling job, working for a foundation like that. They must do so much good."

"Which is why his boss fascinates me," Phoebe said.

"Right. Has nothing to do with all his billions," Bentley said under his breath.

FOURTEEN

Phoebe stepped out of the bathroom adjacent to her room on Saturday morning and almost plowed into Teddy. On reflex, he extended his arms, and his hands landed on her shoulders, bringing her to an abrupt stop. His hands remained on her, and they stared intently into each other's eyes. The pair was alone in the hallway—alone except for the two ghosts who had arrived minutes earlier and were watching them with curiosity.

"Oh my, I remember that look," Eva observed, still watching the pair.

"Do you now? How long has it been?" Marie teased.

"A hundred years, more or less." Eva snickered. "But I still remember what it means when a man looks at a woman like that."

"The man is an ass," Marie said dryly, also watching the pair's intense silent exchange. "You should see how he treats his poor wife in private."

"When a man looks at a woman like that—a woman who is not his wife—we shouldn't expect he will treat his wife with respect in other regards," Eva noted.

"Why did you come here?" Teddy whispered harshly, dropping his hands from Phoebe's shoulders.

"Because Seraphina wanted me to come," Phoebe told him. "I'm her assistant."

"After Barry, you have a lot of nerve coming here. I have a good mind to tell Seraphina you lied."

"You won't tell. Because then I'll have to tell your wife about us." Phoebe leaned closer and whispered, "It's too bad you signed that prenup." Phoebe laughed and then turned away from Teddy, leaving him standing red faced as she returned to her room.

"Oh my, that is interesting," Marie muttered.

Eva shook her head and said, "Some things about this business never change."

"Watch this," Marie said with a giggle after Phoebe returned to her room, leaving Teddy still standing by the doorway to the bathroom.

"What are you going to do?" Eva asked apprehensively as she watched Marie move to Teddy.

"It's called a wedgie," Marie told Eva. "Adam and his brother were always doing this to each other when they were little; used to drive me nuts!"

Before Eva could tell Marie to stop, Marie reached her hand down the back of Teddy's pants just as he turned toward the bathroom. Grabbing hold of his underwear's waistband, she gave it a quick tug upward. The expression on the startled man's face and the way he let out a holler set both Marie and Eva into a fit of giggles. The two ghosts watched as Teddy ran into the bathroom, slamming and locking the door behind him.

"That was so juvenile," Eva choked out between spurts of laughter. "But so amusing!"

"YOU GAVE HIM A WEDGIE?" Danielle asked Marie thirty minutes later. She stood with the two ghosts and Walt in the kitchen of Marlow House, while Joanne was in the dining room setting the table for breakfast.

Marie looked at Walt. "I don't like your director, Walt. He is a womanizer, and he's not nice to his wife."

"What is a wedgie?" Walt asked.

After Danielle explained, Walt said, "I've never heard it called that before."

Danielle picked up her cellphone and made a quick internet search.

"Naturally I could have done it without the illusion of my hands, but I wanted to show Eva what I was doing," Marie explained.

Danielle put her cellphone on the counter and looked to Walt. "According to my search results, the term *wedgie* wasn't used until around the time of your death or later."

"I think you should invite Polly to go with you today," Marie suggested. "She seems like such a nice young girl, and her husband treats her atrociously."

Danielle eyed Marie. "Tell me, what did you do to him yesterday?"

Marie looked innocently at Danielle. "What do you mean?"

"Come on. At dinner last night Jackie made a comment about Teddy acting strange upstairs—said something about him looking as if he had seen a ghost. What did you do?"

Marie shrugged. "He didn't see me. I haven't figured out how to do that yet. I imagine materializing would take up a great deal of my energy."

"Marie?" Danielle urged.

With a sigh Marie said, "Okay. I sort of took down one of your paintings and made it fly around the hallway before rehanging it."

Danielle shook her head and stifled a chuckle. "Marie, I know you don't like how Teddy treats Polly. But please stop haunting him. He's only going to be here for a week.

And if you keep doing stuff like that, they might leave."

"Fine. I know this is important to Walt. But I don't like the man," Marie said.

"Thank you." Danielle smiled.

"THANKS FOR ASKING me to go with you," Polly said from the back of the Packard. Bentley sat next to her. "I love your car, by the way."

Danielle glanced to the back seat and smiled. Walt sat in the driver's seat and was backing out of the garage while Phoebe waited in the rental car parked in front of the house, with Birdie, Seraphina and Julius. They would be following Walt's car to the foundation headquarters.

"Certainly. No reason to hang around the house and get bored when your husband and Jackie are going to be locked up in the library going over things for most of the morning," Danielle said.

"I know they plan to get out and look for some possible shooting sites, but knowing

Teddy and Jackie, they don't want any of us going along," Polly said.

"I understand you're an actress," Walt said from the driver's seat as he steered the vehicle down the alley.

"She is a very talented actor," Bentley added.

Polly smiled at Bentley. "Thank you." She then looked toward the driver's seat and said, "Yes, but I haven't been in anything for a couple of years now."

"Are you giving up acting?" Danielle asked.

"I hope not," Bentley said.

Polly let out a sigh and gazed out the window. They had just turned down Beach Drive, and up ahead was the rental car with Phoebe and the others, waiting for Walt to drive by so they could follow him. "I never planned to give up acting. Actually, I miss it. But I suppose life got in the way. Teddy—well, he is always so busy, and my acting does not always fit into his schedule."

"Oh pshaw, he can stick his schedule in his ear," Marie blurted the instant she materialized in the back seat, sitting between Bentley and Polly.

PHOEBE STOOD by the side of the rental car and looked up at the massive building housing the Glandon Foundation. The modern structure—a mixture of glass, steel, and clean lines—sat on beachfront property. The neighbors were all residential houses, albeit impressive ones, with a few that might be described as mansions. Seraphina chatted with Birdie as she followed Bentley, Julius and Polly up the walkway, trailing behind Walt and Danielle.

Phoebe lingered, taking in the neighborhood and imagining herself living in these surroundings. By the time she entered the front gate, the rest of the group was already on the front porch. Phoebe was halfway up the walkway when she spied a pit bull barreling in her direction, full speed. She froze.

"Don't worry, she's a sweetheart," came an unfamiliar female voice. Phoebe glanced to the right of the building and saw a young woman with long black braids, straight cut bangs covering her eyebrows, and purple lipstick walking in her direction.

"Hunny, come," the woman called out, giving her tight black leather pants a firm pat on the thigh, making a slapping sound. The dog stopped and looked to her, its tail wagging.

"You scared the crap out of me," Phoebe said as she came in earshot.

"Sorry about that. But you are on her turf," the woman said, now standing a few feet away.

Phoebe glanced up to the building and saw they had all gone inside. *They've all left me out here with a pit bull and someone who looks like she's auditioning for a role in a horror movie,* Phoebe thought.

"I'm Heather Donovan. Chris Johnson's assistant. I assume you're with the movie crew?" the woman asked.

Phoebe relaxed. "I'm Phoebe Greda, Seraphina's assistant."

"Nice. Another assistant."

"I guess this means you work for Chris Glandon?" Phoebe asked.

"Yeah, I suppose. Indirectly." Heather shrugged and leaned down, giving Hunny a scratch behind her ears. The dog sat obediently by her side.

"Does he come to Frederickport often?" Phoebe asked.

"Often enough, I suppose." Heather shrugged again.

"Walt told us he's sort of awkward."

Heather arched her brows and smiled. "Awkward? What else did he say?"

"That he's socially inept—insecure. I find that sad."

Heather grinned. "Yeah, that pretty much describes him."

"And he doesn't have a girlfriend?" Phoebe prodded.

"Girlfriend?" Heather laughed. "Hardly. I mean seriously, I don't care how much money a man has, sometimes it's simply not worth it. If you know what I mean."

"Is he that bad?" Phoebe asked.

"Maybe if you could convince him to take a shower more than once a week, or at least wear deodorant. But he's into all this natural stuff. And then his breath." Heather cringed.

BY THE TIME Phoebe made it in the building, she found Chris Johnson chatting with Birdie and Seraphina in the front lobby, while Polly stood at the perimeter of the area with Julius, checking out the artwork hanging along the wall. She didn't see where Bentley had gone. Walt and Danielle sat on one of the sofas with Heather, who had come into the building right before Phoebe. The three chatted, yet Phoebe could not hear their conversation. The dog, who had terrified her minutes earlier, now curled up by Walt's feet on the floor.

Phoebe joined her employer's small group just as she heard Chris promise to deliver Birdie's letter to his boss. Standing quietly by Seraphina's side, she observed Chris's solicitous behavior toward both the older woman and Seraphina. They chatted for another ten minutes or so before Chris offered to take them on a tour of the building. While they did, Phoebe watched Chris. The way he kept eyeing Seraphina, it was obvious he was interested—just as she could tell Sera was attracted to Chris.

Perhaps I was hasty, Phoebe told herself. *If Sera and Chris were to become an item, what better way to ensure an introduction to Chris Glandon? I don't care what he smells like or looks like. By Heather and Walt's description, I think I could handle him.*

After touring the building, Chris took the group outside to enjoy the spectacular ocean view. He was with them for a good fifteen minutes when Heather, who had not joined the tour, sent him a text message about a phone call. Chris excused himself, leaving the group outside while he went to take the call.

"YOU TOLD HER I SMELL?" Chris asked Heather after he finished his phone call, and she recounted the conversation she'd had with Phoebe. The pair was alone in his office, the door leading to the hallway ajar, while they assumed the others were still outside.

"Only because you don't wear deodorant and never shower," Heather quipped.

"I shower," Chris argued. "I even wear deodorant."

"I didn't give an explanation for your bad breath."

Chris rolled his eyes.

"Anyway, you should probably talk to Walt. He started this. Although I'm not sure what he said about you—not you exactly, but about Chris Glandon.

"I am Chris Glandon."

"You know what I mean." Heather giggled.

PHOEBE HAD BEEN LOOKING for the bathroom when she heard voices from the office behind the partially opened door. She had paused a moment when she heard Chris say, *"I am Chris Glandon."*

FIFTEEN

When the group returned from the Glandon Foundation later Saturday afternoon, they found the screenwriter, Chase Wilks, in the library with Teddy and Jackie. Wilks had checked into the cottage he had rented for the week, before coming over to Marlow House. Walt joined the three to discuss *Moon Runners*, while Danielle went to the kitchen to make some coffee. Polly joined her.

As for the other guests, Julius left for the beach with his camera. Birdie retired to her room to take a nap, while Seraphina and Phoebe headed upstairs to their rooms. Bentley started to join the others in the library to take notes for Jackie, when she sent him upstairs to retrieve some papers he had left in his briefcase.

After sprinting up the stairs, Bentley made his way to the room he shared with Phoebe. Once there, he started to open the door when he heard voices. Phoebe was not alone. Instead of going inside, he gently re-closed the door, leaving it open a crack so he could hear what they were saying.

"THIS IS A NICE ROOM TOO," Seraphina said, glancing around.

Giddy, Phoebe sat on the edge of her mattress, barely able to contain herself. "Something exciting happened!"

Seraphina sat down on a nearby chair facing her assistant. "I thought you were dying to tell me something. You've been distracted since before we left the foundation office. I figured that's why you wanted me to come see your room."

"It's about Chris Johnson," Phoebe said.

Seraphina raised a brow. "Chris? What about him?"

"Remember when you guys were still outside, and I came in to use the bathroom?" Phoebe asked.

Seraphina nodded. "Sure. What about it?"

"When I came out of the bathroom, he was in the hallway alone. He approached me, told me he wanted to ask me out, but that he didn't want to make me uncomfortable if I wasn't interested."

Expressionless, Seraphina stared at Phoebe. "He asked you out?"

"Yes! And I told him I would love to go out with him!" Phoebe giggled.

"I…I thought you didn't feel he was good enough?" Seraphina asked.

Phoebe rolled her eyes and laughed. "Silly, I said he wasn't good enough for you. Goodness, he is so out of your league it isn't even funny." Phoebe paused a moment and silently studied Seraphina.

In her best dramatic performance, Phoebe abruptly stood from the bed, "Oh, Sera, if you are seriously interested in him, then I'll tell him I don't want to go out with him. Fact is, I'm sure he would rather go out with you anyway. Heck, he probably just figured you would say no, so he asked me. But I can tell him no."

Seraphina didn't respond immediately but just sat quietly. Finally, she began shaking her head and said, "No. Don't do that. He was nice to me, but if he asked you out, then it's you he's interested in."

"But I'm sure he's interested in you," Phoebe insisted.

Seraphina stood. "No. It's fine. Chris is a nice guy, and I hope you have a great time with him."

BENTLEY STEPPED BACK from the doorway just as Seraphina walked into the hallway. She barely noticed him standing there and didn't seem to realize the door had not been closed all the way. When Bentley walked into his room a moment later, he found Phoebe sitting at the dressing table, humming and brushing her hair while admiring herself in the mirror.

"You're a scheming little number, aren't you?" Bentley asked in disgust, closing the door behind him.

Phoebe glanced over to her roommate. "What are you talking about?"

"I don't believe Chris asked you out."

"She told you?"

"I overheard. You're spinning lies again, Phoebe," Bentley accused. "Chris isn't interested in you. I saw how he looked at Seraphina."

Phoebe shrugged and looked back into the mirror. "Men always look at Seraphina that way. It doesn't mean they aren't also interested in me. Look at Barry."

"I wonder if I ask Chris, what will he say?" Bentley asked.

Phoebe swung around on the vanity stool and glared at Bentley. "You wouldn't dare!"

"I wouldn't? Watch me."

A smile curled the corners of her lips as she set the brush she had been holding on the vanity top. "Then I will just have to tell Jackie about Vegas."

The smile faded from Bentley's face. "You don't know what you're talking about."

"You know that *'everything stays in Vegas'* slogan? Not true," she smirked.

Bentley licked his lips nervously and stared at Phoebe, his expression blank. "You don't know anything. You're bluffing," he challenged.

The next moment she told him exactly what she knew. Upon hearing, Bentley glared at Phoebe. "You are a piece of…"

"Now, now," she interrupted. "Be nice. I will keep your secret if you keep mine."

"I don't know what you think you're doing. But it's not going to matter anyway. I don't have to say anything to Chris. Not sure why you want him in the first place. I thought you were interested in his boss. I would think getting Seraphina and Chris together would make it easier for you to meet Glandon. But if you're dating Johnson, doesn't that mess up your plans?"

"See, smart guy, you don't always know everything. Don't try to figure me out. I'm always going to be a step ahead of you. Now what are you doing up here anyway? I thought Jackie wanted you in the library with them so you could take notes?"

Glaring at Phoebe, he turned abruptly and walked to his bed, grabbing his briefcase off the mattress.

SERAPHINA FOUND Danielle and Polly sitting at the kitchen table, chatting. What she couldn't see was Marie, who also sat at the table.

"Can I join you?" Seraphina asked softly.

"Certainly," Danielle said, immediately standing up and pulling out the empty chair for Seraphina. If the woman thought Danielle was simply welcoming her, she would be wrong. In truth, Danielle didn't want her guest sitting on Marie.

"Would you like a piece of double fudge chocolate cake?" Danielle asked, still standing. "It's homemade."

"Oh…I probably shouldn't," Seraphina said unconvincingly. "As it is, I missed my morning jog. Can you recommend a good place to go?"

Danielle laughed. "Do I look like I jog?"

Seraphina glanced Danielle up and down. "You look great. But you know that camera, they say it puts on twenty pounds, and I need to keep in shape for the movie."

"You met Heather today," Danielle said.

"Yes, what about her?" Seraphina asked.

"She jogs just about every morning. I'm sure she would be happy if you joined her. She lives one door down from here."

"That would be great," Seraphina said.

"If you're going to go jogging, you sure you don't want a piece of that cake?" Danielle teased.

"It really is good," Polly said, picking up the empty plate in front of her to show Seraphina. A sprinkling of chocolate cake crumbs and a smudge of chocolate frosting decorated the plate.

Seraphina flashed Polly a smile and then looked to Danielle. "Actually, I need a little chocolate right now."

A few minutes later, after Danielle had brought Seraphina a slice of cake and cup of hot tea, she sat down and asked, "Is something wrong? When someone needs chocolate, usually they have a problem…Although now that I think about it, I always need chocolate." Danielle grinned.

Stabbing the slice of cake with the tip of her fork, Seraphina let out a sigh and said, "It's nothing, really. And I probably shouldn't say anything anyway."

Polly reached out and touched Seraphina's wrist. "Oh, please do. I was just whining to Danielle about how I need to rejuvenate my acting career. Now tell us, what is the problem?"

She looked up from her plate and glanced from Polly to Danielle. "Promise you won't say anything?"

"Promise," both Polly and Danielle agreed, each adding a nod.

Seraphina looked to Danielle and said while cringing, "I think your friend Chris is nice. He's different from other men I meet. I like him."

Danielle grinned. "I know he likes you."

Seraphina looked embarrassed. "I just thought we might be able to get to know each other better this week."

"I know he'd like that," Danielle said.

Seraphina smiled sadly. "I don't think you understand. I was interested in your friend…I mean not just as a new friend."

Danielle laughed. "Well, good. Because I'm pretty sure Chris would like that too."

"No." Seraphina shook her head. "Chris is interested in getting to know Phoebe better, not me. At least not like that."

"No way," Danielle blurted. "Seriously, no. Chris is definitely interested in you. Although, I'm starting to feel like I'm back in high school again." Danielle laughed.

"He's asked Phoebe out. And that's okay. They're both great people, and maybe something will come of it beyond this weekend."

"I don't know where you got the crazy idea he asked Phoebe out," Danielle said. "I understand she is a beautiful woman, and she seems quite nice, but Chris isn't interested in her. Heck, I don't even think he's noticed her."

Seraphina shook her head. "No, he noticed."

"I know how we can end this nonsense, I'm going to ask Chris," Marie announced before vanishing.

Danielle said, "Listen, Chris is one of my closest friends. He made it very clear to both Walt and myself that he would love to get to know you better. As Marie would say, he's rather smitten with you."

"Who is Marie?" Polly asked.

"Umm…" Danielle looked over to Marie's now empty chair. "Just an old friend. But the point is, I know for a fact Chris would be interested in getting to know you better. And Chris isn't a player. He's not the type to decide you wouldn't be interested—after all, you are Seraphina Bouchard—and then seek out a substitute."

"Chris is also extremely good looking and seems like an interesting guy," Polly added.

"True," Danielle agreed and then went on, "But he's not one to simply give up and settle on some other woman he feels he has a better chance with. Just not going to happen. Serious about this."

"I agree with Danielle," Polly said. "I saw how he looked at you today. He could not take his eyes off you. And you were always making each other smile. I was a little jealous…"

"Over Chris?" Seraphina asked.

"Not like that," Polly said. "I just mean, I kept wondering if Teddy and I ever looked at each other like that. I know we don't now." She looked over at Danielle and said, "I notice you and your husband look at each other that way."

The next moment Marie reappeared. Only Danielle could see or hear her.

"Chris is not interested in Phoebe," Marie announced. "And he certainly did not ask her out. He may be calling you in a minute to ask what in the heck is going on. Once I got him to answer the question, I headed back here."

Danielle looked to Seraphina. She reached out and took her hand, giving it a slight squeeze. "I can't say how I know, but Chris did not ask Phoebe out—he has no intention of asking her out, even if you aren't interested in him. I don't know where you got that idea, but trust me on this one."

The next minute Danielle's cellphone rang.

SIXTEEN

After leaving Polly and Danielle in the kitchen, Seraphina started to go to her bedroom when Birdie walked out of her room. Instead of going upstairs, Seraphina retreated to the parlor with Birdie.

"So how was your nap?" Seraphina asked Birdie after the two were alone in the parlor, its door shut.

"To be honest, I never nap when I say nap. I was reading."

Seraphina smiled. "You could have just told us you wanted to read."

"True. But I've found when people think you're napping, they tend to leave you alone

—but not so with reading. I had a book I wanted to finish."

"Did you?"

"I did. And I wasn't even able to guess the killer until the last chapter," Birdie said, sitting down on a chair.

"Ahh, you were reading a mystery." Seraphina sat on the sofa, Danielle's black cat, Max, sleeping by her side.

"Yes. My favorite genre. Now, what have you been doing the last couple of hours?" Birdie sat primly facing Seraphina.

"I was visiting with Danielle and Polly." Seraphina absently reached over and stroked Max's back. He woke up, lifted his head, and meowed.

"He is the most beautiful cat," Birdie cooed. Max turned his head and looked at Birdie. "I've never seen a cat with markings like that. All black but with white-tipped ears."

"You like cats, don't you?" Seraphina asked.

"Oh, yes. I always considered myself a cat person. But Randy was allergic." Birdie gave her lap several pats, trying to coax Max to her. Taking her invitation, he stood up, walked to the edge of the sofa cushion and jumped down to the floor. He sauntered to Birdie and then jumped up on her lap, making himself comfortable. She began to pet him as he closed his eyes and started to purr.

Seraphina watched Birdie and Max for a moment and then asked, "Can I ask you something?"

"Why certainly. Anything," Birdie said.

Seraphina then went onto recount the conversation she'd had with Phoebe, and then the one with Danielle and Polly, about Chris.

"I didn't tell Danielle and Polly that Phoebe was the one who told me Chris had asked her out. I don't think Danielle knows her friend as well as she thinks."

"Or perhaps you don't know Phoebe as well as you think," Birdie suggested.

"You think she lied?"

"I believe Phoebe has a problem with the truth," Birdie said softly.

"But why? Why would she lie about something like that?"

"She obviously has her sights set on Chris. That's probably why she was so dismissive about him in the beginning. She didn't want you to get interested," Birdie suggested.

"Doesn't she realize I could find out the truth?" Seraphina asked.

"I don't think Phoebe considered that. Another thing I've noticed about the girl, she doesn't think these things through. Look at Barry."

"I was wrong about that," Seraphina said. "Nothing happened. Barry instigated it, and I just walked in at the wrong time. I feel horrible I never listened to her when she tried to explain. She has always been there for me, always. I trust Phoebe. It was all my fault."

"Why was it your fault?" Birdie asked.

"I knew how Barry could be. He promised it would never happen again—the cheating. I just never thought he would try to force himself on someone. I should have protected Phoebe—she worked for me. I put her in situations where she was alone with Barry. Instead of protecting her, I fired her."

"I'm sorry, dear, but that's not what happened. I was going to say something earlier, but then I saw her, and she did seem to be trying. And I know how much she has always meant to you. Everyone deserves a second chance, so I didn't say anything. But I think I need to now."

"What are you talking about?" Seraphina asked.

"Phoebe lied. She lied about all of it."

"She didn't," Seraphina insisted.

"After you kicked Barry out, he came to me. Begged me to talk to you. He wanted you back. Claimed he had made a mistake. He said he knew he had a problem and was willing to go to counseling—therapy if you wanted—if you would try to work it out with him. Of course, I told him I wouldn't help him."

"I'm glad you didn't. Trying to force himself on her was more than a mistake."

"That's not what happened. The reason I know Phoebe lied to you, she called him when he was with me. She didn't know he was with me at the time. Barry let me listen in on the phone call; he wanted me to know her part in all of it."

POLLY AND DANIELLE were in the midst of laughing about something one of them had said when Walt walked into the kitchen. Danielle's laughter subsided, and she glanced up at the kitchen clock and saw that she and Polly had been talking for almost two hours.

"Are you guys finished for now?" Danielle asked, no longer laughing. "Or have you just come for sustenance?"

"We're finished for now, but sustenance would be nice." He walked to the cake pan and lifted its lid, finding one lone piece of double fudge chocolate cake. He looked to Danielle, silently asking permission.

"Go ahead," Danielle told him. "Polly and I each had a piece, but you'd better grab it before someone else does."

Walt didn't need to be told twice. He reached into an overhead cabinet and snatched a small dish.

"Is Teddy still in there?" Polly asked, watching Walt plate the remaining slice of cake.

"He's in there with Chase, but when I left them, they were talking sports, not the movie.

Jackie and Bentley went upstairs, I think," Walt said.

Polly stood up. "If you will excuse me, I think I'll go see if Teddy would like to take a little walk on the beach before dinner."

By the time Polly left the kitchen, Walt was sitting at the kitchen table, eating his chocolate cake with Danielle and Marie.

"I really like Polly. She has a great sense of humor," Danielle told Walt.

"She's a sweet girl, but that husband of hers is a putz," Marie said.

Danielle looked at Marie. "About that. I wish you would withhold some of your comments when you're sitting in on a conversation. It would be different if Polly could hear you. You have no idea how difficult it was sometimes to pay attention to what Polly was saying while you constantly made cracks like *your husband is a jerk* and *you can do better*."

"As long as she isn't saying that to you, I don't see what the problem is," Walt teased as he took another bite of cake.

"Well, he is a jerk, and I do believe she can do better," Marie insisted.

IN CHASE WILKS'S youth he had played high school football. He wasn't particularly good at it, but those hours of practice helped keep his weight off, something that had been difficult for him to do in his forties. Sitting at the computer hours a day, along with his junk-food habit, didn't help the situation. He only wore loose-fitting button-up shirts with his slacks to help conceal his girth. His height, standing over six three, played to his advantage. His shortly cropped beard was his reaction to thinning hair, which was also kept short like the beard.

Chase sat in the library, talking with Teddy. "I wanted to tell you, I'm impressed," Chase said.

"Impressed? What do you mean?" Teddy asked.

"Takes some cojones to spend a week with your wife and girlfriend under the same roof." Chase laughed.

"Please, Phoebe is hardly my girlfriend," Teddy said with a snort. "I can hardly stand the woman."

"That's not how I remember it," Chase said.

"And we both moved on. It was fun while it lasted," Teddy said.

An audible gasp came from the doorway. Both men turned to see who it was. When they did, they caught a glimpse of Polly, who had just run from the room.

PEARL HUCKABEE STOOD at her bedroom window, looking over at Marlow House. Those movie people were there. Cars had been driving up and down the street all day—looky-loos trying to get a glimpse at some celebrity.

Three unfamiliar vehicles were parked in front of the house, and people had been coming and going all day long. Just minutes earlier a young woman with short dark hair came running from the house and headed toward the pier. The silly thing didn't even have a jacket on; she was going to catch pneumonia if she wasn't careful. A few minutes later a bearded man came running out of the house after her. Pearl could tell he was calling for her. Either the woman couldn't hear him, or she was ignoring the man. Pearl watched as the pair ran down the street, heading for the pier, the woman a good distance ahead of him.

Pearl shook her head in disgust and turned from the window.

TEARS STREAMED DOWN Polly's face as she ran down the street—her destination unknown. She just knew she needed to put space between her and Teddy so she could think. Eventually she slowed to a walk and then stopped when she reached the pier. Using her fingers to wipe tears from her eyes, she jumped when a hand unexpectantly seized her upper left arm and jerked her around.

"Teddy!" Polly said in surprise, her face just inches from her husband's.

"Who in the hell did you think it was? And why were you running?" Teddy asked, slightly out of breath.

Yanking her arm from his hold, she rubbed where he had roughly gripped her.

"That's what you have to say to me?" she asked angrily.

"Chase didn't know what he was talking about. It was just guy talk. You don't need to get all dramatic about it."

"Did you or did you not have an affair with Phoebe?"

"Of course I didn't! You know I can't stand the woman. She's a user," Teddy said.

"Did she use you? Is that why you hate her? Did she drop you for Barry?"

"You don't know what you're talking about," he snapped. "It's cold out here, and you didn't even have the sense to put on a coat. Let's go back to the house."

"I want to know, did you have an affair with Phoebe? Don't lie to me. I can ask Phoebe."

"And you don't think that will make the week a little awkward?"

"I know what I heard," she said stubbornly.

"I tell you what." Teddy used a calmer voice. "Walt said there's a nice café on the pier. Let's go get a cup of coffee, warm up, you calm down, and I'll explain exactly what Chase and I were talking about. Trust me, Polly, I would never touch that woman."

THE WAITRESS with the purple and pink hair set a cup of hot cocoa in front of Polly and filled Teddy's cup with coffee. When she left the table, Polly said stubbornly, "Okay, you explain."

"Remember when we went to Vegas to promote the first film Seraphina was in?"

"Yes. I couldn't go. I had the flu. Is that when it started between you and Phoebe?"

"Nothing happen between us, but Phoebe made an obvious play for me in exchange for a part in a film."

"And you turned her down?" she asked.

"You tell me, have you seen Phoebe in any of my movies?"

Polly considered the question. Uncertain, she looked at Teddy and asked, "Then why did you tell Chase you both moved on, that it was fun while it lasted?"

Teddy reached across the table and took Polly's hands in his. "It was a joke. Nothing more. It was a stupid ill-timed joke."

Polly studied her husband's expression from across the table, her hands still in his.

"That was about a few months before Seraphina caught Phoebe with Barry, wasn't it?"

She felt Teddy's hand tighten momentarily and then relax. He smiled across the table and said, "I suppose."

I know your fake smiles, Teddy, Polly thought. *That is a fake smile if there ever was one.*

SEVENTEEN

Moving slowly up the staircase to the second floor of Marlow House, her hand on the rail, Seraphina failed to notice Bentley coming down the stairs.

"Earth to Seraphina," Bentley said good-naturedly.

She paused and looked up and found Bentley standing a few steps ahead of her.

"I'm sorry. I was just thinking," Seraphina said.

Bentley grinned. "Must have been some pretty heavy thinking. I have a feeling if I hadn't said anything and kept coming down the stairs, you would have walked right into me."

"Just a lot on my mind," she said. "Umm, is Phoebe upstairs in her room?"

"You mean our room," he said dryly.

Seraphina smiled up at him. "How is that going? Sharing a room with her?"

He shrugged. "No problem."

"So where are you off to?" she asked.

"Jackie wants me to go find Julius. He went out to take some photographs, and he hasn't come back yet. He's not answering his cellphone."

"She doesn't think anything is wrong, does she?"

Bentley laughed. "No. Julius is notorious for forgetting to charge his phone. So, if you will excuse me…" He flashed her a smile as he passed her on the stairs, continuing on to the first floor.

Seraphina stood midway up the staircase for a moment, watching Bentley head for the front door. After a moment she turned back around and continued up the stairs.

"DO you need me to do something?" Phoebe asked when she let Seraphina in her room a few minutes later.

Seraphina didn't answer immediately. Instead, she walked all the way into the room and then turned, facing Phoebe, waiting for her to close the door for privacy. What neither woman knew, someone else had walked into the room with Seraphina, Marie's ghost.

"Is there a problem?" Phoebe asked as she closed the door and turned to face Seraphina, noticing her stoic expression.

"I know Chris never asked you out," Marie said to deaf ears before taking a seat on an imaginary chair.

"I know Chris never asked you out," Seraphina said.

Marie arched her brows. "I just said that! Can you hear me?"

"What are you talking about?" Phoebe asked.

"I know you lied. Chris didn't ask you out," Seraphina accused.

"Who told you that?" Phoebe demanded.

"Chris," Seraphina lied.

Color drained from Phoebe's face as she

stared into Seraphina's dark eyes. Licking her lips nervously, she swallowed and then said, "I can explain."

"Please do," Seraphina said calmly.

"I…I was just attracted to Chris immediately. There is something about him. But men, they always like you best. It's always been that way, even when we were teenagers. You were the pretty one, the talented one."

"We were both awkward teenagers. The only thing I had back then was my voice. And look at you now. You're gorgeous," Seraphina reminded her.

Phoebe let out a harsh laugh. "Maybe, but I could never compare standing by you. I've been in your shadow since we were kids."

"Then why did you stay, if you felt I stole all the attention?" Seraphina asked.

"Because you were the closest thing I had to a sister," Phoebe said. "I was proud of you. I knew what incredible talent you had. I wanted to see you succeed—I always knew you would."

"I still don't get why you lied about Chris."

"You have to understand. I saw Chris, and

I knew I wanted him. But I could never compete with you, so I lied."

"Is that why you lied about Barry?" Seraphina asked, her voice toneless.

Phoebe looked as if she had been slapped and took a step backwards. "What are you saying? I explained all that."

"No, you lied. You lied about Barry forcing himself on you. You wanted Barry like you want Chris now," Seraphina said.

"How can you say that? You told me you believed me!"

"Birdie told me."

"Birdie?" Phoebe frowned. "What does Birdie have to do with this?"

"Birdie was with Barry when you called him. She heard what you said to him, how you told him it was probably for the best that I'd caught you. That now you could move in with him."

"Birdie heard all that?"

"What happened between you and Barry?" Seraphina asked.

"I thought you just said you knew all about it. Birdie told you."

"No, I mean later, after I fired you and

broke it off with Barry. At the time I assumed you two were together. But then you didn't go to his funeral. And when I ran into you and asked you why you didn't go, you asked me why you would go to the funeral of the man who tried to rape you. You convinced me you hadn't seen him since that day I walked in on you." Seraphina paused a moment and then let out a harsh laugh, shaking her head in disbelief.

"What?"

Looking Phoebe in the eyes, Seraphina shook her head in disgust. "You are a good actress. You didn't need to hitch yourself to my wagon to get where you wanted, you had all the talent to do it on your own."

"What are you talking about?"

"Your performance. Your cold, calculated, and rehearsed performance, convincing me the man who you had been involved with—a man who had just tragically died—was someone you hated and had never been involved with. It was quite the performance. I believed you. I felt guilty for not believing you the first time. I hired you back."

Phoebe stared at Seraphina. Finally she said, "I did you a favor."

"How do you figure that?" Seraphina asked.

"You were better off without him. All he wanted to do was drink."

"He's dead. Don't you feel anything?" Seraphina asked.

Phoebe shrugged. "Not really."

"How can you say that? As much as Barry hurt me, I felt bad when he died. It was so senseless; he was so young. It was such a stupid and foolish way to die. How could you not feel something?"

"It was his own fault. If he hadn't had so much to drink that night, he'd still be alive. I told him if he opened the other bottle of tequila, I was leaving. Booze and pills don't mix, but he would never listen to me."

"You were there that night? The night he died? I thought he was alone?"

"I wasn't there when he drowned. He was still sitting in the spa, alive when I left. Idiot opened the bottle right in front of me and started guzzling."

"And you just left him?" Seraphina gasped.

"I wasn't his keeper. I didn't make him take all those pills. And I certainly didn't pour that second bottle of tequila down his throat."

"You might as well have killed him!" Seraphina shrieked.

The next moment, to Marie's utter surprise, Seraphina leapt on Phoebe, and an instant later there was a full-blown girl fight taking place on the bedroom floor. Marie's chair floated upward, with her still seated, allowing her a view from above. She didn't feel the need to intervene, not quite yet. There was significant hair pulling, cursing, but no biting, and the two women rolling around on the floor didn't look like they were going to break anything, aside from a few nails.

She watched as they rolled into one wall and stopped, with Seraphina on top. Seraphina took advantage of the position and managed to straddle Phoebe, sitting atop her. Marie cringed the next moment when Seraphina gripped two fistfuls of blond hair and used them as makeshift handles as she began slamming Phoebe's head on the floor while shouting, "You killed him! You left him to die!"

Marie thought it time to break up the fight before real damage was done. She didn't know how much pounding Phoebe's head could take. But before she could intervene, the bedroom door flew open and she heard a man yell, "What the hell?"

Bentley and Julius rushed into the room, and the two men did what Marie was about to do—they broke up the fight. Bentley took hold of Seraphina and pulled her off, while Julius grabbed Phoebe, who was preparing to go after Seraphina now that she was free. The two women hurled insults at each other while the two men held them apart. When they finally calmed down, Seraphina jerked her arm from Bentley's hold and, without offering an explanation, marched from the room.

"She's crazy!" Phoebe called after Seraphina, no longer being held by Julius.

"What happened?" Bentley asked.

Out of breath and red faced, Phoebe glared at Bentley. "None of your business! And just get out of my room, both of you!" she shrieked.

A moment later, Bentley and Julius stood alone in the hallway, looking at the now closed door of the room they had just exited.

"What brought that on?" Bentley asked, still staring at the closed door.

"I don't know, but I think you just got kicked out of your room," Julius said.

HAND ON THE RAIL, Seraphina hurried down the staircase, her long black curls waving behind her like a flag. The last person she had expected to walk in the front door of Marlow House was Chris Johnson, but that was who entered the house. Considering he hadn't knocked and just walked in, Seraphina had to assume he was as close with the Marlows as Danielle had claimed.

CHRIS WAS MIDWAY in the entry hall when he spied Seraphina hurrying down the stairs. He smiled at her and was somewhat surprised when she rushed in his direction, grabbed one hand, and pulled him back to the front door.

"Where are we going?" Chris asked, mildly amused.

"I don't know. Just take me somewhere, anywhere," she told him.

Thirty minutes later, Seraphina and Chris sat in his car in the pier parking lot, looking out at the ocean. Seraphina had just told Chris everything that had happened back at the bedroom at Marlow House.

"I really can't see you in a girl fight," Chris mused.

"It's been a long time. But it all came back to me." Seraphina chuckled.

Chris looked to Seraphina, studying her profile as she looked out to the ocean. "You've been in girl fights before?"

Seraphina looked to Chris and smiled. "If it makes you feel any better, I've never been involved in a bar brawl. And the only girl fight—or any physical fight, for that matter—was with Phoebe."

"You and Phoebe have done this before?" he asked incredulously.

"Yes, but not since we were eleven."

"You've known her that long?" he asked.

She nodded. "We were in foster care together. I suppose we were like sisters back then, at least the only sister I ever had. And that included the occasional knockdown. Do you have any siblings?"

"I have an older brother," Chris said.

"Did you guys ever knock it out when you were kids? I've always heard stories of how brothers go at it."

Chris shook his head. "No. He was much older than me. Plus, we were raised in foster care and separated when I was very young. I only recently hooked up with him again."

Seraphina's eyes widened. "You were raised in foster care too?"

Chris nodded. "For a time. But when I was six, I was adopted by a very nice couple, and they raised me."

"Did you love them?" Seraphina asked in a soft voice.

"Very much."

"Did they love you?"

Reaching out one hand, Chris brushed the back of it across Seraphina's left cheek and said, "Yes. They were wonderful parents."

"You were lucky."

Dropping his hand back to his lap, he said, "How about you let me call Danielle, tell her I'm taking you out to dinner."

"I think I would like that."

EIGHTEEN

A chair had been removed from the dining room table to make more room for Chase, who sat between Birdie and Bentley, where Seraphina and Phoebe's chairs had been. Danielle thought the table might be a little crowded had Phoebe and Seraphina joined them for dinner. But Phoebe was still upstairs in her room, the door locked, and Seraphina had gone out with Chris.

"I'm not sure what shocked me most—that Seraphina hired Phoebe back in the first place, or that the two had a brawl," Jackie said as she grabbed a roll from a nearby basket. She looked over to Teddy and said, "What is it you always say, keep the drama in front of the camera?"

"I don't know what Seraphina was thinking when she rehired Phoebe after all that drama with Barry," Teddy grumbled.

About to take a bite of mashed potatoes, Birdie paused and looked across the table at Jackie. "I don't think we should be gossiping about Seraphina and Phoebe. It is their business."

"They made it our business when my husband and Bentley had to break up their fight," Jackie said. "And now poor Bentley has been locked out of his room."

"It's okay," Bentley assured her. "Danielle said I could sleep in the parlor tonight on a blow-up bed. I can grab my things from the room when Phoebe comes out to use the bathroom. I'm sure she's going to need to use the bathroom eventually. And it's probably only going to be for one night."

"What makes you say that?" Julius asked.

"Obviously, when Seraphina comes back, she's going to officially let Phoebe go, and when she does, there's no reason for Phoebe to stay any longer. I don't expect her to leave tonight. She'll have to arrange some transportation back to Portland, since she came here in Birdie's rental car," Bentley explained.

"I have to say, I am a little jealous of you and Julius," Chase said with a gruff laugh as he picked up his glass of wine.

"Why is that?" Julius asked.

"I wouldn't have minded walking in on those two rolling around on the floor. But I don't think I would have been so anxious to break them up, if you know what I mean." He laughed again.

Birdie glared at Chase. "That is a crude thing to say."

"Just speaking the truth. But it's probably best if Phoebe left." Chase glanced across the table and looked at Teddy, flashing him a smile.

Teddy met the smile with a brief glare before turning to Walt and changing the subject. "I was wondering if we're going to be meeting Jon Altar. You know, in all these years, I've never met the man, but I have great respect for his work."

"That's right," Chase said dully. "Altar is a

friend of yours, isn't he?"

"He and his wife live across the street. But to us, he's Ian," Danielle said.

"Ahh, yes, Altar is a pen name. Never understood that. Like you're not proud of your work, you have to hide behind a fake name," Chase said.

"I imagine he's proud enough of his work," Teddy countered. "How many Emmys has he won?"

Chase, who had never even been nominated for an Emmy, glared up at Teddy, who only chuckled in response.

"I'm sure you'll be meeting Ian," Walt said. "If it wasn't for him, we all wouldn't be sitting here right now."

Turning his attention from Teddy to Walt, Chase said, "Actually, what I'm more interested in hearing about is that tunnel. Is it real?"

"I assume you're talking about the tunnel that runs under Beach Drive—from our house to one of the neighbors' up the street?" Walt asked.

Chase arched his brows. "So it is true?"

"Yes. Frederick Marlow, a distant relative,

originally had this house built and at the same time put in the tunnel," Walt explained.

"I'd love to go inside the tunnel," Chase said. "Talk about raw material!"

"I'm afraid that's not possible," Walt said.

"Why not?" Chase asked.

"It's no longer accessible," Walt explained. "Both ends have been sealed off."

"Walt and Danielle showed us the entrance to the tunnel, quite fascinating," Birdie said. "But we weren't able to see anything other than a locked door."

"I'd love a peek inside. Can't you unlock the door?" Chase asked.

"I'm afraid not. Might be dangerous," Walt said. "It could come down on us."

"I bet it would be perfectly safe. Didn't I read you were wandering around in there for hours, and it never fell on you?" Chase asked.

"It's practically impossible to get that door open. But I'll be happy to show you the entrance to the tunnel," Walt offered. "But I'm afraid you'll be disappointed. Nothing much to see."

Birdie, who had just finished her dinner, glanced across the table at Polly, who sat quietly, pushing her food around her plate with her fork. "Polly dear, is everything alright?"

Polly looked up to Birdie and smiled. "Yes, thank you. I'm afraid I'm just a little tired this evening."

Teddy looked at his wife. "You don't look very good."

"Teddy!" Jackie snapped. "That is a terrible thing to say to your wife!"

"I just meant she looks tired. She should probably go up and turn in early tonight," Teddy said.

Polly stood up. "I think Teddy is right. I hope you all don't mind if I go up to my room now." She looked to Danielle and said, "The dinner was delicious. I'm sorry I didn't finish it all, but I'm quite exhausted."

POLLY COULD HEAR the voices in the dining room as she slowly made her way up the stairs. When she reached the second floor, she paused a moment and looked down to the first floor. She noticed the Marlows' black cat leisurely strolling across the entryway from the kitchen toward the parlor. She watched the cat a moment and then turned, making her way upstairs.

Once she came to the second floor, she headed for the room they had given Phoebe and Bentley. When she arrived at their door, she glanced over her shoulder toward the stairway leading to the first floor and then looked back to the closed door. She knocked. A moment later, Phoebe opened the door.

"What do you want?" Phoebe asked, peeking out into the hallway. Polly couldn't tell if Phoebe was dressed for bed or still wearing the clothes she had been wearing earlier. What she did notice, the woman had a black eye.

"I was wondering if we could talk," Polly asked.

"What about?" Phoebe asked.

"Not here. I was hoping we could meet later tonight, after everyone has gone to sleep. I don't want to be interrupted. Teddy or any of them could walk up here at any minute. I thought perhaps we could meet downstairs, in the kitchen. At midnight? I imagine everyone will be in bed by then."

"Maybe I'll be in bed by then too," Phoebe said.

"It's important. I just want to talk to you. Please."

Phoebe looked Polly up and down and then let out a sigh. "Fine. I can't ever get to sleep before midnight anyway, and I imagine I'll be hungry by then. You think they'll have something in the kitchen I can eat?"

"Why didn't you come down for dinner?"

Phoebe let out a snort. "Come on, don't pull that naive act. I'm sure Sera and I were the talk at the dinner table tonight. That's why I didn't want to go down. I know she isn't here. I saw her leave with Chris Johnson, and she hasn't come back, has she?"

Polly shook her head. "No."

"I bet everyone is expecting Sera to can me for good when she gets back, aren't they?"

"You don't think she will?" Polly asked.

Phoebe shrugged. "Sera and I go back a long time. Maybe she will; maybe she won't.

But okay, I'll meet you in the kitchen at midnight." Phoebe closed the door.

"I APPRECIATE THIS," Bentley said as Walt set up the inflatable mattress in the parlor while Danielle waited by his side with an armful of bed linens.

"No problem," Walt said, watching the mattress inflate.

"The sofa is not very comfortable," Danielle said. "I remember Lily's brother camped out on it one night when they were here for her wedding. It's too short. So we picked this up a while back for an extra bed."

"I'm surprised with a house this large you'd need extra beds often," Bentley said.

Danielle smiled. "That's why this inflatable bed is perfect—for those few times we do."

After making up the blow-up bed, Walt and Danielle left Bentley alone in the parlor watching television, while they went to the library, closing the door behind them. Waiting in the room was Eva and Marie.

"Chris still hasn't brought Seraphina back?" Eva asked. She sat with Marie on the sofa and watched as Walt and Danielle took the chairs facing them.

"Maybe he's not bringing her home," Danielle said with a grin.

"Surely you're not suggesting she's staying with him at his house," Marie asked primly. "They just met each other."

"That house has practically a hundred rooms. I'm sure he'll give Seraphina her own," Walt teased.

"Yeah, right." Danielle snickered.

Eva smiled over at Marie and said, "Marie dear, I know you were young once—I remember when you were born. Surely when you were Seraphina's age, you…well…you know."

"When I was her age, I was married," Marie said.

Eva shrugged in response.

"I can't believe those two women actually got into a fight!" Danielle said.

"I can't say I blame Seraphina. I almost decked Phoebe myself," Marie said.

"I'm just glad Chris and Seraphina are

getting to know each other. I worry about Chris," Danielle said.

"Worry, why?" Eva asked.

Danielle shrugged. "Chris, he never goes out. Half the town thinks he and Heather are an item, because she's the only woman they ever see him with."

"You do know Heather has been seeing that fisherman from Astoria?" Marie asked.

"Of course. I told you about it," Danielle reminded her. "But most of Frederickport doesn't know that, and Chris might as well be a monk."

Eva let out a sigh. "That's not exactly true."

"I don't see Chris as a monk," Walt said. "Don't they usually have bald spots? Chris has too much hair to be a monk."

Ignoring Walt's comment, Danielle looked at Eva and asked, "What do you mean?"

"Chris has a social life. Just not in Frederickport," Eva explained.

"He does?" Danielle asked. "He would have told me."

"Love, I have no problem with your close friendship with Chris. But expecting him to confide in you about his sex life," Walt began.

"Chris has a sex life?" Danielle asked.

"We need to change the subject," Marie said.

Eva laughed. "I'm just saying Chris has been on dates. There are a number of women he sees casually in Portland. Casually in that he hasn't felt compelled to share with them his real identity."

Danielle looked to Walt. "Did you know this?"

Walt shrugged. "Well…yes. Chris has talked to me and Ian—"

"Ian knows too?" Danielle asked.

Walt only smiled in reply.

Danielle let out a sigh and slumped back in her chair. "I guess I understand. You guys are all friends, and there are things I talk about with Lily that I would never share with Chris."

"Would you share it with me?" Walt asked.

Danielle looked at Walt and considered his question. "To be honest, I can't think of anything I haven't shared with you. So the answer is probably yes."

Walt smiled again.

"Chris isn't seriously interested in any of these women he's been seeing in Portland?" Danielle asked.

"I imagine not, considering he's out with Seraphina at the moment," Walt said.

NINETEEN

Danielle woke Sunday morning to the gentle patter of rain on the rooftop. Eyes still closed, a smile on her face, she rolled toward Walt and snuggled up against the warmth of his back. She could tell he was still asleep by the rhythm of his breathing.

She continued to lie there, enjoying the heat radiating off Walt's body, when she had the eerie sensation that someone was watching her. Had Max jumped up on the bed and she hadn't noticed, and was he trying to wake her so she would let him out? When there were people in the house, Walt and Danielle normally slept with their bedroom door locked. It was a habit Danielle had gotten into when running the bed and breakfast.

But then Danielle remembered Max had been sleeping in the living room when she and Walt went to bed last night. It was possible Walt had let Max in their bedroom sometime during the evening when she was sleeping.

It would not be the first time she awoke to a stare-down by the feline. Unable to shake the sensation, she sleepily fluttered open her eyes and lifted her head from the pillow, looking down to the foot of the bed where Max liked to sleep. She fully expected to find him perched near her feet, staring in her direction. But it wasn't a cat sitting on the mattress, staring up at her and Walt. It was a man.

Danielle bolted up with a scream.

"What?" Walt said groggily, sitting up in bed.

Danielle managed to get a grasp on her fear, because she realized just moments after letting out a scream that it was not a man exactly—it was a ghost. The same ghost who had come into the kitchen—not the ghost she had caught looking in the kitchen window.

"What are you doing here?" Danielle asked, her heart still racing. "You scared the crap out of me!"

Rubbing sleep from his eyes, Walt glared down the bed at the ghost, who sat cross-legged on the foot of the mattress, looking up at them.

"I've been waiting for you to wake up, of course," the ghost said.

"You'd better have a good reason for being on our bed," Walt growled.

"Really?" the ghost said, cocking his brow. "And what exactly will you do about it?"

Walt narrowed his eyes, still staring at the intruder, and the next moment a bronze bookend came flying off a nearby shelf in the ghost's direction. The surprised spirit widened his eyes and watched as the bookend flew through his chest and then landed on the floor with a thud.

"Impressive," the ghost said. "But like I asked, what are you going to do about it?" He looked over at the bookend and cringed. "I think you just dented your floor."

"Why are you here?" Danielle asked, reaching over, giving Walt a reassuring pat, wanting him to calm down. "Are you going to finally tell us who you are? Who might be in danger and why? And most of all, who is the killer?"

"I'm here to tell you it's already too late," the ghost said as he got up and began pacing the bedroom floor.

Walt and Danielle, now sitting up, the blankets pulled up to their chests, watched the ghost.

"What do you mean it's too late?" Danielle asked.

The ghost stopped pacing and looked at her. "Isn't it obvious? The killer struck again."

"Are you saying one of our guests was murdered?" Danielle squeaked.

"Right here at Marlow House," the ghost said.

Walt cursed and then climbed out of bed. Shirtless, he wore a pair of flannel pajama bottoms.

"Noooo…" Danielle said with a groan.

"I warned you," the ghost said before vanishing.

"That is one annoying ghost," Walt said as he hastily changed his pajama bottoms for slacks and pulled on a clean shirt.

Danielle rolled out of bed. "I don't want to find a dead body."

"You stay here. I'll go check the house," Walt told her. "Hopefully his annoyance extends to making up stories."

"I need to go with you."

NOW DRESSED FOR THE DAY, Walt and Danielle stepped out of their bedroom with trepidation, neither knowing exactly what to expect. When they reached the second floor, they came face-to-face with Teddy coming out of his room, heading for the bathroom.

"Good morning," Teddy said cheerfully. "You're up early."

"Yes, the rain woke us," Danielle said. "Umm, is Polly still sleeping?"

"Yes. Dead to the world," Teddy said before continuing to the bathroom.

When Teddy closed the bathroom door a moment later, Danielle cringed and said in a whisper, "I hope that was just a figure of speech. I like Polly."

"Me too."

"Do we knock on everyone's door? Say, hello, are you alive?" Danielle asked.

Walt looked down the hallway at all the closed doors. Other than Teddy, it didn't sound as if anyone else was awake. "Not unless you can come up with a good reason to be knocking this early."

Danielle glanced at her watch. "Joanne should be here in about thirty minutes to start breakfast. We should check downstairs first. I don't want her to walk in on something, in case it happened down there."

Walt gave a nod and then headed to the staircase with Danielle. When they reached the first floor, all was quiet. The door to the parlor where Bentley had spent the night was still closed, as was the downstairs bedroom. They swiftly went through the rooms with no guests, the kitchen, living room, dining room, library and guest bathroom. Nothing appeared to be out of place. No dead bodies in sight. Together they went down to the basement, and they found nothing unusual there.

Once back on the first floor, they headed to the kitchen to make coffee. They walked into the room at the same time that Max entered through the pet door from the side yard.

"Max," Walt said, before asking him if he had seen anything. He hadn't. The cat told Walt he had spent most of the night sleeping in the library and prowling outside during the early morning hours.

"All we can do is wait for them to come down for breakfast, and hopefully they will. But there is one bright spot," Danielle said.

"What's that?" Walt asked.

"If someone was murdered in the house, I would expect their ghost to greet us," Danielle said. "So that's a good sign."

"True," Walt agreed.

"Oh crap," Danielle groaned.

"What?" Walt asked.

"How do we know Teddy isn't a ghost?" Danielle said.

"I doubt Teddy is a ghost. He didn't walk through the bathroom door, he opened it with the doorknob."

"True. I wish Marie was here. We could

get her to check out the bedrooms and see if any of our guests have been murdered."

"That sounds rather gruesome," Walt noted as he made the coffee while Danielle continued to fret.

"I guess I should be careful what I say. I'd hate for one of our guests to walk in and hear me say something like that."

Walt chuckled. "True. It would put one ill at ease."

"No kidding."

WHEN JOANNE ARRIVED on Sunday morning, Walt and Danielle had already made the coffee and set the dining room table for breakfast. After helping Joanne get the breakfast started, Walt and Danielle retired to the dining room to wait for their guests—each praying none would be missing and none would show up as a ghost.

Birdie arrived at the table first. Danielle and Walt were fairly certain she was not a ghost when she pulled her chair out to sit down. While it was possible for a ghost to move objects, it was rare for someone who had just passed over. But when Joanne brought a basket of cinnamon rolls and said good morning to Birdie, their thoughts were confirmed.

The next one to show up for breakfast was Bentley.

"I went ahead and deflated the blow-up bed," Bentley told them. "I have a feeling I'll be back in the upstairs room tonight." Danielle and Walt exchanged glances while Birdie greeted Bentley.

A few minutes later they could hear chattering voices coming down the stairs. When the people attached to the voices arrived in the dining room, Walt and Danielle counted the Staffords and Larimores safe. All four appeared to be healthy and alive.

"Did Seraphina get home last night?" Jackie asked when she looked over to the empty chair. When Walt and Danielle had set the table that morning, they had returned the chair they had removed the night before to make more room for Chase.

"Yes, I heard her come in rather late last

night," Bentley said. "I was still watching TV."

"That might explain why she isn't down here yet," Jackie said with a chuckle. "Out partying last night."

"I see Phoebe isn't here either," Teddy noted. "Do you know if she's still in her room, or did Seraphina give her the boot last night?"

"I doubt it. But I wouldn't have heard her leave anyway," Birdie said. "First thing I do when heading to my room at night is take off my hearing aids."

Again Danielle and Walt exchanged glances. Just as Joanne brought the platters with breakfast, Seraphina walked into the dining room.

"Sorry I'm late for breakfast," she apologized.

"We're just starting," Julius told her.

"Is Phoebe up?" Polly asked Seraphina. "I was wondering if she's coming down to breakfast this morning, since she missed dinner last night."

"I knocked on her door," Seraphina said as she sat down at her seat and then grabbed the napkin and shook it out before placing it on her lap. "I thought we should talk this morning, before breakfast, but she didn't answer. I assumed she was down here. Since she's not, she's obviously ignoring me."

Danielle stood up. "I think I'll go see if she's coming down. Like Polly said, she did miss dinner."

Seraphina shrugged. "She's a big girl. She knows what time breakfast is being served."

"I'm still going up," Danielle said.

Walt stood. "I'll go with you. "I need to get something from our room anyway," he lied.

"PLEASE DON'T LET Phoebe be dead," Danielle said under her breath as she and Walt hurried up the stairs.

"If the ghost was telling the truth, it has to be her," Walt said.

"Gosh, I hope not. Because you know who looks like the guilty party," Danielle groaned.

"Seraphina," Walt said.

Danielle nodded. "They had a physical fight yesterday. But dang, Chris seems to like her. I don't want her to be a killer. Crap, a serial killer."

Walt paused at the second-floor landing and looked at his wife. "Who said anything about her being a serial killer?"

"How many people do you have to kill to be a serial killer?" Danielle asked. "That ghost is one…Phoebe would be two."

"*If* Phoebe is dead. I'm still holding out hope the ghost is nothing more than a troublemaker. After all, if Seraphina is his killer, I don't see why he would want to protect her."

Danielle reached out and grabbed Walt's right hand for a moment, giving it a brief squeeze. "I love it when you're optimistic."

Together they continued down the hall to the room they had given Bentley and Phoebe. When she reached their door, Danielle knocked.

Nothing.

She knocked again, this time saying, "Phoebe, it's Danielle. Are you up?"

Again, nothing.

Before trying the door, Danielle went to

the bathrooms to see if she might be in one of them. They were both empty. She returned to Phoebe's bedroom and knocked again. When there was still no answer, Danielle took a deep breath and opened the door, Walt right behind her.

She was surprised to find the room empty.

"There's no one here," Danielle said as she walked into the room, Walt following her.

Danielle glanced around. She couldn't tell if the unmade bed had been slept in, as Joanne did not make up the beds during the guests' stay.

"There's a note," Walt called out, picking up a note from the dresser. "It's from Phoebe."

"What does it say?" Danielle asked. She looked over Walt's shoulder and read the note.

Sorry for everything, Sera. I got a ride to the airport. Phoebe.

TWENTY

Their guests were in the midst of a lively conversation around the breakfast table when Danielle and Walt returned from Phoebe's room, note in hand. After they walked into the dining room, all the guests stopped talking and looked at them.

"Is she coming down?" Polly asked.

"I don't think so," Danielle said. She walked to Seraphina and handed her the note. "I think this is for you."

Seraphina silently read the note and then shook her head. "She must have called an Uber."

"She left?" Birdie asked.

"It looks that way," Seraphina said, handing the note to Birdie.

"Does it look like her handwriting?" Danielle asked.

Birdie handed the note back to Seraphina. "Who else's handwriting would it be?"

Danielle glanced around the table and found them all looking at her as if she had asked the lamest question, which from their perspective, she had.

"Silly question," Danielle muttered as she sat down at the table with Walt.

"You didn't talk to her when you got back last night?" Teddy asked.

Seraphina looked to Teddy, her face expressionless. "Didn't I already say that?"

"It's for the best," Jackie said, picking up her cup of coffee. "Those personal dramas just get in the way of our work."

"Who's going to drive my rental car now?" Birdie asked.

"I'm perfectly capable of driving the rental," Seraphina said.

"I don't know. Are you on the insurance?" Birdie asked.

"Seriously, you're worried about that?" Teddy said with a snort.

Birdie turned a frown to Teddy. "A person in my position can't be too careful. Someone out there always wants to sue you, and it is in my name."

"I'm sure you can add Seraphina to the rental car's insurance," Julius said.

"Or you could drive it yourself," Jackie suggested. "I imagine they have you on the policy if you rented the car."

Birdie shrugged. "I don't like to drive."

"Why do you need to drive? You don't want me to drive anymore?" An unexpected voice broke into the conversation. Yet only two people in the room could hear it.

Walt and Danielle both looked to the doorway and saw Phoebe standing just inside the dining room, wearing a pair of jogging pants and a T-shirt. By the way the others continued chattering on, it was obvious they couldn't hear the new arrival.

Danielle looked to Walt, who was still staring at Phoebe. She cringed.

Hands on hips, Phoebe stepped closer to the table and looked from one person to another, her brow furrowing into a frown. "Hello!"

"Bentley, looks like you get the room to yourself," Jackie told him. "No more sleeping in the parlor."

"He didn't have to sleep in the parlor last night," Phoebe snapped. "No one said he couldn't sleep in the room. But don't expect me to sleep in the parlor."

Phoebe started to say something else when something unexpected caught her attention—snow. It fell from the ceiling. Wide eyed, she looked up and started to point. "Look! Look, you guys!"

Everyone at the table—except Walt and Danielle—continued talking, oblivious to the snow falling on their breakfast plates and disappearing. The next moment Eva and Marie appeared, and together floated down from the ceiling, landing on the center of the dining room table.

"That was rather fun!" Marie laughed. "I don't know why I didn't try that before!"

"Holy crap!" Phoebe stammered, her eyes wide as she stared at the two strange women.

Marie glanced over at Phoebe and said,

"Eva, I think she can see us!"

"Perhaps it's your energy!" Eva said excitedly. She quickly looked around the table. Yet all the seated guests were talking amongst themselves, and none of them seem to be aware of her or Marie.

"What is going on?" Phoebe shrieked.

"Goodness, I think she's a ghost," Marie declared.

The next moment Phoebe disappeared.

Danielle stood up. "If you will excuse me, I forgot I have to call my friend Eva Marie."

"I'll go with you. I need to talk to her too," Walt said.

"SHE'S DEAD, ISN'T SHE?" Marie asked after she and Eva joined Walt and Danielle in the parlor, the door closed for privacy.

"It certainly looks that way," Danielle said with a groan as she slumped down on the sofa.

Walt took a seat next to Danielle. He reached over and patted her knee while saying, "And she doesn't know it yet."

Danielle shook her head. "No. She definitely doesn't know it yet."

"How did she die?" Eva asked.

Danielle then explained their morning encounter with the mystery ghost.

"Oh dear, I saw Chris this morning, and he was quite enamored of Seraphina. I hope she isn't the one," Eva said.

"And you have no idea where her body is?" Marie asked.

"We looked around the house. But if she was murdered here, as the ghost said, maybe her body is in one of the bedrooms we couldn't check. After all, if one of those people out there bumped her off, maybe her body's in their room," Walt suggested.

"The ghost never said anything about two killers," Danielle said. "So if the killer has her body in their bedroom…then it would be Birdie or Seraphina. After all, if Jackie or Julius is responsible—or Teddy or Polly—would they be able to hide a body in their room without their spouse seeing it? And none of them looked especially anxious at breakfast. And Bentley slept in here, and I don't see a dead body."

"I would assume if your husband or wife murdered someone and made you help hide the body in your room, the innocent spouse would be quite shaken," Marie said.

Eva stood up. "We need to check those bedrooms."

"Please, while they're still at the breakfast table," Danielle said. "And if you see Phoebe, find out who killed her."

"She doesn't even know she's dead yet," Marie reminded.

When Marie and Eva left the parlor to go check out the bedrooms, Danielle remained on the sofa with Walt. She leaned against him as he put his arm around her shoulders.

"She could be somewhere outside," Danielle suggested.

"I doubt she's in the side yard; Joanne came in that way. But if Marie and Eva don't find anything, then we should go check," Walt said.

"Seraphina seemed so nice," Danielle moaned.

"You think it's her?" Walt said.

"It has to be. And I handed her that note.

Silly me," Danielle said. "I should have taken it back."

"At this point, that would have looked odder than you asking if the handwriting was Phoebe's."

"I know," Danielle agreed, still leaning against Walt. "But that note is evidence. Whoever wrote it is obviously the killer."

"Unless, of course, Phoebe wrote it," Walt suggested.

"Why do you say that?" Danielle asked.

"Maybe she was going to leave. After that embarrassing confrontation, perhaps she decided to slip out last night when everyone was sleeping so she wouldn't have to talk to anyone. She did hide out in her room the rest of the day after the fight. Maybe she wrote that note, and before she left, she had an altercation with the killer," Walt said.

Marie and Eva reappeared in the parlor, sans the glitter snow.

"There's no sign of her anywhere," Marie announced.

"We need to go check outside," Danielle said, starting to stand up.

"Don't bother," Eva said. "We did that

after we checked the bedrooms—got a nice aerial view of the neighborhood—no sign of a body anywhere. I also looked in your garage, and Marie looked in their cars."

"And we checked all the closets," Marie added. "The hidden staircase."

Danielle settled back down on the sofa and asked, "How about pink suitcases?"

"Pink suitcases?" Marie asked.

"Phoebe checked in with two pink suitcases. They weren't in her room when we found her note. And it looks like all her clothes are gone too," Danielle explained.

"No. We didn't see any pink suitcases," Eva said.

"If that ghost hadn't said she was murdered in the house, I would assume she was killed somewhere else, like on her way back to Portland, maybe in a car accident. With no body, none of her suitcases in sight, it seems as if she had to have been killed somewhere else, but her confused spirit found its way back here."

"The only problem with that, the ghost insists she was killed in the house," Walt reminded them.

"THERE IS no way Seraphina murdered Phoebe," Chris insisted. He sat with Walt, Danielle and Heather in his office in the foundation headquarters, Hunny sleeping by his feet. While it was Sunday and Heather's day off, Danielle thought it best if they circle all the wagons, so she had given Heather a call before leaving to see Chris, telling her they were picking her up—there was another ghost in the neighborhood.

Marie and Eva had stayed back at Marlow House. Their duties included being on the lookout for Phoebe's ghost while eavesdropping on all the suspects.

"How do you know that?" Heather asked.

"Because Seraphina and I talked for hours last night," Chris told her.

"Only talked?" Heather teased.

He flashed her a glare. "Shut up."

"I don't think you can get to know someone after spending just a few hours with them," Danielle said.

"I just know she wasn't upset with Phoebe," Chris said.

"She gave her a black eye," Danielle reminded him.

"True, but that doesn't mean she'd kill her," Chris said.

"What are you going to do?" Heather asked.

"I think we need to talk to the chief," Danielle said. "Let him know what's going on."

"And what, tell him you think Seraphina killed two people?" Chris snapped.

"Someone killed her and whoever that ghost used to be," Danielle said.

Heather sat back in her chair, considering the possible scenarios. "I think I know how she did it."

"She didn't do it," Chris said.

"When she got back to Marlow House, she found Phoebe had packed and had written that note," Heather began.

"She didn't do it," Chris repeated.

Heather flashed Chris a *shut up* look and then continued. "She offered to drive Phoebe somewhere. After all, you say Phoebe didn't have a car, and according to the note, she was going to call an Uber."

"No, she didn't say she was calling an Uber," Danielle corrected. "She just said she was calling a ride, Seraphina suggested that's what she had done."

"We should be calling Uber and see who picked her up last night," Chris said.

"Let me finish," Heather snapped.

"According to the ghost, she was killed at Marlow House," Danielle reminded her.

"Yes, I get that," Heather said, sounding annoyed. "Anyway…they are sitting in the car right in front of the house, and Phoebe pisses Seraphina off again, but this time she whacks her with something. Maybe her cellphone. You should check her cellphone for blood. And—"

"Your scenario doesn't work," Chris argued. "According to the ghost, she was killed in the house."

"Wait a minute, Chris," Danielle interrupted. "I'm not sure if he said she was killed in Marlow House—or at Marlow House."

"What difference does it make?" he asked.

"I see what you're saying," Walt said. "He might have just meant on our property—or the general location. In front of the house could be interpreted as being bumped off at Marlow House."

"Exactly," Heather said with a nod. "And then after Seraphina realized she had just bashed her friend's head in, she drives her somewhere and dumps the body and suitcases. Which is why her spirit wasn't there this morning when you guys first got up. She was on her way back to Marlow House from wherever she was dumped."

"If it happened that way, Seraphina isn't the one who did it," Chris insisted.

"When you see her, ask to see her cellphone," Heather said.

"Why?" Chris asked with a frown.

"To see if it has blood stuck in its cover or around the edges, of course. Or maybe she already threw the cover away, or tossed the cellphone in the ocean!"

"You seriously think the murder weapon is a cellphone?" Chris asked dryly. "Based on what evidence?"

"Do you have a better suggestion?" Heather asked.

TWENTY-ONE

Police Chief MacDonald leaned back in his recliner, his hands folded together and resting on his chest, as he peered at the three people sitting on his living room sofa looking at him expectantly. What they wanted from him he had no flipping clue. He would like to toss them out of his home and never deal with them again.

Each had caused him more problems than any other Frederickport resident. Since meeting them, murder stats for Frederickport had risen, and one or more of them had been involved in each one of those recent murders. If he could run them out of town on the proverbial rail, he would. There was only one problem; they were his friends.

"Well, Chief? What do you think?" Danielle asked, leaning forward, waiting for his response. To her right sat Walt and to her left Chris.

"I think you three should take a long trip," the chief said.

"A trip?" Danielle frowned. That was not the answer she had expected.

The chief sat up in his chair. "Maybe buy an RV, go cross-country."

"What are you talking about?" Danielle asked.

"Or maybe a trip to Europe. I hear Paris in the spring is beautiful." The chief grinned.

"You don't want to deal with this, do you?" Chris asked.

"I just wanted a peaceful Sunday," the chief began. "And now you tell me there's been a murder, but you have no idea where the body is. And there is no crime scene."

"I'm sure there is a crime scene. We just can't find it," Danielle said.

"Any possibility she wasn't a ghost? You said she got in a fight with the singer, and two of them had to break it up. Maybe they were just ignoring her?" he asked hopefully.

"She saw Marie and Eva," Danielle reminded him.

"Maybe she's a medium? You have to admit, we have a lot of mediums around here. Frederickport seems like a regular medium magnet," the chief said.

"She disappeared before our eyes," Danielle said.

"Have you been drinking?" MacDonald asked.

"In the morning?" Danielle countered.

"Bloody Marys? Mimosas? You know that Hollywood crowd." The chief grinned weakly.

Danielle rolled her eyes and slumped back, crossing her arms over her chest.

MacDonald glanced to Walt and Chris, who looked at him with bemusement and a hint of sympathy.

With a sigh, MacDonald sat up straighter. "Okay, okay. There has been another murder. And you're sure you have looked everywhere on your property for the body? You said the first ghost claimed the murder happened at Marlow House?"

"We looked everywhere," Walt said. "Marie and Eva went through all the guest rooms, including closets. We checked the hidden staircase and the entrance to the tunnels. Nothing. And no sign of anything."

"I know it looks bad for Seraphina," Chris said. "Considering their fight the night before. But I don't believe she had anything to do with it. We talked all last night. She and Phoebe go back to when they were kids. She was practically her sister. That's why she hired her in the first place, to give her a job."

"A sister who fooled around with her boyfriend," the chief reminded him.

"Seraphina was hurt, but she seemed willing to give Phoebe some slack," Chris said.

Danielle turned to Chris. With a frown she said, "Come on. I like Seraphina too, but seriously, give Phoebe slack for sleeping with her boyfriend? I'm sorry. When I was in that position, I didn't feel that way, and she was dead."

"True, but she wasn't someone you looked at like a sister," Chris reminded her.

"Thank god for that!" Danielle said. "It's enough of a betrayal having someone you think you love betray you, but with a sister figure?"

"Seraphina understands how Phoebe is broken. I get that. Being raised in foster care can leave a scar. And Seraphina told me Phoebe was given up by her mother, who had drug and alcohol issues, and she refused to sign any papers to relinquish her rights. She kept insisting she was going to get her act together and come back for Phoebe. But she never did. And she never made an effort to see her. And when Phoebe turned eighteen, the woman dropped out of sight completely. Seraphina told me Phoebe thinks her mother went AWOL because she was afraid she would be asked for money or to help support Phoebe now that she was on her own."

"She told you a lot," the chief said. "Didn't you just meet her?"

"Come on, Chief, you know how it is sometimes when you meet a woman, and you just click. And you start talking about everything?" Chris said.

The chief shrugged. "Can't say I do. It's been a while."

"What you're suggesting, Chris," Walt said, "Seraphina basically felt sorry for Phoebe, which is why she kept forgiving her, and that she had forgiven her for her most recent transgressions?"

Chris nodded. "Pretty much. Seraphina admitted she was furious at first. Hell, they got into a girl fight. But after she simmered down, she got over it. I don't think she went back to Marlow House and killed her. No way."

"Someone killed her," Walt reminded him.

"If it wasn't Seraphina, then do you have any other theories?" the chief asked Chris.

"Actually, Heather had a good theory," Chris began.

Danielle looked to Chris. "Her theory was that Seraphina killed her."

"Not that part. But maybe one of the other guests offered to take her to the airport, and then they killed her when she got into the car—which could explain why your ghost claimed she was killed at Marlow House. Once in the car, the killer dumped her body and suitcases. There is a nice big ocean out there. Good place to dispose of a body," Chris said.

"All we can do at this point is wait for her body to show up. Hopefully her ghost will come back and tell you where to find it. But until that happens, there is absolutely nothing I can do. Not until someone files a missing person report on her, and chances are, that won't be done until they get back in California. Then it'll be out of my jurisdiction. At this point, there's no indication of foul play," the chief said.

STANDING in the women's bathroom at Pier Café, Carla dried her hands on a paper towel while admiring her reflection in the mirror. The burgundy was a good look, she thought, inspecting her recent hair dye. Tossing the wadded-up paper towel into the trash can, she turned toward the door and froze a moment when a young woman walked into the bathroom. She gasped. It was Seraphina Bouchard.

"Oh my god!" Carla said excitedly, jumping up and down. "It's you, it's really you!"

Seraphina smiled and looked more embarrassed than annoyed.

"I'm such a fan," Carla squealed. "Can I have your autograph?"

"Umm…" Seraphina eyed the toilet stalls. "I guess."

Carla glanced from Seraphina to where she was looking and then grinned. "Oh, I bet you want to use the toilet, don't you? I mean, this is a bathroom and everything. I'll go and let you use it. I imagine someone like you doesn't want a fan hanging around when you're trying to pee, do you? I'll catch you when you're done!" Carla rushed out of the bathroom.

Giddy with excitement, Carla wanted to linger by the bathroom door so she could snag Seraphina and get her autograph, yet when she came out, she was greeted by a group of seven people milling nearby, just inside the front door, looking around for a table large enough to accommodate them.

Stepping up to the group, she asked, "How many?"

"There are eight of us," one of the women said.

Carla did a quick head count, but came up with only seven.

"There's another one in the bathroom," another woman said. "She'll be right out."

"Oh!" Carla grinned. "You must be the people staying at Marlow House. I saw Seraphina in the bathroom. She is absolutely gorgeous and so nice!"

"So you have a table?" the first woman asked, sounding slightly annoyed.

"I'll put two together. Just give me a minute!" Carla said excitedly, rushing to prepare the table.

"Really, Jackie, you didn't need to be so impatient with the waitress," Birdie chastised.

"I have a horrible headache," Jackie said. "I didn't get any sleep last night."

INSTEAD OF GOING with the others when Carla came to take his party to their table, Chase turned to make a trip to the restroom. Before reaching the door, Seraphina stepped out of the women's bathroom. He stopped a moment to talk to her.

"I've got a beautiful beach house right on the ocean," he told her. "You are more than welcome to stay. There are plenty of extra bedrooms. You can stay in any one you want. And I mean any of them." He smiled.

"I guess you heard Phoebe left," Seraphina said.

"If she was still here, there would have been plenty of room for her too." He grinned.

"Thanks, Chase, but I'm pretty comfortable where I am."

When Seraphina arrived at the table, she took the empty seat next to Birdie. "I think Chase just hit on me," she whispered to the older woman.

Birdie arched her brows. "You aren't serious?"

"Remember what Phoebe told us about him," Seraphina reminded her.

"What did he say?" Birdie asked.

"What are you two whispering about over there?" Teddy called from across the table.

Before Seraphina could answer Birdie or respond to Teddy, Carla showed up at the table to claim her autograph.

THE WAITRESS with the burgundy hair had taken their orders, delivered their food, and returned to the table countless times to see if they needed anything. Plates had been cleared and more coffee poured. Bentley and Chase left the others so they could go outside to have a smoke.

Lingering by the pier railing, each man, with a lit cigarette in hand, looked out to sea.

"So Phoebe left, did she?" Chase asked, taking a puff off his cigarette.

"I wondered if you were the driver that picked her up," Bentley said, flicking an ash over the rail.

"What are you talking about?" Chase frowned.

Turning around, Bentley leaned casually

against the railing. "Last night, I heard a car drive up. I was sleeping downstairs in that front den and looked outside. I could swear the car looked just like the one you rented."

Chase shrugged. "Not sure what that has to do with Phoebe."

"Someone obviously picked her up. Why did you come back last night?"

"It sure wasn't to pick up Phoebe," Chase said. "I had a hole in my shirt pocket and lost my fountain pen. I found it on the front porch."

"You came all the way back at that time of night for a fountain pen?" Bentley asked.

"It wasn't just any fountain pen. It was an Ancora, cost me almost two thousand bucks."

"Whoa, you spent almost two thousand dollars on a pen? I knew you had a penchant for pricy pens, but dang."

Chase shrugged and took another puff off his cigarette.

"I did wonder, thought maybe you had Phoebe stashed over at the beach house with you," Bentley added.

Chase laughed. "I don't think so."

TWENTY-TWO

The plan was for a Sunday night cocktail party at Marlow House, followed by dinner. The intimate soiree included invitations extended to Lily and Ian, and at the last minute to Chris. The plan had never been to invite all their friends, but Teddy and Jackie were anxious to meet Jon Altar, aka Ian Bartley, and considering how Seraphina and Chris had immediately taken to each other, Danielle had asked him to join them.

Danielle and Lily stood alone together on the edge of the living room, their backs to the large picture window that looked out at the dark night. They watched the lively conversation taking place on the other side of the room between Ian, Jackie and Teddy, while several others gathered around and listened.

Lily sipped her martini and asked Danielle in a whisper, "So which one do you think killed her?"

"The one with the most obvious motive is Seraphina," Danielle said. "But Chris insists she didn't do it."

Lily glanced out to the open doorway leading to the hallway and spied Chris and Seraphina lingering there, chatting amongst themselves. "I don't think I've seen Chris look at anyone that way since he kissed you the first time on New Year's Eve."

"Oh, shut up," Danielle said.

Lily took another sip of her drink and looked around the room. "Where are Marie and Eva?"

Danielle nodded to the sofa. "Marie is sitting between Polly and Bentley. Eva is over there next to Ian."

"Speaking of Marie, I rather miss my babysitter. You guys have been monopolizing all her time."

"Sorry, but we've needed her and Eva to

eavesdrop. You mentioned Kelly is watching Connor tonight. I thought Heather was going to?" Danielle asked.

"Heather called me this morning and told me she's coming down with a cold and doesn't want to give it to Connor. I really don't need a sick kid. So I called Kelly at the last minute."

"Glad she could watch him. But you could have brought him with you," Danielle said.

"I appreciate that. But I was looking forward to an adult night. Yet I'm not sure how Kelly is going to do."

"What do you mean? She's not still locking Sadie out of the nursery, is she?"

"No. She doesn't do that anymore. But now she's all paranoid Connor is going to leap out of his crib. Before we left, she was taking all my pillows off my bed and piling them up around the crib—you know to provide a soft landing when my gymnast son makes his great escape." Lily chuckled.

"Oh no." Danielle laughed. "And you let her?"

Lily shrugged. "If it makes her feel better.

Whatever. I'm just going to have to change all my pillowcases when I get home, now that they've all been on the floor."

"At least you know she's probably going to keep a close eye on him."

Lily smiled and then asked, "Have Eva and Marie learned anything in their ghostly sleuthing?"

"Just that while Seraphina is the obvious suspect, it looks like a few of them had issues with Phoebe. So maybe Chris is right."

"Such as?" Lily asked.

"Marie heard Polly say something to Teddy about his girlfriend taking off in the middle of the night."

"His girlfriend? Are you saying Teddy and Phoebe were a thing?"

Danielle shrugged. "According to Teddy they weren't, but the comment turned into a fight, but after they got into it, nothing specific was said about Phoebe. According to Marie, Teddy doesn't treat Polly very nice when they're alone. Yet Eva told us it was Polly who was the instigator in that argument, and Teddy who kept trying to appease her."

"If you think your man is cheating on you, then yeah, bring it on," Lily said.

"YOU LOOK BORED," Bentley told Polly, unknowingly looking through Marie, who sat between them.

Polly shrugged. "I should go over there and strike up a conversation with Julius; that will stir things up a bit." She took a sip of wine, her eyes on her husband, who stood across the room, still involved in the animated discussion.

Bentley looked over to Julius, who sat next to Birdie, talking to her. He looked back to Polly and asked, "What's wrong with talking to me?"

"You're gay, obviously." Polly downed the rest of her wine.

Bentley raised his brows. "What does that have to do with anything?"

"I'd like to know that too," Marie said to deaf ears.

Polly flashed Bentley a grin. "Teddy doesn't worry about you hitting on me. But for some reason he's convinced Julius is some player, and I'm on his to-do list."

"Julius? He seems like such a nice man," Marie said, sounding disappointed.

"Julius? He's Jackie's lapdog. Loyal as they come. Not sure where Teddy got that idea," Bentley said.

"Projection," Polly said, setting her empty wineglass on the nearby coffee table.

"Is that what your argument with Phoebe was about. Teddy?" he asked.

"Polly argued with Phoebe?" Marie looked to Polly.

"What are you talking about?" Polly asked.

"Oh my, he did pull your chain with that one," Marie muttered. "I do like you. I would rather you not be the killer."

"Come on, I slept downstairs, remember? I heard you and Phoebe in the kitchen. Surprised no one else did."

"No. I don't want it to be you," Marie said.

"Do you think Birdie heard?" Polly asked.

He shrugged. "I doubt it. Not unless she had her hearing aids on."

"I thought we were being quiet," Polly said.

"You guys weren't that bad. I only heard you because I got up to get a drink of water. But that was some heated discussion you two had going on."

Polly eyed Bentley. "Did you hear what we were talking about?"

"What? What were you talking about?" Marie asked.

"A little. Enough. I imagine you're glad Phoebe left. Did you know she was leaving?" he asked.

"I have a favor to ask you," Polly told him.

"What?"

"Please don't tell anyone that you overheard me talking to Phoebe last night. Please."

"Oh dear, that does not sound good," Marie said.

"Why?" Bentley asked.

"Teddy would be furious with me. I don't want him to know. And now that Phoebe is gone, there's no reason to bring it up."

"What about when we get back to California?" Bentley asked.

"There is no reason for Teddy and Phoebe to run into each other. After all, she doesn't work for Seraphina anymore. So if she doesn't tell him, he won't find out."

"I'm not sure about that. Did Seraphina say she fired her? All we know for certain is that Phoebe left. They've gotten in fights before. I wouldn't be surprised to see her on the set when they start filming. And we all know she's been vying for a part in the film."

"Phoebe is not an actress," Polly reminded him.

"She wants to be. We all know she's trying to take a shortcut through Seraphina. Which is why she'll do what's necessary to get back in her good graces."

"She won't be back," Polly insisted. "But just promise me, don't say anything to anyone."

"No, that does not sound good at all." Marie sighed.

"I promise," Bentley vowed.

CHASE ARRIVED LATE to the cocktail

party. He made his rounds and, when introduced to Ian, cut short the introduction and moved on to another section of the room.

"Was it something I said?" Ian muttered under his breath as he watched the heavyset man head in Birdie's direction.

"Don't mind Chase," Jackie explained. "I think he's a little intimidated by you."

"Not sure *intimidated* is the right word." Teddy snickered. "I'd say it's more he feels he has to put up with Walt, and he isn't about to deal with Ian too."

"I was trying to be diplomatic," Jackie said with a laugh.

"I don't understand," Walt said.

"Chase is good at what he does," Jackie explained. "But his ego doesn't like sharing the spotlight with any writers who might be on par—or in Ian's case—superior to him."

JULIUS GOT up from his chair just as Chase walked up. Explaining he was going to go talk to his wife, he offered the chair to Chase. When Julius was out of earshot,

Birdie asked, "Did you make a pass at Seraphina today?"

Chase frowned at the older woman. "What are you talking about?"

"Did you? At that diner today, when we were having lunch," she demanded.

"I simply told her she was welcome to stay at the beach house I rented. It's right on the ocean. You can't see anything from this place except for other houses."

"So you were just offering her a better view?" she asked.

"There were no strings. Anyway, she could do far worse. Barry was a womanizer, and look at that guy she's hanging out with now." He nodded toward the open doorway, where Chris and Seraphina stood in the foyer. "A nobody."

"You've been hired to write the script for *Moon Runners*, not to turn it into your own private dating service."

"Birdie, I know you're funding the project, but I have a contract, and it doesn't include a clause where I need your permission before I see someone personally. Seraphina is an adult. You're not her mother."

"Maybe not, but contracts can be broken, and this one does have a morality clause."

"I'm not sure how asking Seraphina to join me would be a violation of the clause."

"I wasn't thinking of that. I was thinking of Phoebe," she said.

Chase stared at her a moment, his expression unreadable. Finally he said, "I told you already. Phoebe was lying. Nothing happened."

"No. Nothing happened because Teddy walked in."

"I explained what happened. You said you understood," he said.

"Yes. Considering what went on between her and Barry, I gave you the benefit of the doubt. But I will believe Seraphina if she tells me you've stepped out of line."

"I'm sure Seraphina can take care of herself, Birdie. She doesn't need you to intervene. What's the deal, you taking over where Randy left off?"

"What is that supposed to mean?"

"Come on. We all knew she was Randy's pet project. He loved to tell everyone how he discovered her singing in that little club. Hell,

I was surprised he didn't make himself her agent."

"Leave my husband out of this," she said sharply.

"IT MIGHT HAVE BEEN POLLY," Marie said sadly when she joined Danielle and Lily.

"Marie is here," Danielle told Lily before turning to Marie and asking, "Why do you say that?"

Marie recounted what she had overheard.

"What did she say?" Lily asked.

Danielle told her.

"And she doesn't know what they argued about?" Lily asked.

"According to Eva, she overheard Teddy and Polly arguing. Polly did accuse Teddy of having some sort of relationship with Phoebe—which he denied," Marie said.

Again, Danielle played translator.

"So you think Polly confronted Phoebe about her and Teddy?" Lily asked.

"Sort of sounds that way," Danielle said.

Glancing to the sofa, the two women and

one ghost watched as both Bentley and Polly stood up. Polly walked to the door leading to the hallway, while Bentley went in the opposite direction. The three turned their attention to Bentley. A moment earlier Chase had abandoned the chair next to Birdie, and Bentley claimed it. They watched as Bentley leaned close to Birdie and whispered something in her ear.

"I wonder what he overheard last night," Danielle said, her eyes still on Jackie's assistant.

POLLY STEPPED out of the downstairs bathroom and shut the door. She looked toward the doorway leading to the living room. Chris and Seraphina were no longer standing in the foyer talking, and she wondered briefly if they had joined the others in the living room or had gone somewhere else. The sound of voices drifted out from the living room.

A meow distracted her attention. She glanced to the left and noticed the Marlows' black cat walking toward the door leading to the basement. She followed the cat. When she got to the door leading to the stairwell, she spied Max's tail disappear into the darkness.

Polly stood by the open doorway, considering the basement's secrets. After a moment, she turned and made her way back to the living room. She needed another drink.

TWENTY-THREE

Polly sat in the darkness, watching the last flickering of the dying flames in Marlow House's living room fireplace. Sometime during the evening she had switched from wine to gin. When dinner was served in the dining room, she had no appetite, yet she had sat with the others at the table and then later returned with them to the living room. But the Bartleys, Chris Johnson and the housekeeper had all gone home. The others had retired to their rooms, and considering how quiet it was, she assumed they were all in their beds sleeping. She wasn't completely alone, the Marlows' black cat was curled up on the end of the sofa, yet he too was asleep. She had told Teddy she would be up shortly, but that had been over an hour ago. He obviously hadn't noticed his wife had never come upstairs.

Morbid and vengeful thoughts danced in her head. She thought of all the ways she could kill the man she loved. And she did love Teddy. She would not have endured all his emotional abuse had she not loved him. Although, she had never considered it emotional abuse, not until recently. Until recently she had never—not even for a moment—considered her husband had been unfaithful. After all, he was the one who had fits of jealousy if she so much as smiled at another man.

Polly took another sip of the gin and then swished the remaining contents in the glass. Those times Teddy displayed fits of jealousy—as he had over her casual friendship with Julius—had reassured her of his love. After all, would a man who didn't love her care if she had an affair?

Even Teddy's interference in her career was because he adored her—or so she had thought. He didn't want to share her with the world. Those times he had been short with her, she attributed to the stress of his demanding job—a job that provided her with every luxury imaginable, especially for someone who had come from a lower middle-class family.

A voice interrupted her thoughts by asking, "Are you ever coming up to bed?"

Polly looked to the doorway and saw her husband. He stood just inside the room, wearing a bathrobe over his silk pajamas.

"I don't think so," she said sharply, looking away from Teddy and back to the fireplace. She took another drink of gin.

Teddy marched into the room and grabbed the glass from Polly's hand, sending its remaining contents splashing out on her and the sofa. Polly made a little yelping sound of protest, waking the sleeping cat from his slumber. Max eyed the two humans with annoyance and then jumped to the floor and headed out of the room.

"You got that all over me and the couch!" Polly said.

"How much have you had to drink?"

"Not enough," she snapped back.

"What is wrong with you?" He set the empty glass on the coffee table.

Polly glared at Teddy. "I put up with a lot from you. But I won't tolerate you cheating on me."

"We've already gone over this. Nothing happened between me and Phoebe. Nothing," he insisted.

Glaring at her husband, Polly said, "That's not what Phoebe told me."

"What are you talking about?" he asked.

"I spoke to Phoebe before she left. She admitted there had been something, briefly. She told me there have been others besides her. She wasn't the first, or the last."

Expressionless, Teddy stared at Polly for a moment before asking, "What do you intend to do?"

"Sue you for divorce," she told him.

"You are not going to divorce me," he said.

"Watch me."

"And then what? How are you going to support yourself? You don't have much of an acting career anymore. I suppose you can move in with your brother while you try to get it going again."

"Are you forgetting that prenup you made me sign?" she asked.

"Obviously I'm not. You seem to forget that according to the prenup, you don't get a dime of my money in a divorce."

"And the clause my brother insisted be included? The clause that says if you cheat, then half of your assets are mine."

He smiled. "You can try it, but you have to prove I've been unfaithful. You can't."

She glared at him. "I have Phoebe."

"No. You have Phoebe admitting—when the two of you were alone—that maybe something happened. You can't take that to court, and I guarantee you, you'll never get Phoebe to testify against me. Ever."

"How can you be so sure?" she asked.

"I just know."

Polly cleared her throat and looked Teddy in the eyes. "What now?"

"Now we forget this little conversation ever happened, and we go upstairs to bed."

"Do you want to be married to me?" she asked.

He frowned. "What kind of question is that?"

"How you treat me, for one."

"You've never complained before," he said.

"I have. You haven't listened."

"I work in an extremely stressful profession, long hours to provide you everything you could ever want. You, on the other hand, aren't required to do anything aside from look beautiful and be by my side when needed. I don't understand why you would complain. Your only job is to make me happy, and if you feel I mistreat you in some way, then perhaps I'm not happy, and you're not doing your job. I give you everything—a beautiful home, clothes, jewelry, trips…"

"What about the other women?" she asked in a quiet voice.

"If I'm turning to other women, perhaps you aren't doing your job there either."

"What do you want from me, Teddy?"

"I want you to stop this nonsense and go upstairs. And I don't want to hear about Phoebe ever again. Do you understand? Or I will instigate the divorce, and I will make certain you leave our marriage without a penny. And that non-career of yours? Don't count on reviving it. Because you will never work in this business again. Do you understand?"

Polly nodded silently and stood up. She walked past Teddy to the open doorway to the foyer. He followed her. When they stepped out of the living room, Polly stopped a moment and looked around. The main lighting had been turned off when the Marlows had gone upstairs, yet they had left some lights on so their guests would not be stumbling around in total darkness. She looked toward the basement and considered her options and remembered the fantasies she had been playing over in her head before Teddy had come downstairs.

"Are you coming?" Teddy asked.

She turned to him. "The cat."

"The cat what?"

"I promised Danielle I would make sure the basement door was closed before I went upstairs. She doesn't want her cat going down there at night, and he just left the living room. I'm afraid he might have gone down there."

"Why wouldn't she have just checked it herself before coming upstairs?" he asked.

"Please, Teddy. It'll only take a minute. Will you come with me? It's kind of scary down that back hallway."

Teddy let out a sigh and then said, "Fine. Let's check and then go to bed. I'm exhausted."

"Thank you," she said in her most timid voice.

WHEN THEY REACHED the door to the basement, they found it open—open like it had been when Polly had looked into the basement earlier that evening. Teddy walked into the stairwell and flipped on the lights.

"Is the cat in there?" Polly asked.

"I don't know," he snapped. "Go look."

"Please, Teddy, just look down there for me. This place creeps me out."

Teddy took a deep breath. He didn't feel comfortable poking around in the near darkness. There had been that incident of the painting floating down the hallway, practically hitting him in the face. Shortly before it had happened, he had consumed some chocolate infused with cannabis. He had assumed it had all been some drug-induced episode—although he had never hallucinated with pot before. Since then he had been on edge, so much so that he imagined his underwear had briefly taken on a life of its own.

Standing on the landing, looking down the stairs, he said, "I don't see the cat. I don't really want to go down there."

In the next moment Teddy learned we don't always get what we want when a hand shoved his back, catching him off balance and sending him tumbling head over feet down the stairwell, until he landed with a thud on the cement floor below.

HE HADN'T EVEN SCREAMED. She had expected him to scream after she pushed him. But she wasn't too worried about anyone hearing. Birdie wore hearing aids, and everyone else was upstairs. However, there was one thing she hadn't considered—the blood. As he tumbled like a hapless rag doll down the stairs, it suddenly occurred to her that when he hit the floor, the fall could crack open his head and spill blood all over the concrete floor. Head wounds were known to bleed excessively. How would she ever clean it up?

But to her surprise, there was no blood. Not a single drop. When he landed, he didn't hit his head on the floor, yet she was fairly certain by the angle of his head that he had snapped his neck.

Holding onto the railing, she slowly made her way down the stairs. While she was fairly certain the snapped neck had done the trick, she needed to make sure. After reaching him, she hesitantly felt for his pulse. Nothing.

For a brief moment she considered leaving him there for someone to find. It would look as if he had tripped—it was all a horrible accident. But then she thought better of it. They would wonder why he went down to the basement. And hadn't he gone upstairs before her? Plus, Bentley knew she had argued with Phoebe over her husband's infidelity. There was no guarantee he hadn't told someone what he had overheard, regardless of his promise. No, there would be too many questions. She glanced over to the hook holding the key to the tunnel entrance and smiled.

I'll tell them he couldn't sleep and told me he was going to go for a walk on the beach. When they ask me what time it was, I'll tell them I don't know. I was asleep when he woke me up to tell me he was going. I can do this. I'm an actress. I can play the convincing role of a concerned wife, she told herself.

Polly stepped over Teddy's broken body and retrieved the key from the hook. She unlocked and opened the first door blocking the tunnel. She peered inside—it was dark. She entered the opening and used her hands to feel for the padlock. Had she thought to bring her cellphone, which was upstairs in her room, she could use it as a flashlight. The overhead lighting in the basement did little to illuminate the small space, even with the door left open. In spite of the darkness, she managed to unlock the second padlock.

After returning the key to the hook, she went to Teddy and looked down at him, deciding how best to move him. Grabbing hold of his feet, she tucked one under her right arm and the other under her left arm and tried dragging him toward the tunnel entrance. She managed to slowly drag him across the floor, occasionally changing positions—sometimes walking backwards as she dragged him, and then dragging him behind her.

It took longer than she had imagined it would, but she finally maneuvered him into the first entrance. The trick would be getting him through the second door. It was pitch dark, and she couldn't see inside the second opening to the tunnel. She had no intention of walking into the tunnel and dragging him in. No, she would instead lie on her back and then use her feet to shove his body through the opening.

POLLY STOOD ALONE by the stairwell, looking back to the now locked doorway leading to the first tunnel entrance. She had worked up a sweat and desperately needed a shower, yet she didn't want to wake anyone up. She would have to take a sponge bath before going to bed, she told herself. It might have been backbreaking, but she had managed to shove Teddy into the dark opening.

Dusting her hands off on the sides of her slacks, she made her way up the stairwell. Once she reached the first-floor landing, she turned off the basement light and stepped out to the rear hallway leading to the foyer.

"What are you doing?" An unexpected voice caught her by surprise.

Polly looked up into Bentley's face.

TWENTY-FOUR

Danielle woke up early Monday morning to the sound of a text message beeping her cellphone. She groaned and rolled toward her nightstand. With her sleep-laden eyes still closed, she clumsily reached out for the phone, her hand missing its mark on the first and second tries, aimlessly slapping the nightstand until she found what she was looking for. Opening her eyes and now clutching the phone, she sat up in bed and looked to see which of her annoying close friends chose to send her a message so early. She didn't imagine for a moment it was an emergency.

Had it been an emergency, they would call, not text.

Looking at the phone, she read the message.

Tell Seraphina jog date is on. Allergies. Let me know if she's going.

Danielle let out a grunt and set the phone back on the nightstand.

"What time is it?" she heard Walt say as she climbed out of bed.

"Early, go back to sleep. I have to go downstairs," she explained.

Scooting up in the bed, Walt leaned against the headboard and looked at Danielle. "What's going on?"

"Heather just sent me a text. She wants me to tell Seraphina the jog date is back on if she wants to go. Obviously they did not exchange phone numbers, or she would have texted her."

"I thought Heather was sick?" Walt asked, rubbing sleep from his eyes.

"Lily said Heather thought she was coming down with a cold. That's why the jog date was put on hold. But according to Heather's text, she says it's allergies, and she wants to go now. I'm going to see if Seraphina still wants to join her."

"I thought Seraphina said last night she'd just go by herself?" Walt asked.

"Yeah. Which is why I need to hurry, see if I can catch her."

Throwing on her robe, Danielle dropped a quick kiss on Walt's lips and headed out of their bedroom. A moment later she returned, grabbed her cellphone off the nightstand, and then left again.

When she reached the second floor several minutes later, she went to Seraphina's room. The door was ajar, so she peeked inside instead of knocking. The room was empty. Danielle then checked the bathrooms, but she wasn't in either one, so she headed downstairs.

Danielle found Seraphina in the kitchen, sitting at the table, typing something into her cellphone. "Good morning," Danielle greeted her.

Seraphina looked up in surprise and smiled. "You're up early. I hope I didn't wake you."

"No. We don't hear much in the attic. But

Heather texted me and said she's up to jogging this morning if you still want to join her." Danielle then noticed Seraphina was already dressed to go jogging.

"That's great. Umm, do you know when she wants me to meet her?"

"Let me see." Danielle sat down at the table and sent a text message to Heather. A few minutes later, she received one back. "She said she'll meet you in front of the house in fifteen minutes."

"Great," Seraphina said, yet she didn't sound or look like someone who thought anything was particularly great at the moment.

"Is something wrong?" Danielle asked.

Seraphina, who still held her cellphone, looked down at it a moment, then met Danielle's gaze. "It's Phoebe."

"What's Phoebe?" Danielle asked.

"I've been trying to get ahold of her since last night. She's not answering her phone. And I called Josie, and she hasn't heard from her."

"Josie? Who's that?" Danielle asked.

"She's Phoebe's roommate. They're pretty close. When I talked to her last night, she said she hadn't heard from Phoebe since Saturday morning. Those two normally text throughout the day. But Phoebe's gone silent. I can understand Phoebe blowing off my phone calls and texts, but not Josie's. Josie texted me this morning and told me she still hasn't heard from Phoebe, and she's not answering her calls either. Josie is kinda panicked. She went online and checked Phoebe's credit cards and bank account this morning, and Phoebe hasn't used any of her cards. She never said anything to Josie about leaving. That's not like Phoebe."

"Her roommate has the passwords to her bank accounts?" Danielle asked.

Seraphina smiled. "I told you they were close."

Danielle knew exactly why Phoebe hadn't used any of her credit or debit cards. Ghosts tended not to need cash or credit. Danielle thought Seraphina seemed sincerely concerned over Phoebe's disappearance—either that or the woman was a good actress. And she was an actress.

"What are you going to do?" Danielle asked.

"I'm not sure. When the others get up, I want to talk to them about it. Maybe she said something to one of them."

"Said something like what?" Danielle asked.

"Maybe she told one of them where she was going. And perhaps they didn't want to get involved, so they didn't say anything. Or maybe she mentioned something that they didn't really think about at the time. I don't know. But I have to do something. I can't really call the police. They're not going to do anything at this point."

"Maybe they'll ping her cellphone," Danielle suggested.

"Can they really do that? I see that in movies."

"Yeah. Of course, they have to have a good reason. But I'm pretty good friends with the local police chief. I'll see if he can do anything."

Seraphina stood up. "Would you? That would be great! If Phoebe wants to disappear for a while, I get that. But I just want to make sure something bad didn't happen to her. I don't even know who picked her up."

"Okay, I'll call the chief this morning." She glanced at the kitchen clock. "But I'll wait until he gets in the office."

MINUTES AFTER SERAPHINA left to go jogging, Walt walked into the kitchen. He looked at the coffee pot and frowned. "What, no coffee?"

Danielle stood up from the table. "Sorry, I've been talking to Seraphina; she just left. I'll make some now."

Walt was already removing the pot to fill with water. He shooed her away when she tried to take it from him. Danielle sat back down at the table and told him about her conversation with Seraphina, while he made the coffee.

"At least now the chief will have a reason to ping her phone," Walt said.

"I don't think it's going to help," Danielle said.

"Why do you say that?"

"I hope it will help. That's why I suggested it to Seraphina. And now the chief will have a legitimate reason to do it. But I suspect whoever killed Phoebe got rid of the phone. It's probably at the bottom of the ocean by now, and all the pinging in the world is not going to help. Face it, you don't have to watch many murder mysteries to know the police can track down people using their cellphones. And considering who our prime suspects are, they all know that."

"Good morning!" a voice said brightly, just as the coffee finished brewing. Danielle and Walt looked toward the doorway leading to the hallway and found Bentley standing just inside the kitchen. Neither had heard him enter the room, and Danielle wondered what he had overheard.

"Ummm, morning, Bentley. You're up early," Danielle said. She watched as he stretched and then touched his toes.

"Yes, I am, aren't I? I feel pretty good this morning. I've been having this chronic pain in my lower back. Jackie's been telling me I need to see a doctor about it," Bentley said.

"She's right. You should," Danielle said.

Bentley grinned. "It's gone. I feel great!"

He touched his toes again and then stood up. "Maybe it's the climate up here?"

"Most people complain our damp climate causes aches and pains instead of getting rid of them," Walt said.

Bentley shrugged. "Whatever, I'm just grateful. I think I'll go for a little walk on the beach."

"Do you want some coffee?" Danielle asked as Bentley headed for the door.

"No, thanks," Bentley called out as he went outside.

"Oh crap," Danielle said, staring at the door leading to the side yard.

Walt, who had been busy pouring them each a cup of coffee, turned to Danielle. "What's wrong?"

"Umm, didn't you notice anything when Bentley left just now?"

Walt shook his head. "No. What?"

"He walked through the door," Danielle said dully.

"So? Isn't that how most people go outside? Did you expect him to climb out the window?"

"No, Walt. He walked through the door—as in through the door. He didn't open it."

Walt set down the two cups of coffee he had been holding on the counter and turned to face Danielle. He looked past her to the back door. "Are you saying…"

"We have another ghost," Danielle said.

"And where there is a ghost…" Walt began.

"…there's another dead body. Although, we haven't found the last one."

The next moment Walt bolted from the kitchen, leaving the filled cups abandoned on the counter. Danielle followed him, and together they raced upstairs. When they got to the bedroom Bentley had shared with Phoebe, Walt opened the door without knocking. It was unlocked. Inside the room was empty. There was no dead body—nor did they find Bentley's ghost.

They checked what rooms they could on the second floor without disturbing their still-sleeping guests. When they got downstairs again, they were greeted by Marie.

"Good, you're here!" Danielle said excitedly.

"Nice to be appreciated," Marie clucked. "Eva will be here shortly. You did ask us to stay with your guests when they're up and around." The reason for this, they wanted Marie and Eva to eavesdrop in case one of the guests privately revealed something about the murder.

Danielle quickly told Marie about Bentley. When Danielle completed the telling, Marie went to check the occupied guest rooms for any sign of Bentley—either in physical dead or spiritual form. A moment later Eva arrived, and after they filled her in on what was going on, she joined Marie.

"THERE'S ANOTHER DEAD BODY?" Danielle heard the chief say. She had called him on the phone to give him the most recent update. He was still at home, but considering the new development, she didn't want to wait until he got to the office to call. She and Walt sat alone in the parlor with the door closed, while Marie and Eva continued with their body scavenger hunt.

"Not exactly. There's another ghost. We haven't found the body yet," Danielle said. She heard the chief groan.

"But the good news, now you can ping Phoebe's phone. You said you couldn't do it before. Can't really start an investigation when no one has reported a person missing. But now you can, right?"

"Yes, I can. But whoever the killer is, he or she seems rather adept at stashing bodies and concealing evidence. I'll be surprised if anything pans out with the cellphone," the chief said.

"I know. I told Walt the same thing. But at least we can try," Danielle said.

"What I don't understand, where are the ghosts?" the chief asked. "Why aren't they telling you who killed them?"

"Maybe no one killed Bentley," Danielle said hopefully.

"Are you suggesting he died of natural causes?" the chief asked. "If that was the case, wouldn't his body be, I don't know, still in his bed?"

"I didn't say he died in his sleep," Danielle countered. "Or even in his bed."

"Was he a sickly man?" the chief asked.

"He did say something about chronic lower back pain. But I don't think he was much older than me. Looked to be in fairly good shape. But who knows? I just don't want to think about two murders."

"Now you know how I feel," the chief said.

"Hey, it's hardly my fault. It's not like Walt and I are bumping these people off."

"True. But if you two couldn't see ghosts, I could be contently oblivious to any possible local homicide and enjoy my morning coffee in peace."

TWENTY-FIVE

Shortly before Bentley's ghost jogged into Marlow House's kitchen, Pearl Huckabee was next door peeking through the opening in her bedroom window curtains, looking down to Beach Drive. The sun had just come up, and someone was standing in front of her house. It looked like her neighbor Heather Donovan. She wore a dark-colored jogging suit and her black hair tied up into a gawd-awful messy bun on the top of her head, strands of hair sticking out in all directions.

Pearl then noticed a second person jogging out from the side yard of Marlow House, heading toward Heather. It was a black woman wearing a baseball hat, her hair shoved under its cap. The next moment the woman was touching her toes while Heather did jumping jacks.

"Go do that in front of someone else's house!" Pearl grumbled, turning from the window in disgust.

"THANKS FOR LETTING ME TAG ALONG," Seraphina told Heather as she loosened up for the jog.

"I enjoy the company. I've tried to get Danielle to go jogging, but she'd rather stay in bed with Walt on cold mornings than run with me."

Seraphina laughed. "Well, I have to admit, I kinda understand that."

Heather grinned. "Yeah, I guess. Let's cross the street. I think old Pearl is done watching the show."

"Pearl?" Seraphina asked.

"Just a neighbor I share with Walt and Danielle. I sometimes enjoy annoying her. But only to return the favor."

"I don't understand, return what favor?" Seraphina asked.

"All the times she annoys the heck out of me. I suppose it's petty. But I never claimed to be a good person. We can get to the beach down by the side of Lily and Ian's house." Already running in place, Heather gave a little hand wave for Seraphina to follow her.

After looking both ways for traffic, Heather and Seraphina jogged across the street. The two women then continued down the side path along the Bartley house to the beach. Once there, they started jogging along the coastline, heading north.

"This is so different from Southern California beaches," Seraphina said. "I can't believe how quiet it is."

"Lots cooler too," Heather said, pointing ahead. "That's the house Chris is having built." A moment later they stopped by Chris's new house. Construction was almost complete.

"He told me about his house burning down before Christmas," Seraphina said.

"Yeah, the idiot left a pan on the stove and the burner on. Luckily no one was hurt."

Seraphina looked from the house to Heather. "He also told me who he really is."

Heather didn't respond.

"He told me he's really Chris Glandon."

"He told you that?" Heather asked. According to what Eva had confided, Chris never told the women he went out with who he really was. Eva claimed it was because he hadn't met one he cared enough about to share that secret with. Someone in his position was never sure if the woman wanted him —or his fortune.

Seraphina had money, like Danielle. That was one reason Chris had become comfortable with Danielle—she had her own money. Plus, money never seemed to be as important to Danielle as other women.

Of course, when you had money, it was always easy to say you didn't really care about it, Heather thought. Heather happened to be in another category. She didn't have a lot of money—although she had a comfortable salary, thanks to her job with the Glandon Foundation and Chris. But over the last few years she had been tested—faced with giving up a fortune for the sake of principals and ethics, or keeping it because she needed the cash. Heather had passed the test both times. Although, she had to admit, having enough money to pay your bills sure reduced the stresses of life.

"Are you surprised?" Seraphina asked, jolting Heather's thoughts back to the current here and now.

"Surprised he let you in on his secret?"

"Yeah. He told me he doesn't usually tell anyone. Although he says most of Frederick-port knows—says it is sort of an open secret, one the locals don't share."

"Yeah, that's true," Heather said. "Of course, the Glandon Foundation does a lot for the local community. I don't think they want the golden goose to relocate to another town."

Heather avoided asking the initial question—was she surprised he told her. Yes, actually, she was. Under other circumstances she wouldn't be. But Seraphina, according to Danielle, was the prime suspect in Phoebe's murder. They still hadn't found the woman's body, and until they did, her killer might never be found. Was Seraphina that killer?

Heather wondered. It was obvious Chris was fairly certain she wasn't.

Pushing thoughts of Seraphina being the possible killer from her head, Heather redirected the conversation to Chris's house as opposed to his identity. She discussed the changes between this new house and the old one for a few minutes before suggesting they continue with their morning run.

As they jogged by Chris's neighbor to the north a few minutes later, Heather pointed out it was where the tunnel from the Marlows' led.

"Walt said it was unsafe. Sounded like the tunnel will never be open again," Seraphina said.

Heather laughed. "Yeah, right."

Jogging by Heather's side, Seraphina flashed her a frown. "What do you mean?"

"It's not unsafe. Walt just doesn't like to open up the tunnel. Don't tell them I said that; he'll kill me. Fact is, the historical society has been nagging Walt and the Crawfords, they're the ones who own the house I just showed you, to open up the tunnel for a tour."

"So it's safe to go down there?" she asked.

"Yeah, according to the engineer who inspected it."

As they continued down the beach, it became more difficult to talk and jog, so they each focused on maintaining a comfortable pace and steady breathing. Heather felt a brief pang of regret for being a blabbermouth and telling Seraphina the tunnel was safe when Walt obviously wanted to give the opposite impression. But then she figured, if Chris felt safe enough sharing his big secret with the woman, then the tunnel secret was not that big a deal.

THE JOGGERS APPROACHED the point where Heather normally turned around, when something in the sand ahead caught Heather's attention. It looked like a pile of debris—old clothes and maybe a blanket. It wasn't someone sleeping on the beach, the pile was right at the waterline, being pushed about by the incoming waves.

"Damn jerks," Heather grumbled.

"What?" Seraphina said.

Heather nodded ahead. "Someone dumped some trash on the beach. I hate when they do that."

Several minutes later, as they got close to the pile, Heather stopped abruptly. She reached out and grabbed hold of Seraphina's right wrist, pulling her to a stop.

"Not again!' Heather said with a curse.

"What?" Seraphina asked, rubbing her wrist from the abrupt wrenching. "Why did you do that?"

Heather pointed to the pile. "Because it is not a pile of trash. It is another freaking dead body!"

Seraphina looked from Heather to the pile. "What do you mean, another body?"

"I'd say that is an arm sticking out." Heather pulled out her cellphone, making no attempt to move closer.

"Shouldn't we go check?" Seraphina asked. "Maybe he needs our help. Maybe he's not dead?"

"Oh, he's dead alright," Heather grumbled.

"How do you know?"

"Because I only find dead bodies on the beach. It's sort of my thing. But yeah, I guess we should check." *And I bet it's a she, not a he,* she thought to herself.

Heather and Seraphina approached the body, and just before they could tell if it was a man or woman, Chief MacDonald answered the call.

"Hey, Chief, it's Heather. I'm on the beach jogging. I did it again. I found another body. I think it's her," Heather told him.

"Where?" he asked.

"South from Chris's house," she told him.

When Heather and Seraphina looked down at the body, Heather realized she had been wrong. It was not a woman after all. It was a man.

"Dang, I was wrong, Chief. It's a guy," she told him, still holding the cellphone to her ear as she looked down at the waterlogged corpse.

Seraphina let out a gasp and said, "Bentley," at the same time the chief asked, "Is it Bentley Mason?"

Heather looked from Seraphina to the phone in her hand before putting the phone back to her ear. "How did you know, Chief?"

SHE FELT as if someone had hit her over the head with a hammer. The throbbing wouldn't stop. With a groan, she rested her right wrist on her forehead and then moaned again. Reluctantly Polly opened her bloodshot eyes, dropped her wrist back to the mattress, and looked to the ceiling. It had been a bizarre dream. How much had she had to drink? Teddy had told her countless times to never drink gin. She couldn't handle it. Then to mix it with wine. The thought made her want to puke. She was surprised she hadn't gotten sick. But maybe she had, and she couldn't remember. If she did, Teddy was going to kill her if he had to clean it up.

Polly reached for his side of the bed. It was empty. Turning her head to the right, she looked at the empty spot where Teddy should be.

Now holding her head, she forced herself to sit up in bed. She groaned again. The room began to spin. She was still a little drunk. *Yep, I'm never going to hear the end of this from Teddy*, she thought.

When she finally stumbled out of bed, she glanced at the alarm clock sitting on the nightstand. It was almost time to go downstairs for breakfast. The thought of food made her queasy again. She noticed the clothes Teddy had laid out for the day—something he did religiously before going to bed at night—were still folded on the chair. She didn't see his robe hanging on the hook. *He must be in the bathroom*, she thought.

She also needed to go to the bathroom and splash some water on her face. Luckily for Jackie and Julius, they had gotten one of the two guest rooms with a bathroom. Birdie had gotten the other one. Polly had to use one of the two other bathrooms on the second floor.

Before leaving the bedroom, she glanced down and noticed she was still wearing the dress from the night before. "Wow, I really was drunk," she muttered to herself.

Standing in the middle of the room, she stripped off her dress and then her underwear. She kicked them out of her way and then stumbled across the room nude, looking for her robe.

Exhausted by the search, she plopped down on the edge of the mattress. Now cold, she pulled the top blanket to her, wrapping it around her nude body. She looked over to a mirror hanging on the wall and caught a glimpse of herself. The way her short dark hair stuck up spiky in all directions, one might wonder if she had stuck her finger in a light socket.

Her head spinning again, she let out a loud burp and then looked back to the mirror. She thought about the dream again. She never remembered her dreams, at least not this clearly. She had pushed him down the stairs then shoved him in the tunnel opening. Such a vivid dream. It felt so real.

TWENTY-SIX

The rooms on the second floor were all empty—Polly was alone. Considering the time, she was fairly certain they had started breakfast without her, and she assumed the reason no one had come up to remind her was because Teddy probably told them she was still sleeping. Or dead drunk. Either way, she knew Teddy was going to be pissy with her when she finally got her crap together and went downstairs.

She hadn't showered the night before, so she figured she'd better do it now. It would make her feel better. By the time she was showered, dressed and no longer feeling like a zombie, she decided to head downstairs. First she returned to her room to pick up her cellphone, but then she noticed the battery was almost dead. She had forgotten to charge it the night before. Polly walked over to the desk to plug her phone in when she noticed Teddy's on the charger. It wasn't like Teddy to leave his phone behind. She looked at the cellphone and noted it was fully charged. Unplugging it, she plugged her phone in and slipped his in her sweater pocket. He'd probably want it.

A few minutes later she headed out of the room, first giving herself one final look in the mirror. Her hair was no longer sticking up in all directions. She smiled at the reflection. "Human again," she told herself.

As she reached the staircase, she heard voices coming from the first floor. She started down the stairs, one hand holding onto the oak rail. Once she reached the first-floor landing, she noticed Danielle with a police officer. When they heard her, they turned and looked her way.

"I was just coming up to get you," Danielle said in a solemn voice.

"Sorry I missed breakfast. I overslept." Polly smiled, walking toward Danielle.

"Is Teddy on his way down?" Danielle asked.

"Teddy?" Polly frowned. She stood about six feet from Danielle and the police officer.

"Is he still sleeping?" Danielle asked.

Polly shrugged. "Teddy's not upstairs. He's down here."

"Polly, this is my friend Police Chief MacDonald," Danielle introduced. "Chief, this is Polly Larimore. She's married to the director."

"Ms. Larimore, could you please wait with the others in the living room?" MacDonald asked.

Polly frowned. "What's going on?"

Danielle looked uneasily from Polly to the chief. "There has been an accident. Bentley. It appears he drowned."

"What?" Polly gasped.

"Please, we'll be right in the living room to talk to you all," the chief said.

A few minutes later Polly walked into the living room and found the rest of her party sitting in the room, along with Danielle's neighbor Heather, whom she had met at the Glandon Foundation offices. The only person not in the room was her husband.

She looked around at the sad and confused faces.

"Where's Teddy?" Jackie called out. Polly looked at the woman and noticed her red-rimmed eyes. She had obviously been crying.

"I assumed he was down here," Polly said. "What happened?"

"He's dead…Bentley is dead…" Jackie began to sob again. Julius, who sat by her side on the sofa, wrapped one arm around her shoulders and pulled her closer.

"We found Bentley's body when we were jogging," Seraphina explained from where she stood by the fireplace, wringing her hands.

"I don't understand," Polly said. "Why would he be swimming in this weather?"

"He didn't drown," Heather scoffed.

"That's what Danielle told me," Polly said.

Heather rolled her eyes. "They don't know what the cause of death is. They won't know until they have an autopsy."

"You need to get Teddy here," Jackie demanded.

"Was he at breakfast?" Polly asked.

"We haven't had breakfast," Julius explained. "Seraphina and Heather found the body when they were jogging, and they called the police. Since then we've been in here, waiting."

"They were getting ready to send one of us upstairs to get you and Teddy. I went up earlier, but you were in the shower. I, um… assumed you were both in the shower, since he wasn't in his room or down here," Julius explained.

"If he's not with you, then where is he?" Jackie asked.

Polly shrugged. "I have no idea." A wave of panic hit Polly. She remembered the dream again. *No*, she told herself, *it was just a dream.*

Annoyed, Jackie snatched her cellphone off the coffee table and called Teddy. A phone in Polly's pocket began to ring. Polly removed the phone and looked at it. Jackie hung up the call. The phone stopped ringing.

"Why do you have Teddy's phone?" Jackie asked.

"He left it on his charger," Polly explained. "I brought it downstairs for him."

"He probably went out for a walk," Birdie suggested.

"Without his phone?" Jackie asked.

Birdie frowned to Jackie. "I don't imagine he thought anyone would call him this early. You certainly don't think Teddy had anything to do with Bentley's death, do you?"

"Mrs. Larimore, do you know where your husband is?" Police Chief MacDonald asked from the open doorway.

WALT STOOD QUIETLY by the back wall of the living room, observing his guests. Eva and Marie had just materialized by his side. He listened as the others in the room questioned Teddy's whereabouts, and when—and why—Bentley had left the house the night before—assuming it had been last night and not early this morning.

"We looked everywhere," Marie told Walt. "Perhaps his spirit has moved on."

Walt gave Marie a silent nod and continued to watch and listen to the roomful of people.

"At least they found his body," Eva said. "So Marie might be right. He could have moved on. No reason to stick around now that his body has been recovered."

"What was he doing swimming at that time of night?" Marie asked. "And in his underwear?"

"Perhaps he didn't have a pair of swim trunks with him," Eva suggested.

"But it is freezing out there," Marie said.

"Maybe that's why they found him wrapped in a blanket," Eva suggested, knowing full well that wasn't the case.

"Oh pshaw, I heard Joe say that blanket looked like it had been bouncing around in the ocean for days, not one night. His body just happened to get wrapped up in it," Marie said.

"Oh, I know, I was just teasing," Eva said.

"Not a good time to tease. A poor man is dead!" Marie scolded.

"So? We're dead."

"True. But we're old."

"Speak for yourself," Eva snapped. "I was

younger than that man they found today when I died."

"Goodness, Eva, that was a hundred years ago. You really need to get over it, dear."

Walt cleared his throat, wanting to get the ghosts to stop chatting nonsensically so he could hear what was being said. Getting the message, Eva and Marie went silent.

"I wonder where Teddy went," Walt said aloud. To the others in the room—those who were alive—they would assume he was talking to himself. To Eva and Marie, they understood exactly.

"We'll see if we can find him," Eva said.

"You don't think that young man's death is foul play, do you?" Marie gasped.

"If it was just one dead body, perhaps. But two?" Eva said.

Walt cleared his throat again.

"Walt, you don't have to nag us," Eva said before disappearing. The next moment, Marie vanished.

POLLY SAT in the parlor on the sofa. Her

hands fidgeted nervously on her lap as she looked across to the police chief, who had just sat down in the chair facing her, a notepad in his hand. She was the first one to be questioned.

"Where is your husband?" the chief asked.

"I really don't know," Polly told him. The moment the words left her mouth her stomach churned. The dream. It flashed in her head. Her pushing Teddy down the stairs. Dragging him toward the tunnel. Using her feet to shove him into the dark opening. She closed her eyes and took a deep breath. *Get those thoughts out of your head*, she told herself. *Nothing happened. It was just a dream.*

"Mrs. Larimore? Are you alright?"

Polly's eyes flew open, and she looked into the chief's inquiring gaze. She shook her head nervously. "I…well, to be honest, I had too much to drink last night. That's why I overslept this morning. And…well…I don't really remember much about last night. At least, the last half of the evening. When I woke up this morning, Teddy was already gone."

"Do you remember going to bed with him last night?" he asked.

She shook her head. "Sorry. I don't even remember going to bed myself. I did something really stupid last night. I had some gin, after several glasses of wine. I really shouldn't drink gin. Especially after wine. But even on its own, well, like Teddy says, gin makes me stupid. Fact is, I tend to forget things after I drink gin."

"What's the last thing you remember about last night?" he asked.

She frowned. "I thought Danielle said Bentley drowned. I'm not sure what any of that has to do with Teddy."

"We just want to interview everyone staying here."

"Teddy probably walked down to the pier this morning to get a cup of coffee at that diner," she suggested. "I bet if you go down there, you'll find him."

"They've already checked the pier and diner," the chief explained. "Your husband wasn't there, and no one remembered seeing him."

"You don't really think Teddy has anything to do with Bentley drowning? I don't know why he would. Heck, Teddy doesn't even like swimming in the ocean."

"Mrs. Larimore, we are simply trying to figure out what happened to Mr. Mason. And we need to start by questioning everyone staying at Marlow House. We can't do that if we can't find your husband."

"I imagine Teddy will be back soon enough. You can question him then." Her stomach churned again. *Would he really be back? Why is the dream even more vivid now than when I woke up this morning?* she asked herself.

"I suppose we'll have to wait to question your husband when he gets back. So I will go ahead with your questions."

"My questions? I don't know anything about Bentley's accident."

"Tell me, what is the last thing you remember from last night?" he asked.

Polly considered the question a moment and then took a deep breath before answering, "I was sitting on the sofa, talking to Bentley. Drinking wine. And…ummm…well, he went to get another drink, asked me if I wanted anything. That's when I switched to gin. He brought me the gin, sat down with me; we talked a while. Then I remember I got up to use the bathroom—that's about all. I don't really remember anything after that."

"Do you remember what you were talking about?" he asked.

Polly remembered her conversation with Bentley. She also remembered thinking about killing her husband. And then…she shook her head and said, "No. Everything is a blank."

TWENTY-SEVEN

Their guests had all gone into the dining room to have breakfast. However, by now, it was time for lunch. Joanne was in there with them while Walt and Danielle stood on Marlow House's front porch, talking to Chief MacDonald, who was preparing to leave.

"According to the coroner, it looks like a drowning," the chief told him. "But we'll know more after we get the blood tests back. I suspect we'll find he'd had too much to drink and then got the crazy idea for a late night swim."

"He didn't seem drunk when we went to bed," Danielle told him.

"Did Mrs. Larimore seem drunk last night?" the chief asked.

Danielle frowned. "Polly?"

"Why do you ask that?" Walt asked.

"According to Mrs. Larimore, she had too much to drink last night and can't remember the latter part of the evening, such as going up to bed."

"Really? Wow, she does a good job of hiding it," Danielle said.

"Are you sure it wasn't foul play?" Walt asked.

"I never said that. I just said the coroner felt it was a drowning."

"No suspicious body wounds? No one hit him over the head, shot him or stabbed him. Nothing obvious like that?" Danielle asked.

The chief shook his head. "No."

"Except for the fact he's our second dead body this week," Walt said.

"Correction, your second ghost," the chief reminded him. "We're still looking for that other body."

"It wasn't an accident," a voice declared. The chief didn't hear the words, but Walt and Danielle did. They turned abruptly and found themselves looking at the two ghosts they had seen earlier—the one who had warned them about the possible murders and the one Danielle had seen looking into the kitchen window.

"He was murdered?" Danielle asked the ghosts.

"Are Eva and Marie here?" MacDonald asked.

Danielle shook her head and continued to stare at the ghosts, waiting for one to answer.

"Bentley was murdered," the second ghost announced. He looked to his companion and said, "You could have saved them a lot of trouble and maybe Bentley's life if you had told them everything up front."

"You know why I can't do that," the first ghost argued.

Frustrated, Danielle blurted, "Who murdered Bentley?"

Startled by her outburst, the two ghosts looked to Danielle and vanished.

"You scared them away," Walt said.

"Bentley was murdered?" the chief asked.

"According to the ghosts," Walt said.

"Ghosts? More than one?" MacDonald asked.

"Yes…" Danielle rubbed her forehead with the back of her right hand. Her head was beginning to throb.

"Who killed him? How? Why?" the chief asked.

"We don't know. The ghosts were here one minute and just vanished. But they did say Bentley was murdered," Walt explained.

"Exactly what ghost or ghosts?" MacDonald demanded. "Mason's? Phoebe's?"

"No. I don't know whose ghosts they are. I just know there are far too many of them hanging around Marlow House," Danielle said.

After saying goodbye to the chief fifteen minutes later, Walt and Danielle went back inside and shut the front door. They could hear voices drifting out from the dining room.

"You want to get something to eat?" Walt asked.

Danielle shook her head. "I'm not hungry. Two people staying with us have died—we have no idea why, and we can't even find one of them."

Their conversation was interrupted when Teddy came walking in the foyer from the direction of the kitchen.

"Teddy, where have you been?" Danielle asked.

Teddy came to an abrupt stop and looked from Danielle to Walt. "I…I went for a walk, I guess. Got lost. Kinda freaked me out, if you want to know the truth. Where's Polly?"

"She's in the dining room with the rest," Danielle said. "Umm…I don't guess you know what happened?"

Teddy looked at Danielle and shrugged. "What do you mean?"

"There has been an accident. It's Bentley," Walt told him.

"Something happened to Bentley?" Teddy asked.

"He's dead," Danielle told him, not wanting to draw out the bad news.

Teddy frowned. "Dead? How?"

"It looks like he drowned," Walt said. "They found his body washed up on the beach this morning."

"Drowned? How did that happen?"

"We don't know. Seraphina and our neighbor Heather went jogging this morning, and they found his body. But they'll be running some blood tests, so hopefully we'll find out what happened," Danielle explained.

"I can tell you what happened, that fool got drunk. Not the first time he's done something stupid. But it'll obviously be the last," Teddy said with a laugh. He then turned from Walt and Danielle. Instead of going to the dining room, he headed upstairs.

"Wow," Danielle said when Teddy was out of earshot. "That was cold."

"He didn't seem broken up about Bentley's death. Yet he also seemed surprised. Not shocked, but he didn't act as if he already knew Bentley was dead."

"I have to agree." Danielle let out a sigh. "I should probably call the chief and let him know Teddy's here, if he wants to question him."

"You go ahead and call. I'll go in the dining room and let Polly know her husband is back. I think she's been worried about him."

"Yeah, she seemed pretty anxious," Danielle agreed.

WHEN WALT WALKED into the dining room a few minutes later, he found his guests sitting around the table, eating and talking. The moment they noticed him, they all went silent and looked his way.

"I just wanted to let you all know Teddy is back."

"He's back?" Polly asked, a relieved smile washing over her face.

The others began shooting him questions—where is he, where was he, did he know—but Walt didn't pay attention to the questions; instead he was curiously watching Polly and the array of emotions flickering over her face. *She must have been seriously concerned about her husband's whereabouts*, Walt thought, *judging by her current demeanor*. It was as if the weight of the world had been lifted from her shoulders and she was finally able to relax.

"Where was he?" Jackie asked for the second time.

Walt looked to Jackie and said, "He told us he went for a walk and got lost."

"Lost? How could he get lost?" Jackie asked.

"Did you tell him about Bentley?" Julius asked.

"Yes, we did," Walt said.

"Where is he?" Polly asked.

"He went upstairs," Walt told her.

Polly tossed her napkin on the table and stood up. "I have to go give him a hug."

"A hug?" Jackie frowned.

Polly flashed Jackie a smile. "I was worried about him."

"What did you think he had done, gone swimming with Bentley?" Birdie asked.

Polly shook her head. "No. I just, well, you wouldn't understand." Polly turned abruptly and dashed from the dining room.

"I certainly wouldn't," Birdie muttered.

"I must say, I'm torn between wanting to throttle Bentley for doing something so stupid, and then wanting to curl up and cry again. I don't know what I'm going to do without him." Jackie picked up a napkin and dabbed the corners of her eyes.

DANIELLE HAD JUST FINISHED CALLING the chief, who told her he would be over later to interview Teddy and asked her if she could make sure he didn't go anywhere before he could get there. She was tucking her cellphone in her back pocket when Polly came running out of the dining room, looking incredibly happy.

"Walt said Teddy's back and went upstairs? He hasn't come back down yet, has he?" Polly asked as she stopped by Danielle.

"No, he hasn't come back down," Danielle said as she glanced over Polly's shoulder and saw Walt walking in their direction.

"Thanks!" Polly said brightly, turning and dashing toward the staircase.

"Someone is happy her husband is back," Danielle said when Walt reached her side. They both looked to the staircase and watched Polly run up the steps.

"She certainly is," Walt agreed.

"I hope she doesn't fall. We don't need

any more accidents around here," Danielle said.

The next moment Eva and Marie materialized, sans any glittery snow.

"We couldn't find Teddy," Marie announced.

"That's okay. He's back, he's upstairs," Danielle said. She then went on to tell Marie and Eva about the two ghosts who had been there earlier and what they had told them about Bentley's death.

"I don't understand. In all our lurking, we haven't overheard anything that might incriminate any of them," Eva said.

"Excuse me, have you seen my wife?" a voice asked. They all turned around and found Teddy strolling in their direction.

"She just went upstairs to find you," Danielle explained. "How did you miss her?"

Teddy ignored Danielle's question and instead turned his attention to the two women standing next to Walt—his gaze fixed primarily on Eva.

"Well…hello. And you are?" Teddy said. "I swear, your resemblance to the Gibson Girl is uncanny. Has anyone ever told you that? And I love your costume."

Eva raised her brows and glanced to Marie, who had an equally raised brow.

"I don't feel good about this," Danielle groaned, looking to her husband.

Walt cringed and shook his head.

The sound of footsteps hurrying down the staircase caught their attention, and they all looked in that direction and saw Polly hurrying toward them. They all remained quiet as Polly quickly approached.

"Teddy's not up there," Polly said when she reached them. "Did you see where he went?"

"Are you trying to be funny?" Teddy snapped.

"He's not up there?" Danielle squeaked.

"Obviously not," Teddy said.

"You didn't see him come back down?" Polly asked.

"I think I'm getting sick," Danielle muttered.

"Polly, stop being ridiculous," Teddy snapped.

"She can't see you," Eva told Teddy.

"Who can't see me?" Teddy asked.

"You didn't see him?" Polly asked.

"Your wife, of course," Eva said.

"I need a vacation," Danielle grumbled.

"That is a ridiculous thing to say," Teddy told Polly.

"You never treated her very nice anyway," Marie said. "She's better off without you."

"What are you talking about?" Teddy asked.

"What is wrong, Danielle?" Polly asked. "Has something happened to Teddy?"

"How you treat your wife. You are not a very nice man," Marie said.

"Who are you?" Teddy demanded. "And what do you know about me and my wife?"

"I've been watching you. I see how you talk to that poor thing," Marie said.

Teddy frowned at Marie and then reached out to grab his wife's right hand while saying, "Polly, let's go." His hand moved through Polly's wrist. He froze.

Danielle reached over to Polly and grabbed hold of her hand, gently pulling her away from the ghosts, leading her to a quieter section of the foyer.

"You're dead," Eva explained. "I don't know where your body is, but what you have now is your ghostly illusion, which your wife can't see, hear or touch."

Teddy raised his hands to his face and looked at them. "I don't understand."

"Do you know how you died?" Marie asked.

Teddy shook his head and then vanished.

"WHAT?" Polly asked after Danielle pulled her to the side, away from Walt.

"Umm…I think maybe we were wrong about seeing your husband," Danielle stammered.

"What do you mean wrong? According to Walt, he went for a walk and got lost."

Danielle shrugged. "Maybe Walt meant maybe he went for a walk and got lost?"

Polly studied Danielle, her brow furrowed. "Did you or did you not see my husband?"

Danielle smiled sheepishly. "I really need to call the chief."

TWENTY-EIGHT

The mediums all gathered at the Bartleys' to discuss the recent development. The only Frederickport medium not in attendance was the chief's young son Evan. They preferred to keep him away from the crime spree, considering the current ghost count (they could not say body count, since they hadn't found all those yet). They had a serial killer on the loose. And it looked like it was one of their guests.

Smiling ear to ear, Walt sat on the rocking chair, holding Connor on his right knee, forgetting for a moment their crisis while he encouraged smiles from the baby by tickling his nose and then his ears. Connor's green eyes focused on Walt's playful fingers, giggling in delight over the game. Nearby, Lily glanced in their direction and smiled over the sight and then turned her attention back to what the others were saying.

"I think we can cross Polly off the list of suspects," Heather suggested. She sat on the floor in front of the sofa, leaning back on one corner, as Danielle sat to her left, behind her. Danielle's stockinged feet rested on the coffee table, her ankles crossed, inches from Heather's left shoulder.

"Why do you say that?" Chris asked. He sat on the sofa with Danielle and Lily, with Lily in the middle.

"According to Walt and Danielle, she seemed genuinely happy he was back. I'd think if she was the killer, her more natural response would be, what the hell, why didn't he stay dead?" Heather said.

"You have a point," Danielle agreed. "But I did find something peculiar about her reaction. She was almost…well, too relieved to hear he was back."

"Which makes me think she believes

Teddy was in some way involved in Bentley's death," Chris suggested. "Maybe they left together, and she was afraid Teddy might have drowned too."

"Then why wouldn't she say something?" Lily asked.

Before anyone could respond, a suspicious sound came from the baby, and Walt quickly picked Connor up off his lap, holding him at arm's length.

Lily laughed. "Sounds like someone did something over there."

"Smells like it too," Walt said, looking as if he did not know what to do with the squirmy baby, who was now red faced, making grunting sounds while shaking his legs.

"Let me take him," Ian said, quickly scooping the baby up from Walt and then heading to the nursery.

Danielle looked over at her husband. "Walt, what did you think about Polly's response to Teddy coming back?"

"In what regard?"

"Were you listening to what we were saying?" Danielle asked.

Walt grinned and shrugged. "Not really."

Danielle rolled her eyes and then caught him up on the conversation he had been ignoring.

"I hadn't given that much consideration," Walt confessed. "I'm a little more concerned about when Teddy's body is found and the others start questioning us about seeing him. If we're on record as seeing him alive this afternoon, we could be handing the killer an alibi."

"Not to mention if the coroner's time of death doesn't jibe with when you saw him," Chris said.

Lily looked at Danielle. "So what are you going to say?"

They all turned to look at Danielle, waiting for an answer.

"What do you mean?" Danielle frowned.

"You always come up with a good story in instances like this. What have you come up with?" Lily asked.

"She's right," Chris agreed. "You do have a gift for this sort of thing."

"She does," Walt said with a nod.

Danielle looked from her friends to her

husband and frowned. "I have no idea what I'm going to say. Walt is the one who marched into the dining room and announced to everyone he had just seen Teddy."

Lily looked at Walt and asked, "Which of them acted shocked when you said that?"

"Shocked? How do you mean?" Walt asked.

"If I had just killed someone, and then someone else told me my victim had just walked in the house, I'd be a little freaked," Lily said.

Walt shrugged. "Sorry. I didn't notice their reaction. I was watching Polly. She seemed genuinely relieved."

The doorbell rang.

Walt stood up. "I'll get that. It's probably the chief."

Police Chief MacDonald walked into the Bartley living room with Walt a few minutes later and took a seat. Walt reclaimed the rocking chair, and Ian joined them with Connor a few moments later. He handed the baby to Lily and then sat down on his recliner.

"Are Marie and Eva here?" the chief asked.

"No. They stayed over at our house to keep an eye on our guests and do a little eavesdropping," Danielle explained.

"How are they all doing over there?" MacDonald asked.

"When we left, Jackie was still trying to get ahold of Bentley's mother," Danielle explained. "And Polly said she was going to walk down to the pier to see if Teddy had gone down to the café."

"I don't think she's going to find him down there," Chris said with a snort.

"Everyone in my office believes Mason's death was a foolish accident," the chief began.

"Do you have the blood tests back already?" Lily asked.

The chief shook his head. "No. But the assumption they're making—while waiting for the coroner's report—is that it was an accident. Had he been fully dressed, we might wonder if he fell off the pier somehow and drowned. But he was wearing boxers, and the rest of his clothes were found not far from where his body was discovered. Now, if those tox reports come back showing he wasn't drunk—or using drugs—then it makes us wonder, why would a sober person decide to take a midnight swim in freezing water?"

"Plus, we already know he was murdered," Heather reminded.

"True. But I can't tell my people that a couple of ghosts told us Mason was murdered. Not to mention the fact we can't adequately investigate the other murders until the bodies show up, or when they officially go missing," the chief reminded her.

"Were you able to do anything about Phoebe's phone?" Danielle asked.

"Yes. It looks as if the last call she made was from your house. But we tried pinging it and nothing," MacDonald told them.

CHASE HAD ARRIVED at Marlow House ten minutes earlier. He stood in the living room with the remaining Marlow House guests—the live ones. Eva and Marie hovered overhead on imaginary chairs, eavesdropping.

"Why would he go swimming?" Chase asked after hearing what had happened to Bentley. He sat with Birdie on the sofa, with Jackie and Julius sitting across from them in the wing-backed chairs. Polly anxiously paced the room, gnawing her right thumbnail, while Seraphina sat alone at the game table with a deck of cards, playing solitaire while silently listening to the others.

"He must have had more to drink than any of us ever imagined," Jackie said.

"I did notice he switched to gin during the end of the evening," Birdie noted. She looked at Polly and said, "I believe you did too."

Polly stopped pacing and looked to Birdie. With a shrug she said, "It was stupid of me. I still have a headache."

"I had a friend who said she couldn't drink gin," Birdie said. "Said it made her mean."

"It definitely made Bentley stupid," Chase said with a snort.

Jackie glared at Chase. "I would appreciate it if you didn't talk about Bentley that way. He was a valuable employee, and I'm going to miss him dearly. We've all done foolish things."

"Yeah, well, so far my foolish things haven't got me killed," Chase said. He then looked at Polly and asked, "Where's Teddy?"

Polly stopped pacing and looked at Chase. "I don't know. He was here earlier. After they found Bentley's body, he went out again."

"He didn't tell you where he was going?" Chase asked.

"I'm his wife, not his keeper." Polly stormed from the room.

Seraphina tossed the cards she had been holding on the table, stood up, and ran after Polly.

"What's Polly's problem?" Chase asked, looking at the doorway Polly and Seraphina had left through.

"I think she's annoyed at Teddy, which I don't blame her," Jackie said. "Frankly, I'm pretty sure I know where he is, and so does Polly."

"And where's that?" Chase asked.

"Probably on a bender," Jackie said. "I've always thought a person with a drinking problem needs to stop drinking altogether. Not cut back."

"I never thought he had a problem," Julius said. "It was just that one time, and that was over three years ago."

"Perhaps, but I noticed he was hitting it a little hard last night. I think that whole thing with Phoebe got to him," Jackie said. "According to Bentley, he overheard Phoebe and Polly going at it in the kitchen the other evening. It was the night Bentley slept downstairs. Phoebe admitted everything."

Chase chuckled. "I told him he had some big ones staying under the roof with his wife and Phoebe."

"There was so much I had hoped to get accomplished this week, but now with Bentley gone, I'm not sure how I'm going to handle everything. Perhaps there's a temp agency in Frederickport," Jackie said.

"Why do I get the feeling she's grieving more over the loss of what Bentley could do for her, rather than the man?" Marie asked.

"She's a good actress, I'll give her that." Eva chuckled. "Did you see how she keeps dabbing her eyes?"

"Yes, what about it?" Marie asked.

"Look a little closer. Not a single tear. But just keeps dabbing away like it's waterworks," Eva said.

Marie cocked her head to one side and studied Jackie a little closer. The woman's eyes weren't red rimmed at all.

Seraphina walked back into the room.

"Is Polly alright?" Birdie asked.

"I think it's just her headache. She had way too much to drink last night. She went to lie down." Seraphina returned to the game table, sat down, and picked up her cards.

"Chase, last night you mentioned another project you were working on," Julius said. "I heard you mentioning it to Bentley."

"Ahh…yes, well, it's in the research stage," Chase said.

"I'd hope you would be giving all your attention to the current project," Birdie said primly.

"I am. But one story inspires another," Chase said.

"What do you mean by that?" Jackie asked.

"Meeting that Chris Johnson got me to

thinking," Chase began.

Seraphina looked up from the cards to Chase. "What about Chris?"

"He's about the same age as his camera-shy boss. Same first name. And if you look up the photos of Chris Glandon online, it's not a far cry to imagine they could be one and the same."

"Don't be ridiculous," Birdie argued. "I've seen photographs of Chris Glandon, I knew his parents. He was a homely boy. All that facial hair."

"Shave off the beard, and you'll see something different, I'd wager," Chase said.

"You're saying that handsome young man is Chris Glandon?" Jackie asked with a laugh. "I can't imagine anyone could be that good looking and that rich."

"So what's your story angle? Camera-shy philanthropist hanging out in plain sight?" Julius asked.

Now turned slightly in the chair, watching and listening intently to Chase, Seraphina unwittingly squeezed the cards she held so tight they bent in her hand.

Chase shrugged. "Glandon's plight reminded me how when a kid is put in foster care, their entire future is at the whim of the system. In his case, he was a poor child adopted by an insanely rich couple, yet I imagine there are cases where some kids born of shame from wealthy families are dumped in foster care and end up living in poverty for their entire lives. Am I right, Seraphina?"

Seraphina frowned. "Why are you asking me?"

"Didn't I read you grew up in foster care?"

"She's not exactly living in poverty," Jackie said with a snort.

"Do you remember your parents?" Chase asked.

"Of course I do," Seraphina said. "I was seven when they were killed in a car accident. There wasn't any family to take me in. I never imagined I was a lost princess who'd been taken from her kingdom."

"But did you ever know anyone in foster care that might have come from a wealthy family?" Chase asked.

"Why are we talking about this?" Birdie asked.

TWENTY-NINE

Seraphina stood up. "I think I'll go check on Polly again."

Birdie reached down and picked up her cane. "I think I'll join you." She stood up.

Jackie glanced at her watch. "I think I'm going to try calling Bentley's mother again."

"I'll go with them, if you want to stay here," Eva told Marie.

A few minutes later Chase sat alone in the room with Julius. Marie was also there, yet neither man knew they had an audience.

"I bet you are somewhat relieved this Bentley thing can finally be put behind you," Chase told Julius.

Julius glared at Chase. "I thought you agreed never to mention that."

"It's just you and me," Chase said with a chuckle.

"And me!" Marie added. "But do tell. What did you promise never to mention?"

"I'm very sad Bentley is dead," Julius insisted.

"I imagine you are. You two were…close," Chase said with a snort.

"Chase, I'm not gay. It was that one time. I had too much to drink, and I would rather forget about it."

Chase put up his right palm. "Hey, I'm not going to tell anyone. Promised then, when I walked in on you, and I kept my promise. But with Bentley out of the picture, you don't have to worry about it anymore. Must have been damn awkward, having him working with your wife, seeing him all the time. Must have been awkward for him too."

"We never talked about it," Julius said. "And I'd rather not talk about it now. But I'm certainly not happy he's dead."

WHEN DANIELLE and Walt returned to Marlow House late that afternoon, they found Joanne already in the kitchen preparing dinner. The others were all in their rooms, and according to Joanne, it had been fairly quiet since she had arrived. Not long after Walt and Danielle walked in the house, Marie popped into the kitchen and told them to meet her in the parlor so she could give them an update.

"I must say," Marie began, "all those things I've heard about Hollywood people are even more tawdry than I imagined!"

"I guess I can understand what you're saying, considering they seem to be dropping dead right and left," Danielle grumbled.

"Oh, not that. Sure, we might as well be living in a horror movie, considering the newly departed spirits that have been showing up," Marie said. "I'm talking about the fooling around! Goodness gracious, doesn't anyone respect their wedding vows?"

"Who are we talking about?" Danielle asked.

"Julius for one," Marie said. "And his indiscretion was with someone you've met."

"Who has Julius been indiscreet with?" Walt asked.

"You will never guess this!" Marie said.

"Bentley, right?" Danielle asked.

Both Walt and Marie looked to Danielle and frowned.

"How did you know?" Marie asked.

Danielle shrugged. "Just some vibe I picked up."

"Who else?" Walt asked.

"We already knew about the other. Teddy and Phoebe. But it's shameful. Just shameful."

"Anyone else?" Danielle asked.

"I certainly hope not. Isn't that enough? After all, there are only two couples staying with you, and both of them have broken their wedding vows."

"Actually, we don't know if Polly and Jackie have broken their vows," Danielle reminded her.

Walt glanced briefly to the closed door and asked, "What's everyone doing?"

"Chase went back to his rental house. He told Julius to tell you he would not be returning for dinner. Said he was going to be writing all night," Marie said.

"And the others?" Danielle asked.

"All in their rooms. Eva is with Jackie and Julius. We figure unless the others start talking to themselves, nothing to listen to," Marie explained.

"And no new ghost sightings?" Walt asked.

"None," Marie said. "So what did you all decide? Does the chief have a suspect?"

"They're all suspects," Danielle said.

"But who does he think did it?" Marie asked.

"Chris doesn't like it, but Seraphina is one of the prime suspects—at least she was until Teddy's death. Still trying to figure out why she would want to kill Teddy."

"Why would she want to kill Bentley?" Marie asked.

"He was sleeping downstairs the night Phoebe went missing. Maybe he saw something, and she had to get rid of him," Danielle suggested.

"Of course, Polly is also a suspect," Walt said. "She did have that fight with Phoebe, and she might have gotten rid of Bentley for the same reason as Seraphina."

"Except we don't think Polly killed Teddy," Danielle said.

"No," Marie said, shaking her head. "Polly wasn't responsible for her husband's death. When I went up to her room earlier, she was on the phone calling all the local bars in town, asking if anyone of them had a customer that matched her husband's description."

"No, if she killed him, she certainly wouldn't be calling around looking for him, not unless she was doing it for show. But as far as she knew, she was alone in the room," Danielle said.

"Poor thing. She's going to be devastated when they find his body. Although I don't know why. The man was a putz," Marie said.

As if on cue, someone began knocking on the parlor door. A moment later Danielle let Polly into the room.

"Joanne told me I would find you in here," Polly said.

"What can I help you with?" Danielle asked.

Polly walked all the way into the parlor,

her eyes rimmed in dark shadows. "Teddy still hasn't come back."

Danielle and Walt exchange glances and said nothing.

"Can you tell me again, what did he say when you saw him? Did he seem sober?" she asked.

"He seemed sober," Walt said, then added to himself, *He also seemed alive, and we were wrong about that.*

"You see, Teddy's work is pretty stressful. Ummm…he could be short with me…" Polly began.

"He could be an ass, you mean," Marie said.

"But I understood…well, at least most of the time. Sometimes, well, frankly sometimes I wanted to kill him."

Danielle's eyes widened. "Kill him?"

Polly blushed. "Just a figure of speech. Don't you ever get so mad at Walt sometimes that you might say you want to kill him?"

Danielle looked over to her husband, who met her with his smile. "Honestly? I might say I wanna clobber him…or smack him…"

Walt's grin broadened. "Vicious woman."

"But never ever kill him. I like him on this side." She flashed Walt a smile.

"This side?" Polly frowned.

Danielle shrugged and said, "Umm… nothing…but yeah, I understand we all get mad at our spouses sometimes."

"But I would never in a million years hurt Teddy. I love him."

Danielle frowned. "No one said you hurt Teddy."

"I'm just afraid. He's not back. And like I said, his job can be stressful, and some things that have happened the last few days, I think I might have pushed him over the edge. I even said some things to him that could have made things worse. I'm afraid he might have gone on a drinking binge. And I just want to find him."

"The good news, he didn't take the car," Danielle said.

"The bad news, he's dead," Marie added.

"I just need to know, did he say anything, anything at all? Did he mention where he might go?"

Walt reached out and touched Polly's right hand. "No, he didn't. But we're going to have dinner soon. Why don't you have a nice meal. You're probably hungry because all we had was lunch, and you didn't finish yours. Maybe by the time we finish dinner, Teddy will be back."

"Walt, you know he's not coming back," Danielle said after Polly left the parlor.

"I know, but what else could I say?"

DINNER AT MARLOW HOUSE was a solemn affair on Monday evening. Everyone retired to their rooms shortly after dinner. No one even discussed Teddy's absence, as the silent consensus seemed to be he was out somewhere getting drunk.

Danielle headed up to bed early, leaving Walt to close up the house. As he did every night, he walked through the first floor, locking doors, closing blinds, and turning off overhead lights. When he finally headed upstairs, the only lighting came from the night-lights plugged into random sockets.

When Walt finally walked into his bedroom, he had Max in his arms.

"What do you have there?" Danielle asked, sitting up in bed.

"Max didn't want to be left alone downstairs with a serial killer in the house." Walt tossed the cat on the bed.

"I can't say I blame him," Danielle said as the cat curled up by her feet.

"I just wish they would all go home," Walt said, locking the bedroom door. "I should never have written that book."

"Your book has nothing to do with any of this," she insisted.

"Really?" Walt stood by the side of the bed, unbuttoning his shirt. "Tell me, if I hadn't written *Moon Runners*, would we have those guests downstairs? And would those ghosts be flitting in and out?"

Danielle shrugged sheepishly. "No…but…"

PEARL ROLLED over on her right side and opened her eyes, looking toward her nightstand. The room was pitch dark save for the red glow of the digital numbers on her alarm clock. It was 3:26 in the morning. If she didn't have to pee, she would close her eyes and go back to sleep. But that was not going to happen. Reluctantly she rolled out of bed, grateful she had forgotten to turn the thermostat down when she had gone to bed that night. It was as toasty warm out of her bedding as it was in it.

When Pearl returned from the bathroom ten minutes later, she walked to the window instead of her bed, to look out into the darkness. She hadn't bothered to turn the bedroom light on when she went to the bathroom, so if anyone drove by, they wouldn't see her standing there in her nightgown. *Of course, who would be driving by at three thirty in the morning?* Pearl thought.

As she was about to turn from the window and return to bed, she noticed the kitchen light go on over at the Marlows'. She couldn't see who was in the kitchen, but whoever it was, they were opening the door to the side yard. A moment later, the light went off. She assumed whoever it was had just gone outside —but why?

Believing it was Walt or Danielle, she

looked to the garage behind their house, yet saw no motion. But then she noticed a light turn on in front of the house. Headlights. It was one of the cars that had been parked in front of Marlow House for the last few days. A moment later it drove away.

"It's rather late to go out," Pearl muttered. Letting the curtain drop back into place, she returned to bed and climbed under the covers. Unfortunately, she couldn't get back to sleep. After a few minutes, she turned on the side lamp and picked up the book she had placed there earlier and started to read.

Some thirty minutes later she began feeling sleepy again. Closing her book, she returned it to the nightstand and turned off the light. Cuddling down in the darkness, determined to fall back to sleep, she heard what sounded like a car door slam. Jumping up from the bed, Pearl hurried to the window and looked outside. The car was back, and whoever had driven it had just entered through the Marlows' side gate and was running to the back door. She couldn't tell if it was a man or woman—just a dark figure running to the house under the moonlight.

THIRTY

Adam Nichols, Realtor and owner of Frederickport Vacation Properties and the favorite grandson of Marie Hemming Nichols, was the primary reason Marie hadn't moved on to the other side. She wanted to see him married—and she wanted a great-grandchild. However, she was beginning to think she would have better luck getting a great-grandchild through Adam's younger brother, considering Adam and the woman he was seeing both claimed they didn't want children.

It was a shame, as Adam was a fine-looking young man, Marie thought, fit, good-looking with coal black eyes. Adam had also done fairly well for himself in business, especially for a man in his mid-thirties. Of course, his inheritance from Marie had substantially boosted his bottom line.

ON TUESDAY MORNING Adam sat alone in his office, sorting through his email and drinking his first cup of coffee of the day when his assistant, Leslie, walked into the room. He looked up from his computer and asked, "What's up?"

One hand on her hip, she let out a sigh. "I just got a call from a neighbor across the street from the Marshall house." The Marshall house was one of the properties in Adam's rental program. It was also the house he had rented to Chase Wilks.

"Is there a problem?" Adam asked.

"According to the neighbor, she went to take her dog for a walk on the beach. There's that path that runs along the south side of the Marshall house. When she walked down it, she noticed one of the windows along that side had been smashed in."

"Damn," Adam grumbled. "Did she talk to Wilks? See what happened?"

Leslie shook her head. "She didn't see him and didn't knock on the door. But his car was out front. She thought it was best to call us instead of the police. Figured the renters had broken the window."

Adam groaned. "If it's the neighbor I think it is, she's not thrilled having that house rented out. I'm sure she'd be delighted if Marshall decided to pull it from the program."

"What do you want me to do?" she asked.

"Let me call Wilks, see what happened."

Leslie started to leave the office, but then paused and turned around to face Adam. "Hey, did you hear what happened over at Marlow House yesterday?"

"There's no telling with Danielle. What now?"

"One of their guests drowned," Leslie explained. "I heard it on the radio this morning."

"Drowned? No kidding. Do you know what happened?"

"They aren't sure yet. Looks like the fool decided to take a late night swim and stripped down to his skivvies."

"That water is freezing," Adam said.

Leslie shrugged. "I guess Heather Donovan and one of the other guests found him on the beach when they went jogging."

"Seriously? How many does that make now?" Adam asked.

"I have no idea. I just know if Heather ever asked me to go jogging with her, I'd decline."

"You don't jog anyway," Adam teased.

"Still. If I did, I certainly wouldn't go with her."

"No kidding," Adam said with a snort.

Leslie flashed him a half smile and then turned and left the office.

Several minutes later, after finding Wilks's phone number, Adam tried giving him a call. It went immediately to voicemail. He then called his handyman, Bill Jones.

"I was just getting ready to call you," Bill

said. Bill wasn't just Adam's handyman, they had been friends since high school. "Want to go out to breakfast?"

"Maybe afterwards. But I need you to meet me over at the Marshall house. We just got a call, and one of the windows along the side of the house was smashed in."

"Damn. The north or south side?" Bill asked.

"South, where the path runs."

"Oh crap, not that window. That's going to be a pain. I'll have to special order it. Which means I'll need to take some plywood along to board it up until I can get it fixed."

THIRTY MINUTES later Adam stood with Bill Jones on the south side of the Marshall house on the pathway, looking up at the broken window. Jones, a forgettable-looking man, had shaggy brown hair that needed a trim and good conditioner. His faded blue eyes would never be described as sparkling. He wore denims and a blue work shirt and, as normal, held a lit cigarette in his hand, which accounted for the yellowing of his teeth.

Hands on hips, Adam looked up at the shattered window and shook his head. "I'm surprised Wilks hasn't called me about this."

"Maybe he's planning to get it fixed himself," Bill suggested.

"I suppose." Adam shrugged.

Bill stepped off the path and started toward the window.

"What are you doing?" Adam asked. "Let's go around front and ring the bell. I don't want you looking in a renter's window."

Ignoring Adam, Bill continued to the house and said, "I just want to see if he cleaned up the glass yet." Standing on tiptoes, Bill looked down to the floor inside. "Nope. Hasn't been cleaned up." He then moved to the window of the second bedroom, which hadn't been broken, and looked inside.

"Bill, don't go looking in windows," Adam said. "Like a freaking Peeping Tom. The guy's there."

Now peering in the window, Bill said, "Umm…Adam…how many people did you say are staying here?"

"One, why?"

"A big guy?" Bill asked, still looking inside the house.

"Yes. Get away from there before he walks into the room."

Bill knocked loudly on the window and then said, "Too late. He's already in the room. And either he's out cold…or dead."

ADAM STOOD on the sidewalk in front of the Marshall house, the cellphone to his ear, as a hubbub of activity went on around him. Brian Henderson and Joe Morelli had responded to the call. Someone from the coroner's office had already arrived; however the body hadn't yet been removed.

Bill stood near his truck, chatting with some of the curious neighbors who had showed up to see why all the police cars were there.

Wilks had been dead, alright. Shot in the back, according to what Brian had told Adam.

Adam waited for Danielle to answer his call.

"Hi, Adam. What's up?" came Danielle's voice over the phone.

"Hate to tell you this, but you know Wilks, your guy I rented the house to?" Adam asked.

"What about him?" Danielle asked.

"He's dead," Adam said.

"What? What do you mean dead?"

"What do you think I mean? Dead. You know, no longer alive."

"What happened?" Danielle asked.

"Came over to the house to check on a broken window and found his body."

"I don't believe this," Danielle groaned.

"This week does not seem to be going well for you. I heard about the drowning this morning."

"What happened to Wilks? Heart attack?" Danielle asked.

"Why do you say heart attack?"

"The guy was pretty big, and his food choices when he was here were not the healthiest."

"Says the woman who thinks cinnamon rolls are a food group."

"Hey, you eat them too," Danielle reminded him.

"Well, the cinnamon rolls didn't kill him. Which should make us both feel better. But I suspect it was the bullet to his back."

"Bullet? He was shot?" Danielle gasped.

"Yep. It looks like he was sitting at the desk at his computer, writing. Brian doesn't think he saw it coming."

"Why would someone kill him?" Danielle asked, not expecting an answer.

"The place was ransacked. They found his wallet on the floor by him. It was empty, only had his driver's license. Everything in the bathroom medicine cabinets was on the floor."

"Someone looking for drugs and money?" Danielle asked.

"Looks that way. But the only drugs they would have gotten were any Wilks's brought, if he had any with him. Only thing in the medicine cabinets here are items we leave for our guests, bars of soap, shampoo. No medicine."

"You said Brian is there?" Danielle asked.

"Yeah, he and Joe answered the call. Here comes Brian now. I'll call you back."

POLICE CHIEF MACDONALD stood in the middle of the living room at Marlow House late Tuesday morning, surrounded by its remaining guests, along with Walt and Danielle. Marie and Eva were there too, but only Walt and Danielle could see or hear them.

"I don't believe it," Jackie said for the third time. "Dead. Chase is dead? Who's going to finish the screenplay?"

"Good lord, Jackie, is that all you have to say?" Julius asked.

Jackie looked unapologetically to her husband. "I do have responsibilities, something you know nothing about," she spat.

Julius turned bright red but closed his mouth and did not respond.

Polly and Seraphina sat together on the sofa with Birdie, silently listening to what the others had to say.

"You said he was shot?" Birdie asked. "Why would anyone want to murder Chase?"

"It looks as if he was sitting at his desk when someone broke into the house. We believe they came through a window in one of the bedrooms. He was in the other bedroom at the desk. Apparently working at his computer. The house was ransacked. His wallet was emptied, and whoever it was went through the medicine cabinets in the bathrooms."

"Drugs," Birdie said, shaking her head. "Drugs make people do horrible things."

"That's what it looks like at the moment. But it's too early in the investigation to tell," the chief said.

MacDonald looked at Walt and Danielle and said, "I was wondering if we could talk alone, in the parlor?"

TEN MINUTES later MacDonald sat in the parlor with Walt and Danielle, while Eva and Marie continued to supervise the remaining guests, listening for any clues.

"Do you believe this was some random

killer?" Danielle asked. "We don't have those kinds of break-ins in Frederickport."

"I believe it was made to look that way," MacDonald said. "But considering what has been going on with your guests, I find it hard to believe Chase fell victim to some drug-crazed killer, while others in his group are being killed one by one.

"What doesn't make sense to me," Danielle began. "You said it looked like he was surprised, that someone shot him from behind, and he didn't see it coming. But if the killer entered through the window, how did Chase not hear the glass breaking if he was just in the next room?"

"The television was on in his room. So it's possible the killer broke the window to gain access, and Chase didn't hear him."

"That's not what happened," Chase said, suddenly appearing in the room.

"Chase!" Danielle gasped.

"You can see me?" Chase asked.

"You know you're dead?" Walt asked.

Chase turned from Danielle to Walt. "And you can see me too?"

"Don't tell me, Wilks's ghost is here?" the

chief asked. "If he is, don't let him leave until he tells us who killed him. I'd like to solve at least one of these murders!"

Wilks turned to the chief. "I take it you can't see me."

"Who killed you?" Walt asked.

"I'm rather impressed how well you have accepted your death," Danielle said.

Wilks shrugged. "All this is great material. But unfortunately I won't be able to write about it. And I wish I could tell you who killed me, but I have no idea."

"What did you mean when you said that's not what happened?" Walt asked.

Chase looked to Walt. "The last thing I remember—when I was alive, I was sitting at my computer, writing. And then I felt it. Knocked me clear to the beach. I couldn't figure out what in the heck had happened, but when I went back in the house, there I was sitting at the desk, slumped over, a bullet in my back. And the television was on. I never watch TV when I'm writing. I don't listen to music either. I need quiet."

"So the killer turned on the TV before he left?" Walt asked.

"I sure didn't turn it on," Chase said.

"If you need quiet, didn't you hear the intruder breaking the window in the next room?" Danielle asked.

Chase shook his head. "No. And about that, why break the window to get in? The front door was unlocked. I never locked the front door. Didn't think I needed to. But I guess I was wrong about that, wasn't I?"

THIRTY-ONE

"Chief MacDonald! Oh, Chief MacDonald!" Pearl called out as she pushed open her front gate and hurried out to the sidewalk in front of her house. Wearing a navy blue jogging suit and a knit cap, she hurried as fast as her tennis shoes would take her, making her way to the police car parked in front of Marlow House.

About to get into the vehicle, MacDonald paused a moment and watched Pearl approach.

"Chief MacDonald, did you find out why that man went swimming so late at night?"

Pearl asked when she reached him, slightly out of breath.

"I'm afraid there's nothing I can say at this time," he said. "It's too early in the investigation."

"I know the Marlows are free to have whatever nonpaying guests they want, you remind me of that often enough," Pearl began. "But this coming and going at all hours of the night should be illegal. If nothing else, it's rude. Some of us are trying to sleep. And look what happened to that young man. If he had stayed in his bed, like a sensible person, he wouldn't have drowned."

"Mrs. Huckabee, who exactly is coming and going at all times of the night?" he asked.

"I don't know. I just know it was after 3:30 in the morning. I know that because I happened to look at my clock. But whoever it was got into that car." Pearl pointed to the rental car parked behind MacDonald's vehicle. "And then whoever it was came back about a half hour later."

"Did you see the car leave?" he asked.

"Of course. I looked out my window. Whoever it was came out the back door and got into that car. Later, when I heard them return, I peeked out the window and saw them running like the devil was after them from the street to the back door."

"Was it a man or woman?"

"I couldn't tell. The moon was out, but I couldn't make out who they were. It was just a dark figure."

"And you said they were running?"

"Oh yes. Like the devil was after them."

"Did you notice if they had long hair?" he asked.

Pearl frowned. "No. Whoever it was wore a cap of some sort, and a bulky jacket and dark pants. Like I said, it could have been a man or woman."

"Thank you, Mrs. Huckabee, I appreciate you telling me. One of my officers will be back to take a formal statement from you."

Pearl perked up. "Really? So you're actually going to do something about this?"

"Most certainly," MacDonald told her.

After bidding her goodbye, MacDonald returned to Marlow House instead of getting into his car. When he knocked on the front door a few minutes later, Danielle was surprised to see him again.

"Did you forget something?" Danielle asked, standing at the open doorway.

"I think we need to talk again," he said seriously.

A few minutes later MacDonald sat in the parlor with Walt and Danielle. He had just asked Danielle and Walt to tell him whose rental car was parked in front of his police car.

"That's the car Birdie rented," Danielle said.

"What's this about?" Walt asked.

The chief then told Walt and Danielle what Pearl had shared with him outside.

"Well, it couldn't have been Birdie," Danielle said when he was done. "She uses a cane and doesn't get around that well. I can't imagine that's who Pearl saw running."

"Who else drives that car?" MacDonald asked.

"Phoebe was the one who drove it here. As far as I know, no one has driven that car since Phoebe disappeared." Danielle said.

"You mean since Phoebe was killed?" the chief corrected.

Danielle cringed. "Yeah. I believe Birdie was going to add Seraphina to the insurance so she could drive them back to Portland. Birdie says she doesn't feel comfortable driving anymore, not since her accident."

"What accident was that?" MacDonald asked.

"I'm not sure. I just assume it's why she uses a cane now. As for that car, anyone could have taken it. The keys have been sitting in a bowl in the kitchen since we came back from touring the Glandon Foundation. That's where Phoebe put them, and I noticed them there this morning," Danielle said.

"You think one of our guests went over to Chase's beach house last night and killed him?" Walt asked.

"That's what it's starting to look like."

"Chase did tell us the front door was unlocked," Walt said. "That means, if one of them went over there to kill him, they could have come through the door without even knocking."

"And had it been locked, they could have

knocked and he would have let them in, and he'd be just as dead," Danielle added.

"Except, if that had been the scenario, Chase's ghost could have identified his shooter," Walt reminded her.

"If he remembered. Which is not always the case," Danielle added.

Walt looked at the chief and asked, "What now?"

"I would like to interview all of them again, but I would rather do it down at the police station, one at a time."

"You want me to round up the suspects and send them down there?" Danielle asked.

"Yes. But let them think this is routine," the chief said.

"Okay. I'll get them down there," Danielle promised. "But first, let me tell you everything Marie and Eva overheard."

BRIAN AND JOE stood in the small office, looking through the two-way mirror, watching Julius Stafford, who sat at the only table in the adjacent interrogation room. They guessed he was in his fifties, a pleasant enough looking man, with a full head of gray hair and wire-rimmed glasses.

"Once again the chief is asking the questions. We found the body," Joe complained.

"You know why," Brian reminded him. The chief had told them he had received some anonymous information and felt it best if he asked the questions.

"Have you noticed how he's always receiving anonymous information these days?" Joe asked.

"Only seems to happen when the case involves Marlow House," Brian muttered.

If Joe heard Brian's comment, he didn't respond. The next moment the chief walked into the interrogation room.

"MR. STAFFORD, I appreciate you coming down here," the chief said, extending his hand. Julius stood briefly, shook the police chief's hand, and then both men sat down at the table. The chief set the folder he had been holding on the table.

"This is just horrendous about Chase," Julius said. "Who would do such a horrible thing?" He shook his head.

"Did you know Mr. Wilks well?" the chief asked.

Julius shrugged. "Well enough, I suppose. My wife worked with Chase on another picture. That's when I first met him. In fact, all of us worked on that project. Well, all of those staying at Marlow House."

"You worked on the project?" the chief asked.

Julius blushed. "Not officially. But I usually accompany my wife on business trips, and I help out when I can. I like to think I'm part of the team."

"Do you know anyone on your team who had an issue with Chase?" the chief asked.

"If you're thinking one of us had anything to do with what happened to him, there is no way. Absolutely not."

"So no one had an issue with him?" the chief asked.

"If we killed off everyone we had issues with in this industry, there would be no one left alive in Hollywood."

"Humor me," the chief said. "What was your issue with Chase?"

"My issue? I didn't have a problem with him. He was good at his job. A little obnoxious at times. But nothing worth killing over."

"Not even to keep him from talking?" the chief asked.

Julius frowned. "I don't understand. Talking about what?"

"You and Bentley?" the chief asked.

JOE LOOKED AT BRIAN. "Bentley? Is he talking about the guy who drowned?"

Brian smiled and arched his brows, his gaze still on the two men in the interrogation room. "This is getting interesting."

JULIUS CLOSED HIS EYES BRIEFLY, took a deep breath, and then looked across the table at the chief. "I'm assuming someone overheard Chase's and my conversation last night. But I will assure you, I had no reason to kill Chase to keep him quiet."

"Why should I believe you?" MacDonald asked.

"For one thing, my wife already knows."

"YES, I know about Bentley and Julius's little indiscretion," Jackie said when it was her turn in the interrogation room. "We didn't want Bentley to know I knew. But now, poor Bentley is dead, it's rather a moot point, isn't it?"

"I don't understand. Why wouldn't you want Bentley to know you knew?" he asked.

"It would have been horribly awkward. And Bentley was absolutely the best assistant I ever had. You have no idea how difficult it is to find reliable people you can count on. It was one of those things, too much alcohol. But now…now I have to go through that tedious hiring practice again. I'm not looking forward to that."

"Would you have been upset had Chase

told someone else about Julius and Bentley's secret?" he asked.

"I don't know why," Jackie said. "In the big scheme of things, that is hardly a huge deal, now is it? It's not like we had a prenup like Teddy. But then in that case, it wouldn't really mattered who knew beside me and my husband."

"What do you mean?"

Jackie shrugged. "Polly had to sign a prenup when she married Teddy. Her brother is an attorney and he didn't like the prenup; after all, if Teddy divorced her for any reason, she wouldn't get a dime. But Teddy finally agreed to include a clause that said if he cheated, Polly would get half of his estate. So in their case, infidelity could cost him a great deal."

"Considering how long they've been married, I can't imagine she wouldn't get something in a divorce anyway," the chief said.

Jackie smiled. "Teddy is a shrewd businessman. He runs everything through his corporation—which he set up before he ever met Polly. Even the house they live in he owned before they were married."

The chief asked her a few more questions and then said, "Do you know of anyone who had an issue with Chase?"

"We all had issues with Chase; he was incredibly annoying at times. But the fact was, he was good at his job. And now, with him gone, I'm seriously not sure how we can continue with this project. Especially if Teddy is drinking again."

"Do you know of anyone who would want to sabotage the making of *Moon Runners*?"

Jackie shook her head. "Absolutely not."

"Did anyone staying at Marlow House have second thoughts about the project?"

"Just the opposite. I imagine they'll all be devastated if the movie doesn't move forward. Seraphina is counting on this as her breakout acting role. While she was in another film I produced, and she did amazing—if she hadn't, I never would have considered her for *Moon Runners*—this movie could definitely make her acting career."

"Any jealousy between Seraphina and Polly? I understand Polly used to be an actress."

"Yes, but Teddy sabotaged his wife's career. Of course, Polly let him. It's her choice. As for Polly and Seraphina, they got close during the last film. Polly would help her with the lines."

"Did Seraphina or Polly have any issues with Chase?" he asked.

"Aside from Chase making some not so subtle advances, I don't think there were any serious issues. And Birdie set him straight."

"Birdie?" he asked.

"Since Randy's death, Birdie has become Seraphina's champion. Randy was Birdie's husband, and they discovered Seraphina in a little dive. Randy had all the connections to help Seraphina's career, and after he died, Birdie picked up the mantle. Birdie is a bit of a mother hen when it comes to Seraphina. And if we aren't able to move ahead with *Moon Runners*, I suspect Birdie will be the most disappointed—after Seraphina and Walt, of course."

BIRDIE WAS QUESTIONED NEXT, and

everything she told the chief substantiated what the others had already said.

"By any chance did you hear anyone leave the house last night?" the chief asked Birdie.

Birdie smiled and pointed to one of her hearing aids. "When these come off, I can't hear a thing. They could be having a party outside my room, and I would never hear a thing."

SERAPHINA'S TURN FOLLOWED BIRDIE, and like her benefactor, she had nothing new to add.

"Someone mentioned there had been an altercation between Phoebe and Chase," the chief asked, failing to mention that had been information overheard by a ghost and passed on to him.

Seraphina smiled. "Yeah, when Chase has too much to drink, he can be kind of handsy. We were in Vegas filming, and one night he tried something with Phoebe. He's a big guy, and it got a little out of hand, but Teddy walked in. I've learned to keep my distance."

"And when he asked you to stay with him?" he asked.

"Well, that was not going to happen." Seraphina then took a deep breath and smiled softly at the chief. "I will be honest. While I don't like to speak ill of the dead, and I am truly sorry for what happened to Chase, it's just awful. But the fact is, I didn't care for the man."

"I imagine it would have been a better work environment if they had replaced Chase with another writer," the chief asked.

Seraphina shook her head. "I don't think so. There are a lot of jerks out there, especially in this business. Chase was hardly the worst, and I didn't have a problem dealing with him. I certainly had never campaigned to replace him."

POLLY WAS the last one showed into the interrogation room. She sat alone at the table, waiting for the chief to return. When he walked in the room, she blurted, "I think I'm going crazy!"

The chief took a seat across from her. "I understand. This has been a stressful week for all of you."

"No, you don't understand. I think I killed my husband."

THIRTY-TWO

Polly Larimore wasn't the first distraught wife to make such a claim to Chief MacDonald. Sally Welsh had once frantically called his office, convinced she had killed her husband when he slipped on a peach cobbler she had dropped on the floor, and then he hit his head on the cabinet and had been knocked out. And then there was the time Jillian Bucket had insisted her husband was dead, and it was her fault because they had fought, and he had left the house during a storm and hadn't come home yet. However, in Polly's case, he knew her husband was in fact dead. Yet by her response to Walt after he had claimed to see her husband, it didn't jibe with a woman who had turned black widow.

Chief MacDonald silently studied Polly for a few moments before asking, "What exactly do you mean when you say you think you killed your husband?"

"I would never hurt Teddy," she insisted. "But these crazy images keep popping into my head. They feel so real."

"What kind of images?" he asked.

"I keep seeing myself pushing Teddy down the basement stairs at Marlow House."

"Why would you push him down the stairs?" he asked.

"Oh, I wouldn't. And I didn't. I know I didn't. I would never hurt Teddy. But he left right after they found Bentley's body, and he hasn't come back. I'm so worried about him, and I keep seeing myself pushing him. Why do I keep seeing that? It's driving me crazy."

"You say he left after Bentley's body was found?" he asked.

She nodded. "Yes."

"So you imagined you pushed him after they found Bentley?"

"No, before. Sunday night."

"Why don't you tell me about that," the chief suggested.

"When I woke up yesterday morning, I had these flashes—images. In them I pushed Teddy down the basement stairs at Marlow House. I was starting to think maybe something had happened when I was drinking. I don't do well with gin, and I had a lot. You have no idea how relieved I was when Walt told me he had seen Teddy that morning. Do you think perhaps something has happened to Teddy, and he is sending me messages?"

While the chief knew Teddy was in fact dead, he also knew his body was not in the basement at Marlow House—they had already looked there.

The chief arched his brow. "Messages?"

She nodded. "I've read about this sort of thing. Someone's spirit reaches out, trying to tell a loved one what happened to them. I know I wouldn't hurt my husband. But I keep seeing things. Maybe he's putting these images in my head."

"Did he tell you where his body is?" the chief asked.

JOE LOOKED OVER TO BRIAN, who continued to stare into the interrogation room via the two-way mirror. "That woman is certifiable."

Brian shrugged. "Stranger things have happened." *Don't I know*, he thought to himself.

"I don't know why the chief isn't questioning her about her husband's relationship with Wilks," Joe said. "He obviously had something to do with his murder. Larimore goes AWOL right after Mason's body is found. And then Wilks is murdered, and still no sign of Larimore. Find Larimore, and you'll find Wilks's killer."

"Unless the killer got rid of Larimore first," Brian suggested.

POLLY NODDED AND then closed her eyes. "I see myself unlocking the opening to the tunnel. The key is hanging on a hook in the basement. In my vision I drag Teddy in there. It's horrible. I feel so evil when I do it."

"I don't know if your husband is trying to send you a message, but perhaps you can tell me what his relationship was with the other guests staying at Marlow House. Such as Phoebe Greda and Bentley Mason."

Polly stared down at her hands, now fidgeting on the tabletop. "That's why Teddy and I argued. I found out he and Phoebe had a brief relationship. I was pretty angry. I… well…to be truthful…I was pissed that night, and in my head I thought of ways to punish Teddy. But I'd had too much to drink, and sometimes that makes me think crazy things. I think that's why I keep seeing those ugly images. I shouldn't have had those evil thoughts, and now Teddy is missing."

"What was Teddy's relationship with Bentley?" he asked.

"I think Teddy liked Bentley. They didn't seem to have any issues."

The chief glanced over at the two-way mirror. He knew Joe and Brian were listening, and he also knew they had Teddy at the top of the suspect list for Wilks's murder. They believed he had gone missing after finding Bentley's body. They had no idea the man was already dead. There was no way he had anything to do with Wilks's death. He also knew he had to ask questions as if he believed Teddy was still out there somewhere.

"Did your husband have any issues with Chase Wilks?"

Polly looked up from her hands and met the chief's gaze. "My husband wouldn't kill anyone."

"But did he have any issues with Chase Wilks?"

"Chase knew about the affair with Phoebe. That's how I found out. I walked in on Chase talking to Teddy about it. But Teddy said they were joking around, and that I had misunderstood what had been said."

"And you believed that?"

"I did until Phoebe told me the truth."

"Do you have any idea where Phoebe went?"

"I assume back to California."

"SUCH A SHAME about that young man drowning," Carla the waitress said as she filled the chief's cup with coffee. He had just arrived at Pier Café after completing the interviews with his suspects and now sat at the booth alone. Yet he would not be alone for long. Walt and Danielle were joining him, and they arrived just as she made her comment. A moment later they walked up to the booth and started to sit down across from him.

"You'll be joining the chief?" Carla asked.

"Yes, we are," Danielle said as she scooted to the far side of the booth seat.

"I was just telling the chief how awful it was about that man drowning. He was staying with you, wasn't he?" Carla asked. She spent the next few minutes shooting off questions about the drowning, but after a while she realized they weren't offering up any spicy details, so she took their orders for pie and left the table.

"I don't think Carla's heard about Wilks yet," Danielle said as she picked up her cup of coffee.

"No, she didn't say anything about it," Walt agreed.

"So did you learn anything?" Danielle asked MacDonald.

The chief told them about what had been said during the interviews, and then said, "Julius Stafford implied they may be cutting this trip short, considering all that's happened, and his wife inferred the movie may not be going forward." He looked at Walt and added, "Sorry about that, Walt."

Walt shrugged. "At this point, I don't care about the movie."

"But I did make it clear I didn't want any of them leaving right away. Although, I'm not sure how you feel about possibly having a killer under your roof."

"Fortunately Marie is sticking around, acting as our ghostly watch dog—and then Walt has his own gifts. So I'm not too concerned quite yet," Danielle said.

"What do you think? Is Larimore's ghost reaching out to his wife?" MacDonald asked.

"If she had dreamed it, I would suggest it might have been a dream hop. But why is he showing her as the killer?"

"Maybe he believes she is," Walt suggested.

"He didn't act like she was the killer when we saw him," Danielle reminded. "Remember, he wanted her to go upstairs with him. Anyway, it was not a dream."

"Maybe not, but it might be possible for a spirit to show someone a vision during a waking moment. I never tried it, but we know spirits are capable of showing themselves to non-mediums. And considering Eva regularly gives us a show where we see all sorts of things that aren't there—snow, glitter, furniture—then why not?" Walt suggested.

"And you're sure Larimore's body isn't in the tunnel?" the chief asked.

"He's not in the first opening. But we didn't look in the tunnel," Danielle said.

"What? I thought you told me you did?" the chief said.

"No. But I can't imagine anyone opening that door. I told them all the tunnel could collapse if they tried," Walt said.

"Maybe a killer doesn't worry about those things," the chief said.

"I guess we should have had Eva or Marie check it out. But really, Chief, I can't see someone getting in there. That second door isn't easy to open," Danielle said.

"I think we should at least look," MacDonald said.

"When we go home, I'll have Marie or Eva check it out for us," Danielle said.

THIRTY-THREE

When Walt and Danielle returned to Marlow House after meeting the chief at the pier, they found Jackie in the library with Birdie and Seraphina—with Marie listening in. The three women looked up when Walt and Danielle walked into the room.

"We've just been discussing *Moon Runners*," Jackie told them. "Perhaps you want to join this conversation, Walt."

Danielle glanced over at Marie and said, "I'll leave you guys to talk. I need to go to the parlor and call Marie."

When Danielle left the room a moment

later, followed by Marie, Jackie said, "We've been trying to figure out how we can salvage *Moon Runners*. We have to find someone to finish the script, and I'm not having a good feeling about Teddy. If he's on a bender—which certainly looks like the case—we're going to need a new director."

"I know this is inconvenient, but I believe in this film," Birdie said.

Inconvenient, Walt thought. The situation was a lot of things, but inconvenient wouldn't be how he would describe anything that had happened in the last few days.

"WHAT DO YOU NEED, DEAR?" Marie asked Danielle when they were alone in the parlor a few minutes later.

"Where's Eva?" Danielle asked.

"With Julius and Polly. They went for a walk," Marie said. "Actually, Jackie told her husband to occupy Polly, she wanted to discuss getting rid of Teddy with Birdie, and she didn't want Polly around when she did that."

"I don't think she has to worry about getting rid of Teddy," Danielle scoffed. "He's not coming back."

"I must say, Jackie Stafford is one cool, determined and focused woman," Marie said. "She doesn't seem that broken up over Bentley's or Wilks's deaths, other than it being inconvenient."

"I got that."

"I do wish we would find those two bodies," Marie said.

"About that. I need you to check the tunnel again. It's possible Teddy might be there."

"But we've already looked," Marie reminded her.

"No. I mean actually in the tunnel. You only looked in the first passageway. It's possible he's farther in."

"Okay." Marie vanished.

MARIE STOOD in the dimly lit basement, looking at the padlocked door leading to the first passageway. She glanced up at the overhead light and it turned on. A moment later she was through the door and standing in the small dark space. If not for the ill-fitting door that had been added to replace the original panel, she would have been unable to see anything. Being a ghost didn't mean you had the ability to see in the dark. Just enough light slipped through the edges around the new door, allowing her to see if the space was empty or occupied by a body. As it had been the last time she stood in the passageway, it was empty. She hadn't expected to find anything different. The next moment she stepped through the second locked door.

Surrounded by darkness, Marie grumbled when she realized the area could be piled with corpses and she wouldn't be able to see them. She couldn't even feel around for the bodies—her hands were nothing but an illusion. While she might be able to direct her energy to pick up anything that was around her, if she wasn't careful, her energy might go astray and collapse the tunnel.

I'm going to have to get the key and open the doors to get some light in, Marie told herself. But when she returned to the basement, she discovered she was no longer alone. Polly stood with

Julius by the padlocked first door. Eva stood behind them.

"What are you doing down here?" Eva asked.

Marie explained why she was in the basement, and then said, "I can't very well open the doors with these two down here."

"This room is what you keep seeing?" Julius asked.

Polly nodded and walked closer to the first door and placed her hand on the padlock. "I have a memory of me opening this."

"You don't really think you killed Teddy and then forgot about it and then suddenly remembered? Come on, Polly, that doesn't even make sense."

"I know I didn't kill him. I would never hurt Teddy," Polly said. "It just all seems so real."

"I THINK you'd better come down to the basement," Marie told Danielle when she popped back up to the parlor again.

"Did you find something?" Danielle asked.

"It's darker than a crypt down there," Marie said. "I didn't have a flashlight on me."

"I didn't even think about that," Danielle said.

"And Polly and Julius are down there poking around. It sounds like she has told him about her little visions. Eva is down there watching them."

"I'm beginning to wonder if Teddy is in some way communicating with her," Danielle said as she stood up and started for the door, snatching her cellphone from the desk as she walked by it.

When Danielle and Marie reached the basement, they found Julius and Polly still there. The couple startled when Danielle walked into the room.

"Oh, I guess we shouldn't be down here," Polly said, sounding embarrassed.

"Why are you down here?" Danielle asked.

"I keep having these flashes—visions, sort of. Where Teddy and I are in the basement," Polly explained.

"I told her she's just stressed after all that's gone on the last few days. It's enough to make anyone start imagining things," Julius said. "And with Teddy going AWOL, her mind is seeing all sorts of crazy things."

"You do look tired, Polly. Maybe you should go upstairs and take a nap?" Danielle suggested.

Absently combing her fingers through her short dark hair, Polly nodded in agreement. "My head is killing me."

"Let's get you upstairs," Julius suggested.

When they turned to leave and Danielle didn't follow them, Julius stopped a moment and looked at Danielle. "Aren't you coming?"

"I came down here to find something." She pointed to a stack of boxes on the far wall. "I think it's in one of those."

Julius gave her a nod and then continued up the stairs with Polly, Eva trailing behind them.

Listening to their fading footsteps, Danielle rushed up the stairs and peeked out into the narrow hallway. She didn't see them. Returning to the basement, she looked at Marie and said, "Keep an eye out for anyone.

I'd rather not have to explain why I'm opening the tunnel."

"Are you going to be okay?" Marie asked.

"I'm torn between wanting to find something to help end this mystery—and hoping there is nothing there."

After Marie left to stand guard, Danielle removed the key from the hook and opened the first door. She pulled it all the way open, to allow light in the opening, when she remembered the cellphone she had tucked in her back pocket. Removing the phone from her pocket, she turned on its flashlight app, preparing to unlock the second doorway.

Taking a deep breath, she reminded herself that if she found Teddy behind the door, it was only a body. *Only a body, I have become jaded,* she told herself. Setting the phone on the floor for a moment, she unlocked the second padlock and removed it from the door. Placing the lock on the floor and picking up the cellphone, she pulled open the second door. As she remembered, it did not move easily, but she managed to pull it open.

Even with both doors open and the overhead light on in the basement, it was still difficult to see in the passageway without a flashlight. Shining the cellphone's light into the opening, she let out a gasp. There was Teddy; at least she assumed it was him. His crumpled body had been shoved into the opening, and while she could not make a positive identification from this angle, she was fairly certain it was him.

Lifting the cellphone a little higher, trying to see farther in the opening to get a better look at the corpse, Danielle let out a second gasp. Teddy was not alone. If Danielle was not mistaken, that was Phoebe with him.

Not bothering to close or relock the second door, she left it open and closed the first door, relocking it. She didn't need anyone in there until the police arrived. Tucking the padlock key into her pocket with her cellphone, she hastily told Marie what she had found, before sprinting up the stairs to get Walt before calling the chief.

PEARL HUCKABEE STOOD at the upstairs corner window of her bedroom, binoculars in hand, watching the spectacle below. The police cars had showed up at Marlow House several hours earlier, followed by two official-looking vans. Holding the binoculars to her eyes, she peered out the window and watched as not one—but two bodies were being carried out of the house. She was fairly certain they were dead bodies and not some injured guests, considering the sheets covering whomever they were carrying out.

She watched as one of the guests, a woman with short dark hair, was being put in the back of a squad car. "Are they arresting her?" she wondered.

DANIELLE AND WALT stood together on the sidewalk in front of their house. Walt's arm wrapped protectively around Danielle's shoulders as the police car drove away with Polly in the back seat. Their remaining guests stood some distance away, huddled together and out of earshot.

"They said she wasn't under arrest," Walt told Danielle. "But she knew where he was."

"What I find interesting was how she kept yelling she hadn't killed Phoebe. Does that mean she did kill Teddy?" Danielle asked.

Looking over to their remaining guests huddled together, Walt said, "I wonder if they will find any of their prints?" The police were just finishing processing the scene, looking for evidence.

"I would assume the killer wore gloves," Danielle said.

"You think it's Polly?" Walt asked.

"If it is, she obviously wants to get caught. But with her reaction to finding Phoebe, I don't know, is she that good an actress?"

"If it isn't her, then who?" he asked.

Danielle looked back to the four remaining suspects. "When I was in the basement earlier, I got the feeling Julius wanted me out of there. But Seraphina has a motive too."

"When I was in the library with Jackie and the others, discussing the fate of *Moon Runners*, I got the feeling she didn't have a problem moving forward with a new screenwriter and director. I actually got the impression she was somewhat relieved."

"And then there is Birdie, but I don't think she's physically capable of pulling any of this off. And what is her motive?" Danielle asked.

"Plus, the way she was talking in the library, she argued rather vehemently against Jackie's plan to can Teddy."

THIRTY-FOUR

"I did not kill Phoebe!" Polly insisted. She sat in the interrogation room alone with Brian Henderson, while Joe and the chief watched from the adjacent office. If she had started the day with any makeup on, it was gone now. Her once perky haircut fell limp and dull, and her red-rimmed eyes threatened to shed more tears.

"And your husband?" Brian said.

"I would never intentionally hurt Teddy." Polly broke into a sob.

"Your fingerprints were everywhere. According to Danielle Marlow, the entrance to the tunnel was kept locked, and when she showed it to you, you didn't go inside. So, can you explain how your fingerprints got in there?"

Pulling herself together, she wiped her tears on the cuff of her sweater, looked at Brian and sniffed before saying, "I think I'll stop talking now and speak to my lawyer."

DANIELLE HAD EXPECTED JULIUS, Jackie or even Seraphina to go down to the police station and give Polly emotional support. After all, Julius and Jackie had been personal and professional friends with the Larimores for a number of years, and Seraphina and Polly had seemed close. When down in the basement with Julius and Polly before discovering the bodies, Julius acted as if the idea of Polly killing her husband was ludicrous. Yet, not now. Now the three acted as if they were convinced she had been responsible for the murders—even Chase's. Only Birdie seemed unconvinced and kept saying Polly had always been such a sweet girl, she just couldn't imagine her doing something like that.

Seraphina looked at Birdie and said, "I don't want to believe this. I've always liked Polly. But she knew where those bodies were. It was as if she wanted to get caught."

"And we know, according to the police, someone from this house left in the middle of the night around the time Chase was murdered. I know it wasn't me or Julius. We never left our room," Jackie said.

"And I know it wasn't me," Seraphina said.

"But why kill Chase?" Birdie asked. "I understand Teddy and Phoebe. Crime of passion, it is the oldest motive in the world."

"If Polly didn't kill Chase, then that means one of us did it," Jackie pointed out.

Birdie shook her head. "I don't believe that for a minute. It's just a horrible coincidence. Someone broke into Chase's looking for money and drugs. Isn't that what the police said?"

They argued for another ten minutes while Walt and Danielle silently listened. Finally, Julius looked at Danielle and asked,

"You talked to the police chief. What now? Are they charging Polly with the murders?"

"I know they're holding her. She's asked to see her attorney," Danielle said.

"She should have thought about talking to her attorney before running around telling everyone she had visions of killing Teddy," Jackie said. "Although, maybe she's going for an insanity defense."

"I imagine she called her brother?" Julius asked.

"Yes," Danielle said.

"That's right, her brother is a criminal attorney," Birdie said.

MARIE HAD NEVER EXPECTED her time as a ghost to be so fascinating. She had spent her last ten years of her life dependent on her grandson or the generosity of friends to get around to places like the grocery store or doctors' offices. In fact, doctors' appointments had comprised the bulk of her social calendar. Despite having to rely on others when running errands, she had much to be grateful for regarding her last years. She was grateful she had been able to enjoy one of her passions—gardening—up until her dying day. Although technically, it was up until she broke her hip, which led to rehab in the care home, which resulted in her murder. But still, she had been able to garden for practically her entire life.

Despite being dependent on others to get around, she had managed to keep up on the local gossip, typically discovering the most delicious tidbits even before her grandson. It was a talent. But now, her gift for being in the know was supercharged.

Sitting in the interrogation room with Polly and her brother, Albert Dawson, listening in to their private conversation—one so private even the chief and his officers were not allowed to listen in to—gave her quite the rush. She felt a tad guilty for being so titillated, considering Polly was in a serious pickle, and Marie did like Polly.

PORTLAND ATTORNEY ALBERT DAWSON sat across from his sister, Polly, in the interrogation room, silently listening to her tearful story. When she was done, he asked, "Good lord, Polly, why didn't you call me right away instead of telling anyone—especially the police chief—that you thought you killed Teddy? Didn't I grill that into you? Never talk to the cops. Call your attorney first."

"I was just so confused, and I didn't seriously think I had killed him. But now I know…I did kill Teddy." She broke into tears again. Albert stood up and pushed the box of tissues closer to his sister. Reluctantly she pulled a tissue from the box and then used it to wipe her eyes and blow her nose.

When again composed, she said, "I didn't kill Phoebe. I promise you that. I didn't."

Marie perched on the table's edge, looking down at the siblings, listening to Polly's pitiful tale.

"How did you not know her body was there?" Albert asked.

"You don't believe me?" Polly asked.

"It's not that I don't believe you. I'm trying to understand. How did you not know you killed Teddy—and now you do? How do you hide his body and not see the other one that was already in there?"

"In her defense, it's pitch dark in there," Marie said to deaf ears. "You'd have to see the opening to understand what I mean."

"It was all so surreal. Like an out-of-body experience," Polly explained. "I'd had too much gin."

"You can't drink gin."

"I know. But I was so depressed that night, finding out Teddy had a fling with Phoebe—I mean really, Phoebe? The woman was such an obvious user. What was the attraction? It was humiliating. Bad enough he cheated on me, but with her!"

"For your sake, please do not make those types of comments about Phoebe to anyone else."

"Your brother is right, dear," Marie agreed with a nod. "Does give you a big ol' motive."

"I hated her. Yes, I will admit it. I hated her. I hated her when she cheated with Barry. I never understood why Seraphina would take her back after that. I thought Phoebe wasn't just Seraphina's employee, but one of her oldest friends. And then she fools around with her boyfriend! What kind of a friend does that?"

"Like I said," Albert said dryly, "please don't express your feelings about Phoebe with anyone else. But can you tell me, how is it you killed Teddy and didn't realize it until now?"

"Yes, please, I want to know that too," Marie said, yet neither brother nor sister could see or hear her.

Polly gave a nod, wiped the corners of her eyes with a tissue, sat up straight and then took a deep breath and exhaled. She looked to her brother and said, "Before dinner we had cocktails. I just couldn't stop thinking about what Phoebe had said. She told me that yes, something had happened between her and Teddy, and that she knew it was my ticket to divorce him and break the conditions of our prenup."

"Good lord, did everyone know about the terms of your prenup? Some things should be kept between a husband, wife and their counsel."

"I know you think that way. But you know

Teddy. When he drinks, he says more than he should."

"At least that eliminates your motive for killing Phoebe. Getting her to testify she'd had an affair with Teddy would be more valuable to you than killing her for revenge," Albert said.

"That would only work if she'd testify. She made it clear she was willing to tell me the truth—but she would never testify to the fact. She wasn't going to cross Teddy. She still hoped he would put her in one of his films. I think it gave her some perverse pleasure letting me know she had been with my husband, but I could never divorce him over it—not unless I wanted to lose everything."

Albert groaned. "You just gave yourself a whopping motive."

"But I didn't kill her."

"Okay," Albert said with a nod. "Go back to that night again, the last night you saw Teddy. Tell me everything you remember."

"Like I was saying, we were having cocktails in the living room at Marlow House. I couldn't stop thinking of how Teddy had betrayed me—lied to me. And well, I started imagining ways I could kill him. Not that I wanted to really kill him. I was just fantasizing."

"But you did kill him," he reminded her.

"Your brother has a point," Marie agreed.

"I switched over to gin, and then we all went to dinner. I didn't eat much of my dinner. I just kept drinking."

"Then what?" he asked.

"After dinner, everyone came back to the living room for after-dinner drinks and dessert. When everyone went to bed, I stayed in the living room—alone. I was there for…I don't know how long…a while…when Teddy came downstairs to get me. By that time, I was pretty toasted. And…well…it was almost like an out-of-body experience. Where I am watching myself and Teddy. And I got angry. And then I remembered one of the ways I imagined killing him—by pushing him down the stairs and hiding him in that tunnel Danielle told us about. It seemed like the perfect place to hide a body. After all, Walt claimed it was locked up for good."

"So you just decided to kill him?" he asked.

"It was just—so—detached. Like a dream. Sort of like I thought it was a dream. Haven't you ever done that before? I have. When I'm having a dream, and sometime during the dream I realize none of it is real, so I do things I wouldn't normally do because I know I will eventually wake up and it will have all been my imagination."

"While you were killing him, you thought it was a dream?" he asked.

Polly nodded. "Exactly. I thought I was just acting out my fantasy in my dream. And then the next morning, when I woke up, I was surprised Teddy wasn't in bed with me."

"When did you realize it hadn't been a dream?"

"Part of me knew…but another part of me didn't believe it. I'm not sure you can understand."

"No, I really don't," he confessed.

"But when they found his body, well, something inside me clicked. I knew then, it hadn't been a dream. I killed my husband. I have to live with that, but I didn't kill Phoebe. I promise you."

Albert sat there several minutes in silence,

considering all that his sister had said. Finally he asked, "Is there anything else you remember about that night?"

"Yes. There is one other thing. I never mentioned it to anyone else before."

"What's that?" Albert asked.

"The basement at Marlow House is down a little back hallway, on the north side of the house. After I came up from the basement, I came face-to-face with Bentley."

"Bentley? Jackie's assistant, the one who drowned?" he asked.

She nodded. "Yes. He seemed surprised to see me. I was pretty wobbly on my feet by that time. He assumed I had been heading up to our room but had gotten turned around and lost. He helped me upstairs, but he didn't walk me all the way to my room. And then he went back downstairs. So I guess I might have been the last one to see Bentley alive."

THIRTY-FIVE

Marie hadn't returned to Marlow House, and Danielle was dying of curiosity to find out what was going on at the police station. The remaining guests had all gone to their rooms, and Danielle sat with Walt in the parlor, trying to read a book, but she couldn't focus. Curled up on the sofa with Max by her feet, she kept turning the pages forward and then flipping them back to where she had been, rereading the pages yet comprehending nothing.

Walt, who sat across from her in a chair, holding an open newspaper, glanced up over the pages and looked at her. "You're going to wear that book out."

Danielle peeked up at him and, with a sigh, closed the book and tossed it on the coffee table. "How can you read that paper? I keep trying to finish this book, but I can't focus on what I read and keep having to go back and reread pages. I don't know how you do it."

Walt closed the paper, folding it neatly before dropping it on the floor by his feet. "I'm doing no better than you. I haven't read a single word."

"I wish Marie would get back here," Danielle said. The next moment her cellphone rang. She picked it up and looked at it. It was Chris.

"I was hoping you were the chief," Danielle said when she answered the phone.

"Hello to you too," Chris replied.

"We haven't found out anything yet. Marie still isn't back."

"That's not exactly why I'm calling," Chris said.

"Why, then?" She looked at Walt and mouthed, *It's Chris*.

"I just called Seraphina, offered to take her out to get something to eat. I thought she might want to get away from the house and talk, especially after everything that happened today. I can't imagine how she's processing Phoebe's death."

"I know you believed her when she told you they were close, and she didn't feel she could stay angry with Phoebe because of their history, but I have to be honest with you, she didn't seem all that broken up when she found out Phoebe was dead," Danielle told him.

"She could be in shock. But that's not the reason I'm calling. Did the chief say it was okay if they all leave?"

"What do you mean?"

"I understood that after they found Chase's body, the chief asked them not to leave right away. But according to Seraphina, they're packing up and plan to leave tomorrow. In fact, she told me goodbye. Said she was tired and going to bed early because she and Birdie were leaving first thing in the morning."

"What?" Danielle asked. "No one said

anything to us. And no, as far as I know, the chief didn't say they could leave."

Danielle talked to Chris for a few more minutes while Walt listened. When she finished the phone call, she recounted Chris's side of the conversation that Walt hadn't heard.

"I think we need to tell the chief," Walt said.

Danielle stood up. "First I'm going upstairs to see what Seraphina says. Maybe Chris misunderstood."

After Danielle left the parlor a few moments later, she considered stopping at Birdie's room first to see if they were planning to leave. But then she changed her mind and decided to talk directly to Seraphina, because that was who Chris had spoken to. She hurried up the staircase and once on the second floor started for the room she had assigned to Seraphina. But when she passed her old bedroom, where she had put Jackie and Julius, the door was open, and the couple was in the process of packing their bags.

Stepping to the open doorway, she looked into the room. The Staffords didn't notice her, but Eva, who was in the room with them, eavesdropping, spied Danielle and gave her a little wave. "I was just about to come downstairs and let you know they're planning their escape. They intend to leave as soon as they get packed."

Danielle knocked on the doorframe. Julius and Jackie stopped packing and looked Danielle's way.

"Oh, Danielle, we were just getting ready to come downstairs to say goodbye," Jackie said, closing one of the suitcases on the bed and latching it.

"You're leaving?" Danielle asked.

"Oh, come now, I imagine you will be thrilled to see us go. Heavens, if I were in your position, I would have figured out some way to get us out of the house by now," Jackie said.

"But I thought the chief asked you not to leave yet?" Danielle asked.

"That was before someone was arrested for the murders," Julius said.

"We don't know if Polly has been charged," Danielle reminded them.

Jackie picked her now closed suitcase off

the bed and set it on the floor. She looked at Danielle. "Polly is obviously responsible for Teddy's and Phoebe's deaths. I'm not sure who killed Chase, and I'm beginning to wonder if Bentley's drowning was an accident or another murder. That makes four of us murdered. Four. Nine of us came to Frederickport, and only five are returning. I'm afraid if we stick around, then five might not be returning. Julius and I are leaving."

"You're leaving now? I thought Seraphina and Birdie were leaving in the morning."

Jackie shrugged. "I have no idea what Seraphina's or Birdie's plans are. They can do whatever they want, but I would rather they not come with us. You see, I know I didn't kill Chase. I know my husband didn't kill him because he was with me all night. But I do know someone from this house might very well be the killer. Maybe it's Polly. Maybe she killed Chase too. But I'm not going to take the chance. And if you will excuse me, I need to change my clothes." Jackie slammed the door shut. Danielle could hear her lock it.

DANIELLE RETURNED TO THE PARLOR, and just as she closed the door behind her, Eva appeared in the room.

"I believe Jackie is sincerely frightened," Eva told Danielle.

Danielle then updated Walt on what Jackie had told her upstairs.

"I think she's wondering if Walt or I might have killed Chase," Danielle said.

"What I heard upstairs," Eva began, taking a seat on an imaginary chair, "she believes Polly is responsible for Teddy's and Phoebe's deaths. According to Jackie, Polly had motive and she did practically confess. But she's not sure about Chase—she can't come up with a motive. But she is wrong about Julius."

"Wrong how?" Walt asked.

"Julius could have slipped out and killed Chase. She keeps insisting he was with her all evening, but I was with them that night and then left after they went to sleep. Who's to say Julius didn't wake up and slip out that night, and she slept through it?" Eva asked.

A knock came at the parlor door.

"Come in," Danielle called out, glancing briefly from Eva to Walt.

Seraphina opened the door and stepped into the room. "I'm sorry to bother you, but I wanted to let you know Birdie and I will be leaving first thing in the morning. I hope you understand."

"Umm…yes…" Danielle said.

"Under the circumstances we feel it would be best," Seraphina said. "I'm getting up early in the morning, so I'm going up now to pack and then turn in early. I'm not hungry, so don't worry about any dinner for me—or for Birdie. She wanted me to tell you she's not feeling well and is lying down."

Just as Seraphina stepped out of the parlor a few minutes later, Marie appeared.

"Oh, thank goodness!" Danielle said. "What did you find out?"

AFTER MARIE TOLD them all that she had overheard, it was decided Danielle would go down to the police station to talk to the chief in person. Yet they didn't want the Staffords to leave while Danielle was gone, or before she had a chance to tell the chief everything Marie had learned. They needed to find some way to keep Jackie and Julius at Marlow House, at least for a couple more hours.

"Sabotage their car," Danielle suggested.

"I suppose we could remove the distributor cap," Walt said.

"That won't work, dear," Marie said.

"Why not?" Danielle asked. "I've heard of people doing that before."

"Cars these days don't have distributor caps, at least not recent models, like those rental cars."

"How do you know about distributor caps?" Danielle asked.

"I know all sorts of things," Marie said.

"I suppose we could remove the car's battery. Cars still have batteries, don't they?" Danielle asked.

Marie arched her brow at Danielle. "Was that a serious question?"

Danielle blushed. "Of course not… well…sorta…"

"Removing a battery is going to be far more difficult," Walt said. "And what if one of them looks out the window and sees me messing with their car? It's not dark yet."

"And they will be leaving before it gets dark," Eva added.

"I could do it," Marie said.

"That might work. If they come downstairs to leave, I'll do what I can to stall them while you take care of the battery. When you come back inside, I'll know it was taken care of," Walt said.

"Great, you guys have it all figured out. I'd better get out of here." Danielle gave Walt a quick kiss and then dashed from the room.

PEARL STOOD at her bedroom's corner window, looking down at Marlow House. She spied someone who looked like Danielle Marlow coming out of the kitchen door and heading to the alleyway. Several minutes later she caught a glimpse of Danielle's car backing out of the garage.

She glanced back to the street and noticed the two cars—which she assumed belonged to the Marlows' houseguests—still parked in front of the house. According to what she had heard at Pier Café when she had gone there earlier for fish and chips, three of the Marlows' guests had died under suspicious circumstances, and some guy who was working on the film but staying in another location had been murdered. It wasn't clear if the deaths were all connected, but all Pearl knew, if the Marlows still had their bed and breakfast, this sort of publicity would surely kill their business.

About to turn from the window, she paused a moment when she noticed some motion from one of the cars parked in front of Marlow House. Quickly grabbing her binoculars from her dresser, she put them to her eyes and focused on the vehicle.

The motion had been the car's engine hood opening. She couldn't see who had opened it because the car was parked heading north, with its taillights facing her, and she assumed whoever opened the hood was hidden from her view by the open engine hood. But the next moment she saw an object floating up over the car.

"What the…" Pearl muttered.

What she was seeing made no sense whatsoever. The object looked like a car battery, and it now floated from the car toward the Marlows' fence. It then stopped, hanging in midair over the sidewalk. Pearl looked back to the vehicle just in time to see the hood slam shut. No one was standing there.

Pearl blinked her eyes repeatedly in disbelief and looked back to the car battery and watched it fly over the fence and then land on the roof of the Marlows' garage.

Pearl nervously licked her now parched lips and managed to set the binoculars back on the dresser without dropping them to the floor, despite her shaking hands and the room now spinning around her. Stumbling to the bed, she drew back the covers and climbed in, not caring that the sun was still up and that she was still fully dressed. Once in the bed she mumbled, "I must have gotten some bad fish," and pulled the covers up and over her head.

THIRTY-SIX

Danielle ended up meeting the chief at Pier Café instead of going down to the police station. They sat together in a back booth, with no one sitting in the booths on either side of them.

"Where are the boys?" Danielle asked.

"When I knew I was going to be working late, I called Sissy to pick them up from school. She and Bruce took them out to get pizza, and then she's going to take them back to our house and stay with them until I get home."

"You're lucky to have your sister and brother-in-law to help you," Danielle said.

The chief shrugged. "Since our little adventure in Arizona, the boys prefer to stay at their own house."

Danielle smiled softly. "I get that."

"I imagine you wanted to meet me to find out what's going on with Polly."

"Actually, I wanted to tell you what Marie found out," Danielle began. "She was in the interrogation room with Polly and her brother and—"

The chief put up his hand and said, "Stop right there. I can't know what went on between Polly and her attorney. I would be breaking the law if I listened in, and using Marie would be the same thing."

"You've used inside information before," Danielle reminded him. "I don't think a judge is going to rule your information was illegally obtained by a ghost."

"I think this may be crossing a line," he said.

"Then you should probably know Jackie and Julius are planning to leave Marlow House tonight, and Seraphina and Birdie are leaving in the morning, despite the fact you asked them not to leave."

"I can't make them stay, especially now that we have our suspect in custody."

"Polly is being charged?"

"For all intents and purposes she has confessed to the murder of her husband. While duress and intoxication aren't defenses for murder in this state, her attorney is framing her defense for a lesser charge, and I imagine he thinks with a sympathetic jury it might work. She insists she didn't think it was real when it happened. That it was all a dream," he said with a snort. "What a bunch of BS."

"Actually, she does believe that. At least that's what she told her brother. So unless she's lying to her attorney and a good actress, then that's what happened."

The chief frowned. "No kidding? Well, it doesn't matter. Because I don't think that defense will work on the charges for Phoebe's murder. And while we're in the evidence-gathering stages, there will probably be new charges for the deaths of Bentley and Chase. I don't believe we have two killers on the loose."

Danielle cringed and said, "I think you do, Chief."

"Why do you say that?" he asked.

"That information Marie overheard, it wasn't incriminating against Polly—except for the part about her killing Teddy, which you already know. She was adamant with her brother, she didn't kill Phoebe or anyone else. But we know someone did. And those someones may be getting ready to leave Frederickport."

AFTER LEAVING THE CHIEF, Danielle drove north on Beach Drive, intending to enter the alleyway by taking the road to the north. In doing so, she drove by Marlow House and was relieved to see Stafford's rental car still parked in front, yet was concerned the vehicle Birdie had rented was no longer on the street.

When she got back home five minutes later, she walked in the kitchen and found Walt waiting for her.

"I was getting ready to call you, but I noticed your car coming down the street," Walt said.

"Where's Birdie's car?" Danielle asked.

"Seraphina left not long after you to fill the car with gas and stop at the pharmacy to pick up something for Birdie."

Danielle let out a sigh of relief. "Good. I was afraid we managed to keep one here while the other ones slipped out early."

Walt shook his head. "That's why I was getting ready to call you. The Staffords are gone."

"Gone? What do you mean gone?" she asked.

"I walked them out to their car to say goodbye, and when the car wouldn't start and Julius looked under the hood—there was one thing we hadn't counted on."

Danielle frowned. "What's that? Did they have a spare car battery on them?"

He shook his head. "No. They…as Lily would say…totally freaked."

"Freaked?"

Walt nodded. "Ohhhh yes. Scared senseless, especially Jackie. Convinced someone was out to kill them all. They didn't go back into the house, although I tried to get them to come back inside. Jackie got on her cellphone, called a taxi, and minutes later they drove off. Julius said they'd pay for someone to pick up the rental car. You should have seen them. Reminds me of one of those horror movies Heather made us watch before Halloween. You know, the scene where the victims just realize the guy with the chain saw is about to come through the only exit in the room, and they all scramble frantically to get away."

"On a positive note, I guess that means Jackie is innocent, considering how she's acting," Danielle suggested.

"And it is possible she just drove off with the killer," Walt said. "But Marie went with them, so for Jackie's sake, if Julius is our killer and he decides his wife is next, Marie can intervene. But she's only staying with them until they get to the airport and on the plane. After that, she's heading back here, and if the chief wants to bring them in, he'll know where to find them. At least, until they land in California and they all get off the plane."

"Or the killer is out putting gas in her car," Danielle said. "Where is Eva?"

"She went with Seraphina to get gas, just in case it was all a ruse. Birdie is in her room.

Eva checked on her before she left, told me she was sound asleep. Snoring up a storm. According to Eva she had her hearing aids off, so I assume she's down for the night."

"Must be tired. Kind of early to go to bed," Danielle mused.

"Did you eat anything at the diner?" Walt asked.

"Yeah, I had some fish and chips."

"Since Joanne is not coming back tonight, and you already ate, and Birdie is sound asleep, I hope you don't mind if I go upstairs and take a nap. One thing about being dead, you never get tired."

"You do look exhausted." Danielle reached up and stroked the back of one of her hands across Walt's right cheek.

"It's been a trying week—to say the least." Walt leaned down and brushed a kiss over Danielle's lips.

DANIELLE SAT ALONE in the parlor with the door open to the hallway. Max had gone upstairs with Walt, and she was trying to get into the book she had put down earlier, but like before, her mind would not focus on the written words.

She had called the chief to update him on the Staffords, and Seraphina had not yet returned. The house felt eerily silent. And then it didn't.

Shouts came from the entry hall. A woman's voice. And then a man's. Another man, and then another. Danielle recognized the voices.

She jumped up from the sofa and ran to the open doorway and looked out. There, gathered in her foyer were six people, five men and one woman. Although technically speaking, none of them were people. They were ghosts. Unaware Danielle watched them from the open doorway, they continued to argue amongst themselves. It was difficult to tell what exactly they were saying, as they kept trying to talk over each other, their voices growing louder and louder.

She recognized all of them. There were the two ghosts they had seen earlier but had not yet identified. And then there was Teddy, Chase, Bentley, and Phoebe. After standing quietly for over five minutes and still not getting the gist of the argument, she stepped into the hallway and said in a loud voice, "Please don't leave."

Danielle wasn't particularly concerned about waking Birdie. After all, Eva said she was sleeping and without her hearing aids she was practically deaf.

The ghosts all stopped talking and turned to face Danielle.

"See, I told you she can see and hear us," one of the ghosts said. It was the first ghost Danielle had seen before the others had arrived. In her mind she had named him First Ghost.

"Please tell me what happened to you all." She then turned to the ghost whose identity was still a mystery. "And who are you?"

"If you would have told them that when you first arrived, we wouldn't be in this mess," Chase grumbled at First Ghost.

First Ghost rolled his eyes at Chase and then turned to face Danielle. "I suppose it's time I identified myself. None of this turned out as I had hoped."

"Get on with it, Randy," Phoebe snapped.

Danielle frowned. “Randy?”

First Ghost, who looked like a man in his early twenties, bowed briefly at his waist and said, “The name is Randy Adair. Pleasure to meet you, Danielle Marlow.”

“Randy Adair?” Danielle frowned. “Wasn’t that the name of Birdie’s husband?”

“One and the same,” Randy said.

“If you’re confused about his appearance,” Phoebe said, “the man has always been ridiculously vain. Of course he would come back as a vision of his younger self.”

Randy turned angrily to Phoebe. “I told you, this is not my fault! I didn’t even know I looked like this! It’s not like I can look in a mirror and check myself out now that I’m dead.”

“That’s true,” Danielle said. “A spirit, with some practice, can assume the appearance of his former self at various ages. I suspect the reason you took on your younger version is that’s how you see yourself.”

“Isn’t that the truth,” Bentley said. “Randy never could accept the fact he had gotten old.”

"I'm dead, and so are all of you, so what's it matter now?" Randy asked angrily.

"Dead because of you!" Chase shouted. They all started arguing again.

Frustrated and still no closer to learning the killer's identity, Danielle yelled, "Please stop arguing—and don't leave!"

They grew quiet again and looked at Danielle.

"Sorry," several of them muttered.

"Tell me, who is responsible for your death? Please tell me."

"I suppose I'm the only one who can't blame Randy for the predicament I'm in," Teddy begrudgingly admitted. "Polly killed me. I have to say, I never saw that one coming. Didn't think the girl had it in her. But she should never drink gin. Always makes her mean. Was my own fault for not paying more attention. I walked right into that trap." He chuckled.

"You're not mad at her?" Danielle asked.

"I was for a while, after I realized I was dead and remembered why," Teddy explained.

"Who killed the rest of you?"

All of them, except for Teddy and the remaining unidentified ghost, said at the same time, "Birdie."

Danielle glanced to Birdie's closed bedroom door and then back to the ghosts.

The lone unidentified ghost said, "I should probably introduce myself. I'm Barry Reynolds. Birdie didn't kill me, but considering everything, I'm surprised she didn't."

"Barry Reynolds? Seraphina's ex-boyfriend?" Danielle asked.

He smiled sheepishly and said, "I don't know why I'm here. I've been trying to move on since I had too much to drink and drowned in my spa like an idiot. This is where I ended up."

"Why would Birdie kill any of you—and how could she? She can barely walk," Danielle asked.

"She says she can barely walk," Phoebe said.

"Birdie killed everyone except for Teddy? She was the one who drove over to Chase's that night and shot him? Birdie killed Phoebe and hid her in the basement? But how did she kill Bentley? How did she get him down to the beach?" Danielle asked.

"Maybe I'll tell you," came an unexpected voice. "But first, who are you talking to?"

It was Birdie, who now stood in the open bedroom doorway aiming a revolver at Danielle.

THIRTY-SEVEN

"Oh crap," Danielle muttered, her eyes on the revolver pointed in her direction. She watched as Birdie stepped from the bedroom doorway, unaided by a cane. The pistol-wielding woman seemed taller than before, and by her stride it was clear there was nothing wrong with her mobility.

"Birdie surprises me more than Polly," Teddy said. "Nothing was like I imagined it was."

"Don't do this," Randy moaned, yet Birdie could neither see nor hear him or any of the other ghosts.

"Where's your husband?" Birdie asked in a calm voice.

"Don't tell her," Phoebe said as she lunged toward Birdie, attempting to grab the gun from her hand.

"What do you think you're doing?" Bentley asked dryly as he watched Phoebe repeatedly attempt to swipe the gun from Birdie.

"Umm…Walt's upstairs in our room, taking a nap. Would you like me to go get him?"

"You told her? Why did you do that?" Phoebe asked, making another try for the gun. Her hand moved effortlessly through Birdie's. "Of course she's not going to let you go get him. Are you crazy?"

"Do you love your husband, Danielle?" Birdie asked.

Phoebe looked at her fellow ghosts and said, "Do something. Don't just stand there."

"Of course I do." The nervous flipness faded from Danielle's voice, replaced by a solemn tone.

"Then you don't want him to get hurt. There's no reason to get him involved in all this. Simply do as I say, and the man you claim to love will be fine," Birdie explained.

Taking Phoebe's challenge, the other ghosts jumped on Birdie, a wild tangle of swinging limbs and hands. The scene might have been comical, especially since Birdie stood oblivious in the midst of the melee, her aim steady and sure. Danielle then began to worry that one of the ghosts might manage to harness some energy and, instead of knocking the gun from Birdie's grasp, cause her to pull the trigger.

"Please stop!" Danielle called out. "The gun might go off."

THE GHOSTS UNDERSTOOD Danielle was talking to them, while Birdie assumed she was talking to her. Danielle's comment made her laugh.

"What about Jackie and Julius? They could come down here at any minute. Hardly enough time to kill me and hide my body," Danielle said.

"They aren't here," Randy said.

Birdie laughed again. "They left. I saw

them drive off in the taxi from my bedroom window. They couldn't leave fast enough. And I know Joanne isn't coming back tonight. Seraphina mentioned it when she asked me if I wanted her to pick me up anything for dinner."

"See, she knew they weren't here," Randy said.

"What about Seraphina? She could be back at any time," Danielle asked.

"She wouldn't hurt Seraphina," Randy said.

"I would never hurt Seraphina," Birdie insisted.

"See, I told you," Randy said.

"Is she part of this?" Danielle asked.

"Absolutely not!" Randy and Birdie said at the same time.

"Then what happens when she shows up and finds you holding a gun on me—or me dead on the floor? Let me go in the bathroom; you can barricade the door with the coat rack and take my car. Leave, get out of here before she comes back. Before anyone else gets hurt."

"That might work," Randy said, looking

hopefully at his wife. "Listen to her, Birdie. You don't want to do this, love. Put the gun away."

"Seraphina won't be back for a while. I just got a text message from her. She decided to stop and talk to Chris. She told me not to expect her back for a couple of hours."

"Would someone please go up to my bedroom now and get Walt. Hurry before it's too late. He can see and hear you. Please! Before it's too late! Tell him what's going on," Danielle begged.

"Come on, Bentley," Phoebe said. "Let's go get Walt." The two ghosts disappeared.

"What are you talking about?" Birdie asked. "Are you trying to make yourself sound crazy so I'll just leave? That is not going to happen, Danielle. Somehow you figured it out when no one else did. And I can't leave you here to convince your friend the police chief to start looking in my direction. I suppose it's a good thing you have a penchant for talking to yourself or I would have never overheard you rambling on. Quite fascinating what was going on in that little mind of yours."

"Since we have some time—after all, you

yourself said Seraphina is going to be gone for a few hours. At least give me a dying wish. Explain why you killed them, and how you killed Bentley?"

Birdie laughed. "I know what you're doing. You hope that you can keep me talking, and then I might change my mind. Or perhaps you do want your husband to come downstairs, but I'm afraid you would be unhappy with that outcome. I'm a very good shot. He wouldn't make it down the stairs, and then you'd be next."

"You know, when you shoot me, blood can get everywhere. I've seen people who have been shot before. Are you sure you're going to be able to clean up the blood and dispose of my body before Seraphina gets here?" Danielle asked.

"I was hoping to shoot you in the tunnel," Birdie said with a pleasant smile.

"And exactly how did you plan to get me to the tunnel?" Danielle asked.

"You can go with me, or I will have to shoot you here and then go upstairs and shoot your husband. And when Seraphina returns, I'll convince her some crazed killer came and got rid of you while I was hiding in my closet. Considering all the other deaths, I think I could sell that story."

"That's crazy," Danielle said.

Birdie shrugged. "Perhaps."

"I tell you what. I really want to know why and how. So if you just tell me, then I will walk to the basement, get in the tunnel, and let you shoot me. What do you have to lose?"

"If you want to know that bad, I suppose I could tell you. Let's see…I guess I could start with Phoebe. She wasn't a very nice person. Betrayed Seraphina more than once. She needed to go."

"Good thing Phoebe isn't here to hear this," Teddy said.

"And if she was?" Chase asked. "What could she do? Give her a good sock? She couldn't even knock the gun out of her hand."

"What about Bentley?" Danielle asked.

"Bentley knew too many secrets. Overheard things he shouldn't have. I couldn't risk it. After all, he'd slept downstairs the night I got rid of Phoebe. I needed to get rid of him. It was rather easy. I convinced him to walk me down to the beach. Of course, he didn't want to go. But I sold him some cockamamy story about how I just wanted to walk along the ocean in the moonlight, because that's what Randy and I always did when we visited the beach. Offered to pay him to escort me. Told him it was hard to do it alone with my cane. I needed a man's steady arm. Bentley was never one to turn down easy money."

"How did you kill him?" Danielle asked.

"Of course I insisted we take a cocktail with us. After all, Randy and I always enjoyed a cocktail when walking along the beach at night. At least, that's what I told Bentley. I just slipped a little something extra in his. Hit him not long after we reached the water. He was clueless. Once he was out, I removed most of his clothes, rolled him in the ocean, and kept him facedown until I was certain he had drowned."

"I just don't understand how you did that," Randy groaned. "What happened to you, Birdie love?"

"And Chase?" Danielle asked.

"I have a good idea why," Chase said.

"I considered getting rid of Chase when

he made that pass at Seraphina. Dirty old man. But that's not why I did it. He was getting too close. I wasn't sure if he was just talking off the cuff or if he was baiting me."

"WALT! WAKE UP!" Phoebe yelled into Walt's ear for the second time. The two ghosts stood bedside in the attic master suite.

"Why isn't he waking up?" Bentley asked. "I thought Danielle said he would be able to hear us?"

"I don't know." Phoebe shrugged. "I don't get it. But maybe she was wrong."

They heard a meow and looked to the foot of the bed. There sat Max looking up at them, his black tail twitching back and forth.

"It's their cat," Phoebe murmured before jumping back in surprise. "Bentley! Did you umm…well, feel that?"

"Did he just ask why we're in here?" Bentley asked, staring in disbelief at the cat.

"It's weird. I didn't really hear him—not like he can talk, but—"

"He wants to know. He asked again," Bentley said.

Phoebe stared at the cat and then asked, "Can you understand me?"

Max meowed.

"We need to wake up Walt. But I'm not sure he'll be able to see or hear us."

Max meowed again.

"He said he will," Bentley said.

"This is so flipping weird," Phoebe said.

Max meowed again.

"Because Danielle is in trouble," Phoebe explained. "We need to wake him up so he can rescue her."

Max didn't need to be asked twice. He leapt from the foot of the bed to Walt's chest and began vigorously batting his chin with both paws. It looked as if Max was in a boxing match and Walt was down for the count. Yet after a few moments Walt bolted up in bed.

"Max? What the hell?" Walt sputtered, now awake.

The cat meowed.

Walt turned to his left. There standing

next to his bed were the ghosts of Bentley and Phoebe.

"Can you see us?" Phoebe asked.

"Yes, I can. I can hear you too," Walt said.

"You must sleep soundly, because I was shouting in your ear and you didn't budge," Phoebe told him.

"While I can see and hear you now, the sound of your voice—the voice of a ghost—works differently than the sound of a living person's voice," Walt explained.

"Interesting," Phoebe murmured. "And did the cat really understand what I was saying?"

"Yes. And I imagine you understood what Max was saying," Walt said.

Phoebe grinned. "Wow. That's pretty cool."

"Before you disappear, please tell me who killed you," Walt urged.

"Oh…" Phoebe cringed. "I guess we shouldn't be standing around chatting. You need to get downstairs."

"But she has a gun, so you need to be careful. Probably should call the police," Bentley suggested.

"Who has a gun?" Walt asked.

"Birdie of course," Phoebe said. "Danielle is trying to buy some time, keeping her talking before she takes her down to the basement and shoots her."

Walt leapt from the bed and started for the doorway.

"Wait!" both Phoebe and Bentley called out.

Walt paused a moment and looked back to the ghosts.

"Didn't you hear what we said? Birdie has a gun. You aren't going to help Danielle if you get yourself shot," Phoebe said.

Walt took a deep breath and said, "You're right. Please come with me. You too, Max."

THIRTY-EIGHT

Walt asked Phoebe to go ahead and let him know exactly where Danielle and Birdie were so he would know what he was walking into. He didn't want to go around a corner and come face-to-face with a gun-wielding Birdie. In the meantime, he made his way down the stairs as quietly as possible while Bentley told him everything he had seen regarding the situation downstairs.

When they reached the top of the stairs leading to the first floor, they found Phoebe waiting below, looking up at them. They couldn't see Danielle or Birdie, but Walt could hear Danielle asking Birdie questions.

"If you start down the stairs, Birdie is going to see you," Phoebe called up to Walt. "When you come down here, they're to your right, by the bathroom door leading to the hallway to the basement. That's where Birdie is taking her, the basement."

"I don't understand why you aren't calling the police," Bentley told him. "And what do you think you're going to do? She has a gun. You're unarmed. Do you really want to join us?"

I've already been on your side, no desire to return just yet, Walt thought. He looked down at Max, who stood attentively by his feet, looking up, waiting for instructions. Not wanting to be overheard by Birdie, Walt conveyed to Max what he wanted him to do.

"OKAY, enough talking, I've told you everything you need to know," Birdie said. "Keep moving."

"But you haven't told me why. I don't understand why you killed any of them. What did Bentley know that he needed to be silenced for? And when you said Chase was baiting you, what did you mean?" Danielle asked.

"It's none of your business," Birdie said.

A loud meow caught Birdie's attention. She looked down and smiled at Max, who was now weaving in and out of her legs, purring loudly. "Not now, Max," Birdie cooed, no longer sounding like a coldhearted killer. Still holding the gun and pointing it at Danielle, she reached down and petted the cat under his chin. In turn, Max nuzzled into her hand, headbutting her palm.

"You have the sweetest cat," Birdie said. "Maybe Walt will let me take him when I leave." She looked down at the cat and said in a soft voice, "You would like that, wouldn't you?" Max nuzzled her hand again.

"So what do you plan to do, just let everyone think I vanished into thin air?" Danielle asked.

"I think I'm going to tell them something woke me up, I looked out my window and saw you arguing with someone, and then you got into a car with them and drove away. It was dark, so I couldn't see what kind of car it was.

Walt will probably be grateful to me for taking the cat off his hands. After all, he's going to be busy looking for you."

PEARL OPENED her eyes and shoved the blanket and sheet off her. She glanced down at her body, still wearing the clothes she had put on that morning. *Unless…unless that was actually yesterday morning. How long have I slept?* she wondered. Rolling over to look at her clock on the nightstand, she saw she had only been sleeping a couple of hours. It was still early.

With a yawn Pearl got out of bed. She hadn't forgotten what she had seen, but she tried to make sense of it. Before retreating to sleep, she had convinced herself that it had to have been something she ate. Yet now, after sleeping for a few hours, she didn't think that was it. After all, she didn't feel sick. Pearl walked over to her dresser, picked up her brush, and began combing her hair while looking at her reflection in the mirror.

Thinking about what she had seen, she

began to laugh. "Your imagination is working overtime. You didn't see a flying battery; you saw a box being blown over the fence and onto the neighbor's yard." She laughed again and shook her head, pleased with how she had sorted it all out.

Feeling relieved and hungry, Pearl decided to run out to get something to eat—maybe a hamburger at Lucy's, or some Mexican food at Beach Taco.

"HER BACK IS TO ME," Phoebe called out, still standing by the first-floor landing.

Walt gave her a nod, beginning his silent descent down the stairs, mindful of all the spots in the steps that might creak. He slowly made his way toward Phoebe. One step at a time.

"I hope you know what you're doing," Bentley muttered, following Walt down the stairs.

Phoebe continued to look from Walt to Birdie's back. The older woman had just stopped petting the cat and now stood a little straighter, waving the pistol a bit, pointing the way to the basement and telling Danielle to keep moving.

"Come on, we're wasting time. You don't want me to have to kill your husband too, do you?" Birdie asked. Danielle, who had been frantically thinking up questions, paused after Birdie's last question and inadvertently looked past her as if something had caught her eye.

Nervous herself, Birdie whirled around to face whatever Danielle had seen, gun in hand, and found Walt Marlow walking in her direction. But he wasn't armed, so she smiled, about to aim the gun at his chest and then tell him to get over with his wife when something unexpected happened—her gun flew out of her hand and up into the air, landing on an overhead light fixture. Stunned, Birdie looked up and saw her pistol teetering far above her, out of reach.

Birdie looked frantically from Walt to Danielle. Walt was no longer approaching, and he, like his wife, stood silently watching her. Without hesitation, she turned abruptly and ran to the front door. Walt and Danielle started after her, but before they got halfway across the foyer, she was already out the door, running into the dark night.

"She can run!" Walt said when he and Danielle reached the front door.

"The woman definitely doesn't need that cane," Danielle said.

"Are you alright?" he asked, pausing a moment as he reached for the doorknob.

"I am now," Danielle said, slightly out of breath, her heart racing.

"You stay here. Call the police," Walt said before running out of the house.

BEFORE HEADING DOWNTOWN, Pearl decided to first cruise by her neighbor's and check out what was going on. Considering the chilling turn of events, she didn't imagine anyone was still over there, yet there was one vehicle still parked out front—the one with the faulty engine hood. Driving north down Beach Drive, her attention on Marlow House's living room window, Pearl didn't see the front door open, or the woman run outside and down the front walk. Instead, she kept staring in the house while driving down the street, not slowing down. The living room was fully lit, and the blind was open, but she didn't see anyone inside the room.

Pearl's head turned to see where she was going, and to her horror the headlights of her car illuminated the terrified face of a blond woman just before Pearl's car struck, running the woman down.

IF IT HADN'T BEEN SO dark outside and Walt had seen where Birdie was going, he could have prevented the accident. But like Birdie, he hadn't seen it coming. Walt stood horrified, at the edge of the sidewalk, and watched as Pearl pulled her car to a stop and quickly got out of the vehicle. She didn't exit quietly. No. Screaming at the top of her lungs, Pearl Huckabee repeatedly yelled, "She just ran out in front of me!"

No longer standing mute at the edge of the sidewalk, Walt ran toward the victim, who was trapped under Pearl's car. Danielle, who had just gotten the chief on the phone, dashed out of the house, phone in hand, and told him to send an ambulance.

PEARL WAS STILL hysterical when the police arrived. Danielle stood by her side, an arm around her neighbor, trying to calm her down. Lily and Ian had come over from across the street, and Heather was already walking down from her house after hearing the ambulances arriving. Lily kept glancing across the street to Connor's bedroom window, as she had left him sleeping in his crib with Sadie standing guard.

The paramedics were attending to Birdie when Seraphina drove up and parked her car behind the one the Staffords had rented. Confused, she got out of the vehicle and rushed to Danielle and the others to see what had happened. Unbeknownst to Seraphina, she carried a passenger, Eva. The onetime silent screen star got out of the car and went to get a closer look at the body attended to by the handsome paramedics.

"What happened?" Seraphina asked.

"It's Birdie," Danielle told her, still holding onto Pearl.

"She ran in front of me! It wasn't my fault!" Pearl sobbed.

THE SOMBER GROUP sat in the living room at Marlow House. Pearl had been given a sedative, and the police chief had Officer Carpenter take her home. Lily had dashed across the street and picked up Connor and Sadie. Now she sat quietly in the Marlow House living room, holding her sleeping son with her husband by her side.

Danielle and Walt sat with Heather on the sofa. Police Chief MacDonald and Brian Henderson stood in the center of the room, going over the events of the evening while Seraphina paced the room anxiously. There was just one ghost in attendance, Eva. All the others had vanished moments after the car had hit Birdie.

"I can't believe Birdie was responsible for all those deaths…why?" Seraphina asked, still in shock. Danielle had just filled them in on the details of the evening, including all that Birdie had told her, yet excluding any mention of spirit intervention.

The official story was that Walt had startled Birdie, and she had dropped the gun. Before the police had arrived, Walt had remembered to bring the gun down from the light fixture, not wanting to have to explain that to the police. As it was, guns landing in high places at Marlow House had become oddly commonplace.

"Why would she do it?" Seraphina repeated.

"Unfortunately we may never find out now," Brian said.

"She got off easy," Heather said. "Killing all those people and trying to kill Danielle."

"It wasn't the Birdie I knew," Seraphina said, breaking into a sob.

Chris arrived a few minutes later. Danielle had called him, letting him know Birdie had been killed, and that she had been the one responsible for all the deaths, all except for Teddy's. Danielle thought Seraphina could use a special friend about now.

"I'M GOING to pick her up in the morning and take her to the airport," Chris told Danielle after everyone had gone home.

"I imagine she wants to get far away from here," Danielle said. She stood with Chris by the front door as he prepared to leave. Seraphina had already gone up to her room for the night.

"She's pretty confused. And none of it makes sense. Why would she kill them?"

"Birdie obviously thought she was doing it for Seraphina for some reason," Danielle said.

"That's a little extreme," Chris said. "It's quite a leap from benefactor to raging fan willing to kill anyone you feel has hurt or insulted the person you idolize."

"She was more like a protective mother than a fan," Danielle said.

Chris frowned. "Does Birdie have kids?"

Danielle shook her head. "No. She had a daughter who died a long time ago from drugs."

"Perhaps it was transference," Chris suggested.

“What do you mean?”

“Maybe Birdie saw Seraphina more like a daughter. She couldn’t save her own daughter, so she was willing to kill to keep Seraphina safe.”

Danielle shrugged. “Possible. And if the spirits are gone for good, then we will never know for sure.”

THIRTY-NINE

Danielle felt the light touch of Walt's fingertips as they brushed over her forehead. Her eyes fluttered open and she rolled toward him, welcomed by his arms as he drew her close. He kissed her forehead and whispered, "Good morning, love."

"What time is it?" she asked, snuggling closer.

"Time for us to get up if we want to say goodbye to Seraphina before Chris gets here."

Danielle groaned and tightened her hold on Walt, resting her face against his bare chest.

"Ian did warn me when my agent was

contacted by Jackie that an option was no guarantee the movie would get made. But I have to say, I never imagined it would go this far, only to be cancelled because of something like this," Walt said.

"She's not going to try for another backer?" Danielle asked. The night before Walt had called Jackie. He caught her at the Portland airport, still waiting on standby for a flight home. He told her about Birdie and how she had been responsible for all the deaths except for Teddy's.

"She would have to find another backer, another director, another screenwriter. To say it's put a dark cloud on the production would be a wild understatement. I told her I understood if she wanted to walk away from *Moon Runners*, considering everything that happened. She told me she would talk to me next week, after they get home and sort some of this out. But I don't expect her to change her mind, and I understand."

"I do too," Danielle said. "But I'd like to know why Randy Adair told us *Moon Runners* started all this."

"Maybe just the fact it gathered together

all the players, and he understood the dynamics," Walt suggested.

"I wonder if any of them will be back. I'd like to learn more."

"Hopefully Marie or Eva will learn something before Birdie moves on."

"I don't know what I was thinking," Walt said with a weary sigh. "I could have prevented her death. I don't know why I let her run out of the house. I could have stopped her."

"It all happened so fast," Danielle reminded. "You were running on adrenaline."

"I wonder if she has moved on," Walt said.

"Considering where she is probably headed, I don't imagine she'll be anxious to."

The night before Eva had followed Birdie's body to the morgue. Birdie's spirit hadn't showed up, and since a soul often follows his or her body before moving on, Eva hoped to catch the ghost before she did, to learn more about her motives.

Marie had returned to Frederickport shortly after Walt had talked to Jackie on the phone. She had overheard Jackie recount the conversation with Walt to Julius and understood it was no longer necessary to wait for them to get on the plane.

When back in Frederickport, Marie had taken off to find Eva and keep an eye out for Birdie. Back at Marlow House, Max had agreed to night patrol while Walt, Danielle and Seraphina went to bed. If any of the spirits showed up, Max would wake Walt and Danielle.

They had also called Joanne, letting her know what had gone on and telling her not to come over the next day. Seraphina was leaving early and had told them she intended to eat something at the airport. Joanne offered to come over in the afternoon to start stripping the sheets, but Danielle told her she and Walt just needed some quiet alone time considering all that had happened. Joanne understood, yet the truth was, they didn't really want alone time. They wanted to be available to any of the spirits should they show up again. Danielle wanted to learn Birdie's true motives.

CHRIS WAS ALREADY at their house when Walt and Danielle came down that morning. He was sitting at the table drinking coffee when they walked into the kitchen. "I made some coffee. You want a cup?"

"Danielle, do you think we should call the police and tell them we have a break-in?" Walt asked.

"He did make us coffee," Danielle said, standing by Walt's side near the coffee maker.

"If it makes you feel any better, Seraphina let me in," Chris said.

"I know. We saw her." Walt grabbed two coffee cups and filled them. "She was just setting her suitcases outside her room. I brought them downstairs and set them by the front door. She'll be down in a minute. She was using the bathroom."

"Any ghost sightings?" Danielle asked, taking the cup of coffee Walt had just poured her.

"Nothing here. I was wondering if you saw anyone last night," Chris said.

"No. And we haven't seen Eva and Marie since they left." Danielle took a seat at the table.

A few minutes later Seraphina walked into the kitchen and helped herself to a cup of coffee. "Do you need me to go through anything in Birdie's room?" Seraphina asked as she joined the three at the table.

"The police took everything last night," Danielle told her.

"I never asked…but when you found Phoebe, were her things with her?" Seraphina asked.

"Yes. Birdie had put the suitcases in the tunnel opening with her body," Danielle said. "The police took her things and Bentley's."

Seraphina shook her head and sipped her coffee. "I'll never understand. It was not the Birdie I knew. From the moment I met her and Randy, they were always so good to me—so supportive. I can't believe she would do any of this."

"I'm sorry. Birdie confessed everything to me. But she didn't make it clear why she did any of it. Not really." Danielle avoided mentioning Birdie might have been motivated by a desire to protect Seraphina. She preferred to spare the young woman unwarranted guilt.

TOGETHER WALT and Danielle stood on their front porch and waved to Chris and Seraphina as they drove away in Chris's car, heading to the Portland Airport. It had been arranged to have Birdie's rental car picked up with the Staffords' later that afternoon.

Danielle glanced over to Pearl's house and said, "I wonder how she's doing this morning."

"The woman is unpleasant, but I feel sorry for her," Walt said. "Horrible thing to have to live with."

Danielle let out a sigh. "Let's go inside. I'll make us some breakfast."

The moment they stepped back into the house, they were greeted by Marie and Eva.

"She's here," Marie said proudly. "Waiting in the parlor."

"We tried to get the others to come, but they were anxious to move on and felt there was no reason to stick around," Eva said.

"When you say she's here, do you mean Birdie?" Danielle asked.

"Yes, we explained to her the least she can

do is help you understand why she did what she did."

"The others understand now too, as much as they can," Eva said. "It was rather crowded and lively—in a dead sort of way—at the mortuary last night."

Danielle glanced toward the parlor, where Birdie waited.

"What do you mean?" Walt asked.

"The other spirits. The ones who tried to help Danielle last night. They followed Birdie after she left her body. She didn't go immediately to the mortuary. She went down to the beach," Eva explained.

"The poor dear was so confused," Marie added.

"That poor dear tried to kill me last night," Danielle said. "And she killed three people. That dear is a freaking serial killer."

"Go talk to her, Danielle. She's confused," Marie urged. "Eva and I will stay out here. I think it will be easier on Birdie if she can talk to just you two."

"By all means, let's make it easier on the woman who wanted to kill me," Danielle grumbled, heading to the parlor.

BIRDIE SAT in one of the parlor chairs facing the sofa, her hands on her lap. She smiled at Danielle and Walt when they enter the room.

"I guess this is what it feels like to be dead," Birdie said, sounding far more friendly than she had the previous evening.

"Marie said you would explain why you did it," Danielle said, taking a seat on the sofa with Walt.

"First I want to apologize to you both. Especially to you, Danielle. I feel horrible I put you through all that. I am so thankful Walt intervened."

Danielle frowned at Birdie. The woman—or ghost—seemed sincere.

Birdie turned her attention to Walt and smiled. "Eva and Marie told us all about you. How utterly fascinating! I must say you surprised me with that trick of yours! And poor Bentley and Phoebe, you had them both worried. They had no idea you had special gifts."

"Why did you do it?" Danielle asked, redirecting the conversation back to what she most wanted to know.

"That's the thing, dear. I'm not sure. Which is why I have a favor to ask you," Birdie began.

Danielle arched her brows. "You want to ask me a favor?"

"Well, you and Walt."

"What kind of favor?" Walt asked.

"I'll get to that in a moment, but first, I think I need to explain some things to you." Birdie let out a deep sigh and then said, "Seraphina doesn't know this. But she is my granddaughter."

"Your granddaughter?" Danielle sputtered.

Birdie nodded. "I know most people believe my daughter was lost to drugs. I'm ashamed to say I helped perpetuate that lie for years after she died. It seemed in some way easier, considering things I had been raised to believe."

"So your daughter didn't die of a drug overdose?" Danielle asked.

Birdie shook her head. "No. She never experimented with drugs, at least, as far as I'm aware. But when she was a teenager, she fell in love with a young man who happened to be black. And I am ashamed to admit, back then I believed it would be better my daughter have drug issues than get involved with a black boy. At least with drug problems, we had the money to send her to the best rehab centers. But what do you do when your daughter tells you she's in love with someone you don't approve of?"

Danielle and Walt reserved comment and continued to listen.

"My husband was utterly furious. You have no idea how angry he was. I thought he was going to kill the young man."

"This wasn't Randy?" Danielle asked.

Birdie shook her head. "Heavens no. Randy was the polar opposite of Christie's father. If we'd had children, he wouldn't have blinked an eye if any of them married someone who wasn't white."

"So what happened?" Danielle asked.

"We forbade her to see him, but she was seventeen and went behind our backs. When she turned eighteen, she told us she was pregnant and planned to marry him. We told her that she either get an abortion and never see him again, or we would disown her."

"She didn't get an abortion," Danielle said quietly.

Birdie shook her head. "I never saw her again. In the beginning, I tried to talk my husband into changing his position, but he wouldn't budge. I'm not casting the blame solely on him; I let it happen."

"So Seraphina's parents who died in the car accident, they were your daughter and her husband?" Walt asked.

"No. About a year after Seraphina was born, Christie and her husband were killed in a house fire. The baby survived. Christie's husband had no family, and to our surprise they had a will and had appointed her father and I as Seraphina's guardians should something happen to them. I suspect she did that because she had no one else, and she assumed we would come around and accept our granddaughter if the unimaginable happened."

"But you didn't," Walt said quietly.

Birdie closed her eyes for a moment and then reopened them. If a ghost were capable of tears, they would be running down her face. "Not when Seraphina needed us. But we did arrange for a private adoption with a black family—under the condition that she never be told the true origin of her birth."

"And then they died," Danielle said.

"It was years before I learned that," Birdie said. "My husband forbade any contact with the family who adopted her. But after my first husband died and I met Randy, I had a private investigator find her. I wanted to see how she was. I was shocked to discover she had been raised in foster care."

"So you sought her out?" Danielle asked.

"Yes. She was playing in a little club. I just wanted to make it up to her. But I couldn't tell her who I was. She would hate me. I wouldn't blame her."

"So why did you kill Randy and the others?" Danielle asked.

"That's what I need you to help me figure out," Birdie said.

"I don't understand," Danielle said with a frown.

"I was angry with them. But I don't understand why I felt I had to kill them. It was something I just couldn't prevent—a compulsion is the best I can explain it. And now, now with death, that need, that compulsion, it's gone."

"Start by telling us why you were angry with them," Walt suggested.

"I became jealous over Randy's relationship with Seraphina. It was so natural with him. He was so good with her, and she seemed to look at him like a surrogate parent. I wanted her to see me that way. So I tampered with his heart medication. I killed my beloved Randy."

"He didn't blame you. He tried to protect you even while he wanted to stop others from getting hurt," Danielle said.

"Yes. He told me. He promised to wait for me on the other side when I'm finished here. Even though I'll probably be sent somewhere else, considering what I've done. And I am prepared to pay for my sins; I'm not afraid. But, Randy believes now something physically was wrong with me. He wants you to make sure they do an autopsy on my body. When Randy saw me again on this side, he became more convinced there was a physiological reason for my violent actions."

"And the others? What issues did you have with them?" Danielle asked.

"Phoebe was obvious; she hurt Seraphina. With Chase, I believed he had stumbled on the truth regarding my relationship with Seraphina, and Bentley was starting to ask too many questions, and by some of the things he said, I was afraid he had seen me with Phoebe that last night, yet I had told everyone I hadn't seen her."

"Randy told us *Moon Runners* got him killed. Do you know why he said that?" Walt asked.

"It was because Randy is the one who approached Jackie about *Moon Runners*. He's the one who got Seraphina the role. That sent my jealousy out of control. I wanted to be the one to give her things, not Randy."

DANIELLE OPENED the front door and welcomed the chief into the house.

"Thanks for stopping by. Let's go in the

parlor. Walt's in there," Danielle said after closing the door.

"It was no problem. I was planning to stop by and talk to you after I checked on Pearl, anyway."

"How's she doing?" Danielle asked, leading the way.

"I think relieved, since I told her we recommended charges not be pressed against her."

They walked through the parlor doorway and Danielle said, "But didn't you pretty much tell her that yesterday?"

"Morning, Chief," Walt called out from the sofa.

"Walt," MacDonald said with a nod. He looked back to Danielle and said, "Yes, but she was so hysterical I don't think she heard me."

MacDonald took a seat in one of the chairs across from the sofa, while Danielle sat next to Walt.

"So what did you need to tell me?" the chief asked.

"Birdie was here," Danielle began. She then told him everything that had been said.

"She's her grandmother?" the chief said after Danielle finished the story.

"That's what she claimed."

"Are you going to tell Seraphina? Does Birdie want you to tell her?" MacDonald asked.

"Birdie left before I even considered asking that question," Danielle said. "And I don't know if she's coming back. I have a feeling she moved on. She did what she needed to do, and she said Randy was waiting for her on the other side."

"Randy? That's the husband she murdered?" MacDonald asked.

Danielle smiled at the chief. "When people move over, things from this side look a little different. It's easier to forgive."

"Are you going to tell Seraphina Birdie is her grandmother?"

"I'm not sure. Obviously, if I do, I'll have to say Birdie told me at gunpoint, not after she died. And then figure out a reason why I didn't say something before. I don't know." Danielle shrugged. "But Walt and I talked about it after Birdie left."

"What do you think, Walt?" the chief asked.

"I'm not sure what the point would be," Walt said. "It may not be in Seraphina's best interest. As it is she's having difficulty understanding how her friend Birdie committed such atrocities. But then to discover she was her grandmother."

"But we're going to discuss it with Chris when he gets back from Portland," Danielle said.

"What about the autopsy?" Walt asked. "Would it be possible for them to look a little closer, see if there was some physical reason for her behavior?"

"Chief," Danielle interrupted before he could answer Walt's question, "I think there may be something to this. Birdie didn't seem apprehensive about moving on to the next side—not a typical reaction for someone who has murdered four people."

"I wouldn't think so," the chief muttered.

"One thing I've learned," Danielle continued, "spirits aren't that much different from the person they were when they were alive. Once they pass over and understand they're dead, they may see things from a little different perspective—yet really no more than a person who has broadened their views after traveling to another country or had some profound experience. But with Birdie, she didn't understand why she did those things. That's not a typical response for a spirit, in my opinion. A spirit might feel remorse and regret, but not this type of confusion at this stage. And I would expect her to be feeling some apprehension about moving on, considering what she did."

"I'd assume physiological changes that would alter behavior would take place in the brain. And considering our killer's head injuries, if something is there, the coroner might find it without me mentioning anything. But I will talk to him." The chief then turned to Danielle and said, "I also need a favor."

"What's that?" she asked.

"Polly is being moved today, and she has requested Walt come talk to her before she leaves. But I think you should be the one to do it, not Walt. You're better at this."

Danielle frowned. "I don't understand. Talk to her about what?"

"She wants to know why he said he saw Teddy after she had killed him." The chief glanced at his watch and then looked back at Danielle. "And you have about an hour to make up a story to tell her before they pick her up. By the way, Brian and Joe will be listening in when you tell her. They've also been wondering why Walt claimed to have seen Teddy after he'd been killed."

DANIELLE SAT ALONE in the interrogation room, waiting for Polly to be brought to her. She glanced over at the two-way mirror and frowned. She knew she had an audience for this performance.

A few minutes later Officer Carpenter brought Polly to the room. Danielle couldn't help but feel sorry for her, she looked utterly pitiful.

"Thank you for coming to see me," Polly said, taking a seat across from Danielle. "But I'll be honest, I was hoping your husband would come. I wanted to ask him why he said he saw Teddy that morning."

"That was my fault," Danielle lied. "I told Walt to say that."

"Why would you do that?" Polly asked.

"Umm…well, after they found Bentley's body and Teddy seemed to be missing, I wondered if someone had done something to him."

"But why tell us he saw Teddy?" Polly asked.

Danielle shrugged. "I just figured if any of you were responsible for Teddy going missing, that hearing Walt say he had just seen him would freak that person out, and they would do something to tip their hand. But that didn't happen."

"WHERE DOES Danielle come up with these lame ideas?" Joe asked. He stood with the chief and Brian, watching Danielle and Polly through the two-way mirror.

"Where indeed," Brian said under his breath, his eyes still on Danielle.

"She could have totally screwed up this murder investigation," Joe grumbled. "She and Walt should be charged with giving false information."

"I don't think making a false statement to your guests over breakfast falls into that category," the chief said.

"She doesn't know that," Joe argued.

"I'll have a talk with her," the chief promised before leaving the room.

Joe looked to Brian and asked, "What do you think?"

Brian nodded toward the two women sitting at the table in the interrogation room. "I think the false statement Danielle made was in that room just now."

Joe frowned. "Are you saying she didn't tell Walt to lie? He lied on his own?"

Brian smiled, his eyes still on Danielle. "Not exactly…"

FORTY

It was confirmed the following week that *Moon Runners* would not be made into a movie—at least it would not be produced by Jackie Stafford. While the movie deal had died, Walt's book sales soared due to the recent publicity from the *Moon Runner Murders*. That is what the press had dubbed the series of events. Walt declined multiple offers to appear on morning and evening talk shows to discuss the killing spree. "I guess it's true what they say," Walt told Danielle. "Any publicity is good publicity."

Seraphina also found herself in the spotlight. While Chris had agreed with Walt that telling Seraphina Birdie was her grandmother would just cause her pain, it all proved a moot point. It turned out that Birdie had left her entire estate to her granddaughter, along with a letter revealing their true connection. While Birdie's estate was vast, they all expected the families of Birdie's victims would be making claims against it—how much exactly was yet to be seen.

DANIELLE LOOKED out their front window and glanced up the street. "Chris said his furniture is arriving later this afternoon."

Walt looked up from the book he was reading. "Does this mean he's going to be spending less time at our house and more at his own? *I hope.*"

Danielle turned from the window and said, "Oh, come on, Walt. You like Chris."

"Yes, I like Chris. And I had no problem when he stayed here after his house burned down. Temporarily."

"And he moved out when he knew we

were having guests," Danielle reminded, taking a seat across from him.

Walt closed the book and set it on his lap. "And the minute they left, he has been over here every day—several times a day. I can't recall the last time I got up, and he wasn't in our kitchen, drinking coffee."

"Then you have a short memory, because he didn't come over for coffee this morning."

"That's only because he's moving into his house. He'll be back."

"You have to admit, it's nice having the coffee ready when we get up every morning." Danielle grinned.

Walt made a grunting sound and picked up his book, opening it.

"Chris says he feels comfortable over here; it feels like home to him. I don't want to hurt his feelings."

"But this isn't his home. And we're no longer running a B and B," Walt reminded her.

"If you think about it, when he was living down the street, he wasn't always dropping in."

Walt glanced over his book at Danielle and cocked a brow.

"I'm serious! Yeah, he dropped over a lot —but no more than Lily. It's just since he started staying at the foundation office. It's kinda cold and unhomey over there."

"Is unhomey a word?" Walt asked.

Danielle shrugged. "I don't know, you tell me. You're the writer."

Walt flashed Danielle a smile and then looked back down at his book.

"I think now that Chris is moving into his new house, he's going to be busy getting it in shape. We'll have to start making our own coffee," Danielle said.

"We could change the locks," Walt muttered as he turned a page.

"Marie would just open the door for him," Danielle teased.

"You have a point."

A few minutes later, as Walt quietly read and Danielle picked up the newspaper, a cheerful, "Morning, guys," came from the doorway, and Chris walked in. "Your front door was unlocked. I was wondering if I could borrow some coffee."

Walt looked up from his book and said, "Make yourself at home."

"You're alright, Walt," Chris said before heading for the kitchen.

Danielle chuckled. "You're an old softy, Walt."

"In the head," he grumbled.

LOSING his home to a house fire had taught Chris several lessons. The first, always double-check the burners on your stove before leaving the kitchen after you've been cooking. The second, the vagabond lifestyle was no longer his thing.

After his parents' deaths, Chris had spent some time bouncing around, most notably living on a friend's boat in Dana Point, California, before moving up to Oregon. He then lived at Marlow House before buying his home on Beach Drive.

After living in his own home—one that belonged to him and not his parents or a friend—Chris realized he rather liked having a place to call his own. Permanently moving into a section of the foundation headquarters was never an option. It might be large enough, and it might be able to accommodate necessary office and living spaces, while having a stunning view, but it was never a place he could call home.

When deciding to rebuild on his lot, many warned him it would take over a year to get a new house built. After all, there were house plans to have drawn, permits to take out, not to mention the actual construction. What those naysayers failed to consider was Chris's money, which had a magical way of speeding up the process. Within five months after the fire, he was moving into his new home.

Today was his housewarming party. The guest list included the regulars—his friends on Beach Drive, along with Adam and Melony. He also invited some of the neighbors, such as the Crawfords next door. But he didn't include Pearl. He invited the chief and his boys, who would probably spend most of their time throwing the ball for Sadie and Hunny on the beach. He included Ian's sister, Kelly, which meant her boyfriend, Joe, would be invited. Chris and Joe's fellow officer Brian Henderson had a better relationship these days, so he asked Brian at the last minute, and when he was at Pier Café, Chris extended an invitation to Carla the waitress.

Chris had considered briefly having the party catered, but quickly changed his mind when Lily, Danielle and Heather suggested a potluck. He would buy the steaks and grill, while everyone would bring their favorite dish. He would also provide the beer and other beverages.

CHRIS'S GUESTS who weren't inside the house getting a tour were either sitting on the spacious patio on the back of the house overlooking the ocean, or taking a walk on the beach. Danielle stood with Walt on the sand, just beyond Chris's patio, looking out to the sea.

"Would you like to move to a house with a view like this?" Walt asked.

"Nah. I love Marlow House. If I want to look at the ocean, I can walk across the street and borrow one of our friends' views."

Walt was about to respond when he heard someone calling their names. He glanced behind him and spied Chief MacDonald walking toward them from Chris's back patio.

"Hi, Chief," Danielle said when he reached their side. "Where are the boys?"

"Inside checking out the house. But I have a feeling they'll be out here in a minute." He exchanged a quick handshake and greeting with Walt and then said, "But I wanted to tell you both, I talked to the coroner this afternoon and asked him when we might get the final results back on Birdie's autopsy. He said next week, but unofficially he told me she did have a medical issue that could have definitely affected her behavior."

"What kind of medical issue?" Danielle asked.

"Birdie had a tumor pressing on a section of her brain called the amygdala. It's the region that controls emotion and behavior."

"And that could have turned her into a killer?" Danielle asked.

"I can't say for sure, but from what he told me, there is a definite possibility," MacDonald said.

"This has taught me one thing," Walt said.

"What's that?" the chief asked.

"We had Eva and Marie keeping an eye on everyone, but when they were alone in their rooms, they normally didn't go in with them," Walt said. "But they should have."

"How would that have mattered?" the chief asked.

"Birdie didn't need that cane. I can't imagine she used it when walking around alone in her room," Walt pointed out. "If we knew that earlier, maybe we could have prevented all this."

"True," Danielle agreed with a sigh. She then added, "If nothing else, I think Birdie's medical condition might help Seraphina come to terms with all this. She's been so conflicted since this all began."

"It might impact what type of settlement the families receive against the estate," the chief suggested, "if they can prove Birdie had some physical reason beyond her control that contributed to her actions."

"Chris told me earlier, that's pretty much settled," Danielle said. "Phoebe didn't have any family, so there was no one to sue the estate. Chase just had a brother, whom he wasn't close to. Birdie's lawyers—who are now Seraphina's lawyers—already made an offer to Chase's brother and Bentley's parents—a very generous offer—and they already accepted. Seraphina ends up with the balance of the estate, which is still a fortune."

"Do you think she'll decide to back *Moon Runners* like her grandmother wanted to?" the chief asked.

Walt shook his head. "I would be surprised. With all that's happened, I can't imagine she'd want to come back here."

"Not even for Chris?" the chief asked.

Danielle shrugged. "I know they talk on the phone, but not sure there's a future there for them. They each have very different lives, and I think right now, Seraphina is just trying to sort out hers."

THE PARTY at Chris's had been fun, but all Danielle wanted to do now was go to bed and sleep in until noon. She was exhausted.

Danielle fell asleep within ten minutes of her head hitting the pillow. Unfortunately, not long after dozing off, she found herself sitting in Marlow House's dining room with Birdie, Chase, Phoebe, Randy, Teddy, and Bentley.

"Ummm, hello?" Danielle said uneasily, looking around at the others sitting at the table. "I have to assume this is a dream hop?"

"Is that what this is called?" Phoebe asked.

"It's what I call it." *Yep*, Danielle thought to herself, *definitely a dream hop. Has its own unique feel.*

"I wanted to thank you," Birdie said. "I know now why I did those horrible things. Thank you for finding out for me."

Randy reached over and patted Birdie's hand. "I knew there had to be a reason. It wasn't like you."

"I don't know if I did much," Danielle said. "I suspect they would've found it even if I hadn't asked the chief to look into it. But I do have one more question for Birdie."

"I'll try to answer it," Birdie said.

"Why did you want to come to Frederickport in the first place? Were you…well…did you want them here so you could kill them?"

"Oh, heavens no!" Birdie cried. "I just wanted to spend some time with my granddaughter. And I couldn't figure out anyway to get her to take a trip with me. But things got out of control."

"You could say that again," Chase grumbled. "But considering my last doctor's checkup, I was on borrowed time anyway."

"I'm still annoyed," Phoebe said. "But I understand it was not Birdie's fault. And I suppose I have some blame in all this, considering my actions."

"I certainly didn't want to check out this early," Bentley said, "but at least my back isn't killing me anymore. That's something."

"Do you know how Polly is doing?" Teddy asked. "I might try one of these dream things with her, but I'd like to know what I'll be getting into."

Danielle looked to Teddy. "All I know is her brother is working on some sort of diminished capacity defense."

"Polly is the one thing I feel pretty guilty about," Phoebe said.

"Because she killed me?" Teddy asked.

"I feel guilty she's now facing prison," Phoebe said. "I should have lied and said nothing happened."

"We were both foolish," Teddy muttered.

"Where is Barry, by the way?" Danielle said.

"He didn't want to come with us. He's just thrilled to finally have moved over to the other side," Phoebe said. "He'd been stuck on your side since after his death. Thing about Barry, once he's done with something, he likes to move on."

"I think we should let Danielle get back to her sleep," Birdie said and then looked at Danielle. "I wanted to thank you for everything, and the others wanted to say goodbye, since they didn't get a chance to, after I was hit by the car."

AS DANIELLE DRIFTED from dream hop to sleep and Walt slept soundly by her side, a car pulled up in front of Marlow House for a moment and stopped, its engine still running.

Overhead a moon broke the late night's darkness.

"That's it?" the woman asked the car's driver.

"Yes. And now we need to figure out how to get Walt Marlow to tell us what he knows."

THE GHOST OF A MEMORY

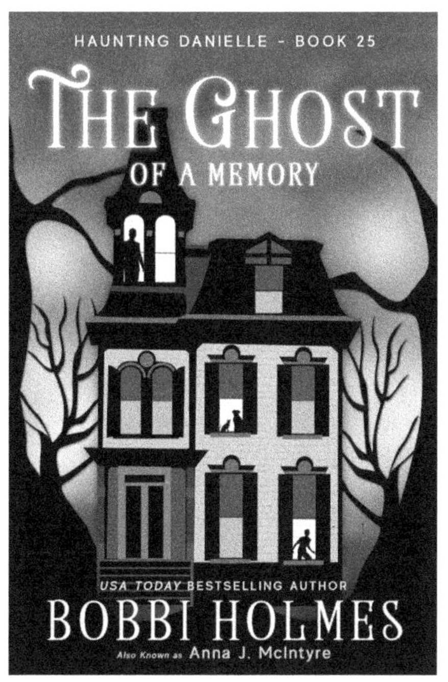

Return to Marlow House in

The Ghost of a Memory

Haunting Danielle, Book 25

Past and present collide when a secret from the 1920s wreaks havoc on Marlow House.

Walt struggles to remember what he may have

forgotten before it's too late.

NON-FICTION BY

BOBBI ANN JOHNSON HOLMES

Havasu Palms, A Hostile Takeover

Where the Road Ends, Recipes & Remembrances

Motherhood, a book of poetry

The Story of the Christmas Village

BOOKS BY ANNA J. MCINTYRE

Coulson's Wife

Coulson's Crucible

Coulson's Lessons

Coulson's Secret

Coulson's Reckoning

UNLOCKED HEARTS

Sundered Hearts

After Sundown

While Snowbound

Sugar Rush

CPSIA information can be obtained
at www.ICGtesting.com
Printed in the USA
LVHW081411250420
654386LV00004B/125

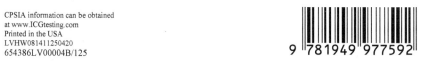